SPIRITED

Spirited

Published by The Conrad Press Ltd. in the United Kingdom 2021

Tel: +44(0)1227 472 874
www.theconradpress.com
info@theconradpress.com

ISBN 978-1-914913-16-7

Printed and bound in Great Britain by Clays Ltd, Elcograf S.p.A

Typesetting and Cover Design by The Book Typesetters,
www.thebooktypesetters.com

The Conrad Press logo was designed by Maria Priestley.

SPIRITED

D. E. HANSON

To my family and to the memories of summer days with Christmas and Mary in Craig Fryn and being chased by that pig...

CHAPTER 1

She wipes the steamy film from the bathroom mirror and her fifteen-year-old features swim into focus.

A slight girl; dark hair, wet from the shower and hair hanging like dank seaweed onto her shoulders. Wide-set eyes, cornflower-blue and striking (or so she has been told) against the dark tone of her skin; a Celtic thing, from her mother. Then her mouth, which she despises. The dentist called it a slight overbite, which was fine for him, he didn't have one. She calls it an aberration.

For years she has practised smiling in different ways, disguising the way her top lip slides back over her front teeth. In the end she settled for a turning down at the corner of her mouth, which her mum said looked like a smirk; disrespectful, Mum added. Beth prefers sardonic, a word she found when reading The Vampire Soul. God, she hates her mouth.

She knows that her upper body is too skinny. Collarbones like handlebars, ribs clearly visible, tiny breasts. She hardly needs a bra when she runs, which she does a lot. The running has toned her legs though; her best feature by a long way. Her friends tell her to wear short skirts to show them off, or skinny jeans because her bum's okay too. She prefers joggers.

Her name is Bethan Mary Gray. She is aged fifteen years and five months. She is yet to have her first period. She is yet to fall in love. She is yet to experience the trauma of paralysing fear.

CHAPTER 2

Beth has never had a boyfriend. Well, actually that's not *strictly* true. She once kissed Kyle Smith. She was fourteen. Her best friend Sienna had practically shoved her in Kyle's direction in Gregg's after school one day.

'What do I say??' Beth had asked.

'You don't *say* anything, durr,' replied Sienna. 'You follow him on Insta, that'll do it…'

Sienna had recently parachuted into her life and had instantly become her best friend, simply by being more outrageous and luminous than anyone else in her orbit. Sienna was slumming it in Beth's state High School having been dragged out of some fee paying one by her capricious mother, Trish. Trish described herself as 'being temporarily between husbands', hence the downgrade. Sienna said she'd had cats giving off less heat than Trish.

And so, to the date with Kyle. Her first date and her first proper kiss. They'd been to see Ready Player One – his choice – and she'd felt him getting restless beside her all of the film. A twitch here, a brush there.

They went to Nando's after. It was only when she'd bitten into her first fiery chicken leg that she thought, 'oh great, what if he wants to kiss me with chicken breath?' She'd sneaked a sideways looks at him chewing away. Greasy-chicken lips, slightly red nose, okay teeth.

Kyle threw the javelin; not always in the right direction, he'd joked. He wasn't particularly academic and, also like her,

8

he didn't really stand out. In many ways, she thought, they were well matched. Her mum reluctantly approved. Her dad said he'd be waiting outside Nando's ten minutes early, engine running and carrying a big stick; he thinks he's hilarious.

She'd looked for his car as they walked out and, as she craned her head around to check out the nearby bus stop, Kyle pounced. It was clumsy and quick and they banged teeth. His head sprang back in shock as he patted at his swelling lip and stared at the culprit; the reason for this humiliation, her aberration. He muttered about catching his bus and practically ran away, her thanks for the chicken aimed at his swiftly departing back and becoming lost in the wind.

Her dad had been joking about being there ten minutes early and she had to wait another fifteen before he turned up, no stick in sight, and asked where her date was. She tried to make light of Kyle's disappearance but Dad was livid and Mum threatened to phone Kyle and have a massive go for leaving her on her own.

Since then, her mum has kept a very close an eye on her (over the 'sex thing') and it's not as if she'd had to beat potential boyfriends off with a real stick. Beth thinks that there's something that puts them off. Maybe it's the sardonic smile, or, to give it its real name, the overbite.

Anyway, she tells herself that she hasn't got time for them. She reads books instead. Lots of books. Maybe that's it, what puts them off? Maybe she gives off this 'I'd rather be reading a book' vibe. And when not buried in books, she's running, hoping that she never gets stuck in front of a psychiatrist; they'd have a field day.

Beth's mum, Eve, was an athlete; she won things. Eve was selected for Team GB to run in the fifteen-hundred metres at the Sydney Olympics. Sixth place in the final proved to be the pinnacle of her career; two years later a ruptured cruciate knocked Eve into a spiral she never fully recovered from.

Eve says she can see herself in the way Beth runs. Herself as a girl, that is, because, according to Eve, Beth's stride needs correcting. Maybe my stride's sardonic too? Beth occasionally thinks.

Dad, Joe, reckons the running isn't the only similarity. Peas in a pod he calls them. Prickly peas, Beth silently adds. He tells people he deserves a medal living in their house; it's a war zone. Dad and Beth's younger brother Max, spend hours on X box, playing COD. Dad reckons it's a less violent environment. He exaggerates. Mum and Beth might argue every now and then, but, when they run, it all stops. It becomes about the breathing. The rhythm. The slap of their shoes. The synchronicity.

Beth has started to win medals of her own, with Eve pushing her every inch of the way.

Beth has the one really close friend, no pets, a brother, and (now) three grandparents. Brilliantly, her grandparents on Mum's side were called Mary and Christmas Williams. Beth still can't get used to thinking of her grandparents in the past tense. Grandma Mary died when Beth was fourteen, a few weeks after that kiss, which kind of put romance (or lack of) in perspective for her. Grandad still lives in North Wales, in a hill farm called Craig Gwaed, which sits in a grass-lush valley, blazing white in the summer sun, like someone's dropped a lump of misshapen chalk into a plump velvet-green cushion. On clear, sunny days you can spot the sea, silver and opal, at the end of the valley.

'C'mon, Beth! I want a piss!'

It's Max, outside the bathroom, saying piss because he thinks it's grown up and dangerous for a nine year old and because he knows no one else can hear him.

She yells back through the locked door, wrapping a towel around her slight chest, shaking drops from her hair.

'Shut up, Max, and stop saying 'piss.'

'Piss, piss, piss…' he yells back.

Beth acknowledges that they all have to 'make allowances' for Max. He's got ADHD and has a Teaching Assistant at school. She has watched as Mum has practically dragged him home from school, having acted out some fresh atrocity. The nastier kids in Beth's year reckon that ADHD is just another label for twat and, if she's being totally honest, there are times when she wants to agree with them.

'You're not still crying 'cos One D split are you?' he yells.

'No Max, I never liked One D…'

'You so do! You want to marry Harry, have his babies…'

She yanks the door open quickly, making him start. He recovers quickly, grinning like a loon, and she breezes past him into her room. Except it's not her room at all. They're in Wales for Grandad's seventy-fifth birthday, and she's in Mum's old childhood room.

It overlooks the farmyard through tiny, leaded windows. She flops back onto the single bed and takes in all the medals, cups and ribbons Mum has won down the years. The place is a shrine to her success and Grandma Mary always buffed the trophies until they glistened and winked at her from the

11

shelves. Grandad Christmas is too old to farm properly now and sometimes employs a local boy, Trev, to keep the yard tidy, whitewash the cottage; odd-jobs. Trev's hair grows thick and low on his forehead, as if trying to meet up with his eyebrows. His arms hang limply at his sides and swing when he walks, sausage fingers looking like they're too fat to form into a fist.

Everything about Trev screams 'slow', but he's not. Beth's seen the light in his dark eyes, and his smile as it splits his huge head; mocking. She's also seen him whip a rabbit from a trap and snap its neck in a heartbeat. He doesn't know she's watched him like this, not many people do. She seems to be able to drift into peoples' space without them realising, all the while watching and learning things.

Trev also doesn't know that she's noticed the way he's looked at her, especially last summer, when she was fourteen. She'd seen that look on his face before – with the rabbit. She avoids Trev, it's easy. Anyway, he seems less interested since he took up with Susie. Susie was last year's May Queen and once Trev clapped eyes on her sitting up on that float, riding high through the town, garlanded with flowers, he was lost.

The whole town of Porthmadog had lined the streets that day under a blazing sun that made everything bright and harsh. It's a small-ish town, once a teeming port, shipping slate all over the world. Now, it's tourist-dependent and practically empty in winter.

Susie was Disney–perfect. Cascades of buttermilk-blonde hair and a bee sting mouth, red as a rose. She preened and swelled with self-importance, but there was a sense of malice about her. She didn't so much smile, as expose her teeth; like a dog does when cornered, so that she seemed like a thorn in all those petals. Something sharp, lying in wait for anyone who, mesmerised by the flowers, dared to reach out. Beth saw Trev catch Susie's eye, saw him lick his lips, then watched as Susie turned her head away, leaving her gaze on him a second longer than was necessary. Then, Beth knew she was safe. Okay, she *thought* she was safe.

CHAPTER 3

B eth swings her legs off the bed and sits at the window, peering into the yard, which is already brilliant in the morning sun. She sees Grandad make his way across the cobbles, a slight swing to his gait, gnarled old stick in his right hand and ratty cap on his head, no matter what the weather's doing.

Seeing the yard, golden with sunshine like this, always pricks her memory of a day from her childhood. In those days they would stay here for the whole summer. Mum would run daily, Dad would play at being a farmer. Max was a baby and she tended the chickens. Until the day the pig turned up.

She was nearly seven years old and had ventured out into the yard, swinging a little rubber bucket, which she'd just filled with seed. The chickens saw her and started their helter-skelter approach, jockeying for position. Then they stopped, some skidding, and turned, beating their wings, squawking and fleeing. She watched them go, and then slowly turned to look behind her. It was a pig the size of a pony.

They stared at each other for the briefest of moments before it charged, head down, horribly sure-footed on the cobbles. She dropped the bucket and began to run for the open farmhouse door. But the pig was too fast and Beth could hear the clatter of its feet, feel its heavy, hot breath on her legs. Then, in an instant she was snatched up and lifted to the sky. She felt strong hands beneath her arms, smelt the warmth of fresh bread; yeast and butter. All the smells that

14

meant Grandma Mary had her, high and safe.

The next thing she knew, Grandad Christmas was there, beating the pig with his walking stick. Whacking it, driving it back across the yard.

'She's old,' Grandma Mary explained to Beth, 'we brought her in from the fields, but perhaps now it's time she went'.

Christmas was baffled, his sow had never behaved like that, he'd said, lifting his cap to scratch at his head. We've had her since birth and it wasn't as if she had any piglets to protect. Mary clutched Beth that morning as if she never meant to let go.

'She didn't mean it. She's a special pig. Like you, Bethan,' Mary whispered, '*you're* special…'

'You saved me, Granny.'

'Yes, dear, I did didn't I?'

She can remember looking into her Grandma's eyes and seeing the depth of the love there, but mixed with something else, some foreboding.

Then the spell was broken as Mum and Dad rushed from the farmhouse to see what all the fuss was about. Mum plucked Beth from her grandma's arms and, as Mum carried her to the safety of the house, Beth held her grandma's intense gaze until they became enveloped by the gloom of the kitchen and she slid from view.

CHAPTER 4

The day after 'pig day,' Grandma Mary took Beth through fields of tasselled, undulating corn to a point, high above the farm. Mary had borrowed Grandad's old stick to see off the sow, should she appear again. Ahead of them, at the crest of the highest hill, there was a small, round copse of silver birches.

'They're like a silver crown!' Beth remembered saying.

'I've always thought that too,' Mary had replied. 'A crown for a queen made from blood, Bethan.' Grandma Mary always used her full name.

Beth didn't press her for an explanation. Grandma often said fanciful things, usually to make her grandchildren laugh.

The climb to the crown of birches was steep and brought Beth's hot breath into her throat.

'There!' said Mary. 'Craig Gwaed...'

Beth peered through the thicket of low branches and trunks to see something squat and dark in the middle of the copse. She stepped cautiously closer to a gap in the trees. Squinting and leaning forward, she gasped when something dark and red blinked back at her. Then a screech pierced the silence and Beth jumped back into Mary, startling them both. Mary pointed to the sky and Beth saw two elegant birds, floating in the hot air.

'They're hawks, sweetheart,' Mary spoke. 'They guard the Blood Queen.'

Mary took Beth's hand. 'Come along now, she won't bite.'

Beth reluctantly stepped through the gap and into a small clearing. Sitting in the middle, and seeming to wink under the overhead sun, was a blood- red rock the size of a small car.

'Craig Gwaed,' Mary said simply. 'Blood Rock.'

It was beautiful. Facets had either been worn or chipped away, and then turned smooth by the weather. They caught the sun as Beth moved around the rock.

'Touch it,' Mary said.

Beth did.

There was a heat there. A smell of iron.

Mary came alongside her and spoke softly. 'Give me your hand, child.'

Beth did.

Mary separated Beth's thumb from her fingers and held it over the top of the rock. Beth heard a rustling as Mary produced a twinkle of metal from inside her voluminous shawl.

'This won't hurt.'

It did. In the blink of an eye Mary had pricked Beth's thumb and proceeded to squeeze some small droplets of her blood onto the rock's smooth surface. Beth watched in awe as the blood simply melted into the rock itself; as if sucked in.

'There,' Mary added. 'My grandmother did this and now I pass it to you…'

'What, Granny?' Beth asked.

'The gift of blood.'

Beth didn't get it. And, to be honest, Mary was beginning to scare her.

'Did my mum do this?' she asked.

Mary replied quickly and with some finality. 'No. Just us

special ones. Your mum's special, but not in this way. You're young. One day I'll explain. When the blood comes to you. Before then, just between us. You understand?'

Beth nodded, wanting away from the Blood Queen. Wanting the fusty warmth of the farm kitchen and non-scary Granny back. The one who baked bread and saved her from pigs.

Mary didn't mention the Blood Queen again for years and Beth never dared ask. She could keep a secret. From that day though, Beth feared the day the 'blood' would come to her. It sounded vile and painful, like the pricking of her thumb had been.

~·~

Then, last year and on the last day of summer, Beth found herself reluctantly climbing the same steep hill with Mary waddling behind her.

'It's time,' Mary had said. 'We should visit Craig Gwaed again.'

By now, Beth had come to understand what Mary had meant about the blood coming to her. Only it hadn't. Not yet. Her mum had sat her down aged twelve and gone through the whole horrible process. Sienna had cemented it days later, only in a more succinct manner.

'You on the blob yet?' Sienna chirruped one day walking home from school.

Beth practically spat out her full-fat Pepsi. The Pepsi was precious and she had to finish it before her mum caught her drinking sugary drinks.

Beth was aware of the blood rising to her cheeks. 'Course I am,' she lied.

'Plug or towel?' Sienna wasn't going to let it go.

'Oh, towel...' Beth replied, not liking the word plug.

'Plugs for me. Hate that waddling around in a bikini feeling like I'm in a nappy.'

Beth's memory of the conversation is interrupted by Mary. 'Shan't be doing this trip for many moons longer,' her grandma spoke between short gasps of breath. 'Too old and fat.'

'You're not fat, Grandma.' She'd dropped saying 'Granny' after the blood chat with her mum; it seemed to belong to another age.

'Liar.'

Beth laughed.

The sharp cry of a hawk drew her glance to the skies. 'Wow, they're not the same ones are they?'

'You remember?' Mary asked.

Beth rubbed her thumb against her finger. 'Yes.'

Mary linked her arm through Beth's and smiled up at her, leading them into the crown of birches.

'They're Ospreys, live up to nine years... so, who knows?'

Craig Gwaed hadn't lost any of its terrible beauty. It seemed smaller now, but, Beth thought, wasn't that the way with all things, given the passing of time?

Mary ran her own hands over the rock and then rested her head on its smooth top.

'Join me,' she said.

Beth cautiously embraced the warm, red surface. She lay across the rock so that she and Mary were looking straight at each other.

'Do you feel the stirring of your blood?' Mary asked.

Beth flushed and Mary caught the look. She raised her head from the rock. 'Oh, poor child… I thought…'

'Not yet, Grandma.' Beth stood too.

'You're fourteen…'

'Nearly fifteen…'

'Eve pushes you too hard, girl.'

'No, it's okay. I love the running and the training. I'm good at it.'

'Even sound like her now.'

'Is that a bad thing?'

'No. Only Eve doesn't have the gift. Never will. It has skipped her. But you… when you were born…'

Mary stopped talking and seemed to come to a decision. Mary slipped a hand into her shapeless cardigan and pulled it free again, something cupped in her palm. Beth was appalled to see that it was a dead mouse.

'Ewww.'

Mary held her hand flat, exposing the small lifeless shape. 'So sad. Death; it diminishes everything.'

Mary slowly slid the mouse from her palm onto the top of the stone. Beth cast a quizzical look at her.

'Don't look at me, Bethan. Look at the Blood Queen.'

There was a gleam in Mary's eyes, some kind of yearning. Then she reached out and began to softly stroke the mouse.

'Quickly now…' Mary flicked a look to the rock and Beth followed her gaze -just in time to see the mouse twitching. It staggered to its feet, tottering there. Beth had ceased to breathe. Mary took her fingers away. The mouse peered over its shoulders to look at the two of them. It squeaked and skittered away, zigzagging over the side of Craig Gwaed.

'Fuck.' The word popped out of Beth, unwarranted.

'Our gift,' said Mary. 'This is in our gift.'

'What? Was it drugged?' Beth stammered.

'No darling. It was dead. Now it's not.'

'Right, so it's magic? A trick?' Beth was almost laughing at the absurdity of what she had seen.

Mary shook her head.

'Are you a witch?'

Mary snorted. 'Witch is such a misused term. We're not witches.'

'*We're* not? As in *us*?'

'Sweetheart. So much to take in and here you are, not yet in blood. I've been too hasty…'

'Grandma? I mean, come *on*…?'

Mary brushed her hands against her cardigan and linked Beth again, this time leading her away from the Blood Queen and through the trees.

'Remember what I said? Between us?'

'But, like, that was terrifying!'

'You mustn't be afraid, Bethan. I can make sense of it all, when you're older…'

'When I'm bleeding you mean?

'If you like.'

'But I don't like!' Beth could feel a chill turning her insides to water.

'Enough now. Forget this,' Grandma said sternly. 'We can wait until the time is right. You will *feel* it then. And I will be there to help you.'

21

Mary squeezed Beth's arm and suddenly lifted her face and kissed Beth warmly on the cheek.

Beth stared at her grandmother but Mary simply looked ahead, down at the farm, a smile slowly spreading across her lips. Beth scanned her face. The wrinkles by the eyes and the deep grooves at each corner of her mouth. The plump roundness of her cheeks, rosied by the years and the wind; the way strands of wiry grey hair refused to be tamed by the many pins and clips Mary stuffed into them. Beth felt suffused by love and fear, in equal measure.

Two weeks later Grandma Mary was dead.

An embolism, the doctor had said. Grandad Christmas said that it was as if his wife had been a puppet and someone had just cut her strings. There had been no illness, no signs, just a crumpling, a collapse and then nothing.

CHAPTER 5

Now, a full year on, Beth watches her grandad slip the latch to the gate and call for his old collie, Rags, to join him as he lurches up the lane, away from the farm. The sight brings a lump to her throat. He never complains. Never wants any fuss, not even for his birthday. No, all that socialising was down to Mary, he's happy just to see his daughter and her family.

'I don't like it, see?' In his singsong voice. 'That was all Mary; gathered friends like you gathered those hens. They'd sit by the hearth all day, cluck, cluck, cluck. And she'd bake enough bread to feed the entire chapel on a good Sunday and fill 'em so full of tea you'd hear 'em sloshing all the way down the lane.'

This cosy, by-the-hearthside, jam and Bara Brith Granny Mary now seems a little at odds with Beth's memory of her. Blood rock, the gift, the dead mouse, Grandma's promise; all these thoughts teem into Beth's mind every time they have driven back to Wales. Not so long ago, she literally couldn't wait to start her period, join the real world. Now, she dreads it and has never ventured near the queen with her crown of trees since.

Beth slips into baggy joggers and an old *Adventure Time* T-shirt she occasionally sleeps in; Marcelline with her guitar. The whitewashed walls of the landing are smooth and cool to the touch, the stairs crooked and worn, creaking with every step. Pushing open a door, she breathes in the cool, buttery wood-smoke air of the kitchen. She notices the dusty windowsills, spotless in Mary's time. Grandad has hung curling, yellowing tape from the hearth, to catch the flies. Several are stuck there, long dead. A bluebottle buzzes uselessly in a spider's web, high above the dresser.

Beth thinks that she really should offer to clean. Perhaps Mum will. But then again, they're only here for a few days, for the party and to spend time with Grandad before their real summer holiday. Since the blossoming of Mum's 'gym bunny' empire (Dad's words) they've had some pretty exotic summers. Mexico, Vietnam, Cambodia and this summer, scuba diving in the Maldives – 'whilst they're still with us,' Beth heard her mum say. She never knew if Mum was referring to them, her children, or the islands. Eve characteristically channelled her athletic prowess into creating a series of gyms, using her Olympic success as a springboard… a brand. Beth's happy that they have a nice life, but, she always feels the shadow of ambition thrown from her mum; stretching all the way forward from that blazingly hot day in Sydney and clipping at every step Beth takes on the track.

Beth contemplates the trapped bluebottle, its buzzing annoying her, when Mum's voice pipes up.

'Remember the old sow?' Eve asks, appearing in the kind of Lycra that would shame other women of her age.

'I was just thinking about that…'

Mum stands, hands on hips. 'Fancy a run?'

'Yeah, sure. I'll just get changed.'

Upstairs, Beth quickly ties her hair back and chooses a vest from Eve's old dresser. Shorts; it's way too warm for joggers. She laces her bright blue Nike road shoes and bounces back downstairs as Mum fills two water bottles at the sink.

'It's getting hot,' Mum says, 'we'll just do five k, yeah?'

Beth smiles. '*Just* five k..?'

'Lightweight,' Mum replies, smiling. 'Come on.'

They jog up the lane away from the farm, which rises gently and is hemmed in by chest high dry-stone walls, all built by Grandad himself. Here and there they have bulged and split and have stayed that way. There was a time when he'd never have allowed a single stone out of place.

They jog along the single line of grass, which runs down the middle of the lane, either side rutted and potholed by the punishing years of vans and tractors rattling along it. The grass is a riot of dandelion clocks and buttercups. They pass Grandad who laughs.

'I'm jiggered just looking at you two!' he wheezes.

Beth can tell Rags wants to run with them; he twitches, tongue out, staring at Grandad, waiting for the word... but all he gets is a 'stay!'

At the top of the lane Beth starts to turn to the left, following the B road away from Beddgelert, the way they always go. Eve tugs at her arm, dragging her in the opposite direction.

'Where are we going?' Beth asks.

'Surprise,' Eve announces, pressing the timer on her smart watch. 'Keep up!'

Eve sets a twenty-minute five k pace and Beth can feel the burn in her calves, but she does keep up, determined not to start breathing through her mouth until her mum does. I'm as bad as she is, Beth thinks.

The road they follow takes them under huge, towering oaks and Beth realises that she's grateful for the shade. Soon they are following the river and the road bends with it. She catches glimpses of the river, bottle green and glassy, snaking through the trees. She can hear the distant muted roar of the Glaslyn pass, where the river crashes down a dizzyingly narrow gorge, stippled with pine trees and gorse.

Eve slows to a jog, then stops and Beth falls into place beside her. The sweat begins to cool between Beth's shoulder blades in the breeze coming off the river. The air is thick with pine and dust.

'Are we halfway?' Beth asks.

'No. I wanted to show you something,' Her mum takes a swig from her bottle and leans over the waist-high stone wall, planting her hands on its top. 'Look...'

Beth leans over too and sees a steep cliff leading down to the river's edge. Here the waters are running deep and green, whirling into pools under enormous boulders. Eve jumps up onto the wall. 'Come on, we're climbing down!'

'Mum?'

'We're going swimming,' Eve says. Like it's the most natural thing in the world at that moment.

'You're kidding, right?'

'*You* can swim in what you're wearing.'

'You're never getting naked, are you?' Beth is genuinely appalled.

'Well, no, I'm not,' Mum adds and Beth sighs with relief. 'Not *this* time!'

'Mum!'

But she's too late and Eve starts to descend, picking her way carefully.

Beth shouts after her. 'What d'you mean, *this* time!?'

'I used to come here with my mates…' Eve calls back up. 'Come on!'

Beth carefully lowers herself over the wall, watching as her mum drops to the ground, some fifteen feet beneath her, and starts kicking off her shoes. Eve skips over the loose stones and begins to clamber up the biggest, closest rock. Beth's down now and sheds her own shoes, tiptoeing to the water's edge. She dips in a toe.

'It's freezing!'

Eve has reached the top of the rock and lifts her head, arms outstretched, swan-like. 'You'll never get in a toe at a time…'

'Muuum?' But Beth watches as Eve springs, a perfect Y shape, and seems to hover for a split second, before swooping into the water, kissing it, hardly making a ripple.

Beth scrambles up the rock, searching the glassy greenness of the pool for sight of her mum, only to have her bob up a dozen feet downstream, whooping like a child.

'Come on!' she yells, 'it's not that cold once you're in!'

Beth shuffles to the edge. 'Honestly?'

'Honestly!'

One deep breath and she dives, the water enveloping her with an icy suddenness that drives the air from her lungs. Under the water, she can see her mum's pale legs kicking to keep afloat, ghostly greenish white. Long weeds sway in the current on the river's bottom, and then, as Beth twists up and kicks, she can see the sun's rays piercing the gloom in brilliant shafts. Bursting through the surface, she gasps. 'Liar!'

'Well, if I'd told you the truth, you'd still be up on that rock, like a complete loser!'

Eve makes the 'L' sign above her head, laughing.

'*Loser!?*' Beth gasps. 'Promise you'll never do that in public, like, when I'm actually there?' But Beth finds herself laughing too, thinking, '*this* is my mum?'

Beth turns to float on her back, letting the river pull her along, the sun blinking through tall trees.

'See, you're alright now,' Eve calls, straddling that tall rock again.

'That's only 'cos all my major organs have shut down.'

'Bet it's ages since you were bombed.'

'Mum, that's not even an appropriate saying anymore… Oh, wait a minute…'

Cackling with delight, Eve leaps high into the air and folds herself into a bomb, hitting the water with a smack and sending up a ridiculously tall flume of spray.

'What are you – like, *ten*!?' Beth suppresses a giggle.

Eve crosses the pool with a languid stroke, barely creasing the fat, viscous surface. As she plants her feet on the mossy stones, Eve slips and places a hand firmly on Beth's shoulder. Beth finds herself instinctively grasping it, helping her mum stay upright.

'Thanks,' Eve smiles at Beth, squeezing her shoulder for a moment.

'We should dry off before we go back,' Eve says.

'Okay,' Beth realises that her mum is making an effort and loves her for it.

They climb up onto a flat boulder and, finding a square of hot, bright sunlight, lie side by side; eyes closed against the glare, backs already warm.

Minutes pass with only the gurgling of the river and the passing of the odd car above them on the road.

There's something nagging at Beth. 'Okay, I'm scared to ask, but I can't let it go... *when* were you ever naked here??'

Eve snorts with laughter. 'I can't believe I let that slip!'

'Well, it's out now...'

'When I was sixteen or so, last couple of summers here before I left for Uni. We'd come down, bring a picnic. Summers always seemed to be hotter back then...'

'We?'

'Yeah, friends, you know?'

'Naked?'

'Skinny-dipping, if you don't mind. It sounds... more reasonable.'

'With your mates?'

'Yes.'

'Boys?'

'Well, Beth, of *course* with boys, where's the fun otherwise?'

'Names!'

'Well,' Eve giggles at some long buried memory. 'Karen, of course. Her boyfriend. I might have had the odd boy in tow.'

'Muuum!'

'Hey, you asked.'

A terrible thought occurs to Beth. 'Oh, no. Not on this rock...?' She sits up.

'No! Nothing like that. We were dressed out of the water. All very proper.'

Beth gawps at her Mum, astonished.

'Karen was your bestie, right?'

Mum nods.

'You don't see her so much?'

'No, not so much. Busy people…'

For a brief second something darker crosses her mum's face and she looks down at the water pooling beneath them. Then, just as quickly, it's gone and Eve looks back at her daughter. Beth spots the change and begins to regret pushing her mum.

'You should see your face,' Eve smiles.

'What?'

'Anyone would think you were *my* mum!'

Eve reaches up and coaxes Beth's hair into a long loop, coiling it and draping it over her shoulder.

'Don't get cold now…'

'This has been great.' Beth finds that she means it.

Eve smiles. 'Yes, it has hasn't it? Come on, your hair will dry on the run back.'

Beth jumps to her feet as Eve holds out her hand.

'Help an old lady up, will you?'

Beth does, surprised at how light she is.

Eve seems impressed. 'Hello, when did you get to be so strong?'

'What can I say, I work out…'

Eve smiles again and then, shoes on, leads the way back up the cliff of the gorge, gently brushing brambles aside and warning Beth not to get scratched. It's only when she's half way up the wall that Beth feels it. A tingling, a vibration. It must be the blood returning to my frozen fingers, she thinks.

Beth casually looks around, taking in the mossy cliff; a snail, secreted safely among the barbs of the brambles. And there, to her left, just out of reach, something glints. She leans away from the rock, steadying herself, shifting her feet slightly to compensate. Now she can see more clearly. It's a coin… is it? She looks down at her feet and sees that, if she can place her left foot six inches or so along the cliff face, she can reach whatever it is.

Beth does this carefully, testing that this new lip in the rock will take her weight. With the fingers of her right hand gripping a protruding stone tightly, she leans as far as she can reach, the fingers of her left hand stretching out, trying to tease the coin into her grasp. Only it isn't a coin. Her fingertips snag a chain, once silver, and loop it slowly into her palm, pulling the prize closer.

It's a medallion bearing the image of a man; stick in hand, walking through shallow water. He's carrying a child. The medallion has scalloped edges and, on its reverse, what looks like a car… a plane… a boat…? She turns it over in her free hand, digging a thumbnail into the grime that has been encrusted into the medallion's crevices. Then that tingling again, only stronger. And a weird taste at the back of her throat – metallic. She feels slightly dizzy. Is the medallion getting *hotter*? She begins to feel her body sway, becoming detached from the cliff face. In a second Beth pitches backwards, only pulling herself close into the wall at the last moment.

'You okay down there?' Eve peers back over the top of the wall.

'Yeah, I'm fine.' Beth breathes deeply through her nose, clearing her head. I must eat more, she thinks. She scrambles back up the wall and sits for a moment.

'What's that?' asks Eve.

Beth opens up her fist.

'Wow, it's a Saint Christopher.' Her mum lifts it from Beth's palm.

'Yeah?'

'Patron saint of travellers. That's Christ on his shoulders.'

'Really?'

Eve sighs. 'Dear God, we've raised heathens…'

'What's he doing, carrying Christ?'

'He didn't know it was Christ at the time. Thought he had the weight of the world on his shoulders. He was supposed to keep travellers safe.' Eve hands it back.

'It was in the brambles.'

'It's lovely,' Eve says.

For a beat Beth just looks at it, trying to imagine who might have worn it and for how long it had lain there, hidden. The metallic taste is still there. Beth licks her lips.

'Thirsty?' Eve asks.

Beth nods and Eve hands her a bottle.

'Just a jog back, yeah?'

'Yeah…'

On the jog they talk. Or rather, Eve does. That's where she fell off her bike. She had her first kiss in that bus stop. See that mountain, that's Cnicht. Beth tells her it sounds like a sneeze. Laughing, Eve tells her there's a lake up there, wild and colder than the river… one day…

'In your dreams!' Beth says,' or maybe in a wetsuit.' All too soon they are at the top of the lane to the farm, still fresh. Beth has an idea.

'Race you the last two hundred?'

Her mum looks genuinely surprised. 'You. Race *me*?'

'Course, I mean, if you're chicken?' Beth makes the 'L' for loser sign above her head.

'Okay...' Eve says warily.

'On my count of five,' Beth tells her as she crouches. 'One, two, five!'

And, as Eve begins her own crouch, Beth's off, hair loose and trailing, snorting with laughter.

'Oi!' Her mum is after her. Beth can hear the sharp slap of her shoes, gaining.

Beth sucks in the hot air, her lungs and elbows pumping; surely her mum will pass her any moment. But she doesn't and Beth raises her arms, crossing an imaginary line. Eve is right behind her.

'I'm getting older and you're getting faster,' Eve says, barely out of breath.

Arm in arm they troop into the kitchen where they seem to surprise Joe, who is sitting at the huge pockmarked wooden table which dominates the whole room.

He looks up from his newspaper. 'Fun, girls?'

'Just a bit...' Eve replies.

Beth looks at her dad and can't help herself. 'Did Mum ever take you swimming up in the Glaslyn?'

'No... Why?' he asks. Innocently.

Beth glances at her mum to see a huge grin spread across her face. 'Oh, no reason...'

So that her dad can't see her smile too, Beth turns to the Belfast sink and runs the tap, holding the St Christopher under the chill water. Eve pushes Joe's chair around so that she can plonk herself in his lap.

'You're all sweaty,' he complains.

Eve acts mock offended, 'That's no way to talk to a lady.'

Beth looks at them, practically cuddling. Grandad appears in the open doorframe and leans his stick against the wall, where its gnarly head rests in a groove worn there. Indoors, the cap comes off.

He raises his sun-wrinkled map of a face and nods at the medallion.

'What you got there?'

'Patron saint of travellers… he's a bit grimy.'

'Brown sauce. That's what you need. Bit of HP.'

'Can you fix the chain, Grandad?'

'Course, lovely. Leave it with me.'

And, ignoring the start of that now familiar tingling, Beth hands it over, rinsing her hands, flexing her fingers, shaking the feeling away. 'I'm off for a shower.'

Joe pipes up. 'Take your mother with you!'

Her mum giggles and the years seem to slip from her face, sitting in Dad's lap; giddy and sixteen again.

As Beth turns to leave she notices that the bluebottle in the spider's web has now been mummified, its struggles over. It's an image that she takes upstairs with her, until, under the stinging rain of the hot shower, it slowly recedes.

Later, at night, Beth is sitting on the bed with the glow from her laptop pooling around her. She thumbs through week-old messages on her phone. Sienna's thinking of dumping Freddy. Sasha's celebrating her first anniversary with George. Is it all about boys? The getting, the keeping, the losing, the leaving? It seems to be that way for her friends; GCSE exams are a hindrance to them in their tireless pursuit of 'the one.'

34

Sienna's mum, Trish has just cast off her third husband at forty; none of them, it seems, being 'the one' for her, even though she's lingered with them long enough to move up the housing ladder – trying for size, Beth guesses; the houses, that is. Every now and then she would stop going round to Sienna's because divorce had settled over the house like a storm cloud; black and about to burst, making them all miserable. Until the next house and picking wallpaper again.

Sienna's dad had embarked on an affair pretty soon after the announcement of the pregnancy. As Trish memorably put it, 'My piss was hardly dry on the fucking tester!' He dumped her for a younger, less pregnant model. It kind of explains her attitude to men ever since, Beth often thinks.

Beth kills off the messages and plugs earphones in, scrolling through her music library for something suitable for lonely fifteen-year-old single girls in the middle of nowhere. Her dad's made a playlist. He's pretty cool for a dad, when it comes to music that is. Even though he calls his lists 'mix tapes.' She chooses something he has labelled 'ambient', then closes the laptop lid to kill off the light and opens the curtains.

The depth of the blackest nights here always impresses her. There's no light pollution and the stars literally go on forever. She lets the music wash over her and stares at the sky until the individual pricks of light become a milky cloud. The stillness is absolute and she slips into sleep within moments.

CHAPTER 6

It's always the same dream here in Wales. In the dream it's always night. Long shadows spill across the farm's yard; spread like butter by a fat, yellowish moon. Beth walks barefoot across the cool cobbles, totally alone and totally silent. Although she cannot see herself, she can feel from the chill on her skin that she's naked. Something catches her eye, looming from a dark corner. That same huge sow, ears slanting forward, over its eyes, making a mask of its face. In her dream it never charges.

A rook or a blackbird, she's not sure, falls from the sky, folding like a small broken umbrella as it silently hits the ground. It lurches onto one foot and turns its beady gaze on her. She walks past it and heads for the barn where the tall doors are slightly cracked open.

She can hear a twitching in the straw inside. A scuffling noise. She slowly peels the barn doors open, allowing pale light to spread across the barn floor until it illuminates something writhing in the straw at the edge of the bales.

Without seeming to move a muscle, she's across the space between her and the shape in an instant. She looks down. It is a new-born baby girl, arms waving, legs kicking… but weakly. It is smeared with what looks like slime and something dark, like blood. Its mouth is open without making a sound, forming a small black hole. There is a cord wrapped around its neck. Twice. The cord is grey and marbled, like a snake. She reaches down and tries to take it with her fingers, but it tightens on her touch. She pinches at it but it's slippy and tough. She can hear a cracking noise coming from the baby's neck. Its twitching limbs slow to a halt. She stoops down to try and use her teeth but, as her face gets closer, the baby's eyes snap open and they're bulging, gorged with blood.

Beth wakes with a start. Always the same dream, yet she never sees it coming, like you're meant to with recurring dreams. It's like she's an amnesiac, living her life over and over.

It's still early and Beth gets that gnawing feeling in her stomach that she usually tries to ignore. Brushing her teeth often helps, it doesn't get rid of the hunger but she feels as if she's using her mouth for something, so that must count. And besides, the paste must carry calories.

She pads downstairs, aware that Grandad will be the only other person up at this time. The kitchen is gloomy despite having no curtains or blinds. The sun hasn't risen high enough to reach the windows here and the furniture and hearth are shapes, barely discernible. She crosses the cool floor to find the light switch by the door but then stops half way there.

She can hear a buzzing; muffled, frantic. Others join it, closer, louder. She hurries to the door and flicks on the switch, flooding the room with sickly yellowish light as the overhead fluorescent tube stutters into life. Up in the corner, by the ceiling, the spider's web bounces with energy as the bluebottle batters its cocoon against the windowpane. The flies in the tape are making it twitch and swivel as they struggle to get free.

She realises that her hand has remained frozen, the toggle of the switch still between her fingers. She can smell a faint tang of disinfectant and suddenly needs fresh air. The door is only on the latch and she slips out, into the yard, breathing deeply through her mouth and closing the door firmly behind her. She can't hear the buzzing out here. Has Grandad replaced the tape, cleaned out the web? Are all these newly trapped insects? She has her back to the yard, staring at the kitchen door, strangely dreading what is inside.

Beth's feet shift and she feels the dirt beneath them, the chill of the early morning pricking at her skin beneath her T-shirt and pyjama bottoms. Without looking she knows she's being watched and slowly turns to face the yard. A fox sits on the outer wall, looking at her, its jaws caked in blood. There's a beating of feathers in the air and a blackbird wheels down from the sky, insanely flapping one wing whilst the other juts uselessly from its body.

Taking its eyes off Beth for a mere beat, the fox leaps up and snaps the bird in its mouth. The bird twitches and caws pitifully until the fox kills it with a toss of its head. The fox cocks its head sideways, the blackbird lolling over horribly from its mouth and then he coolly regards her, before slipping back over the wall, out of sight.

The dream crashes into Beth's thoughts and for a terrible second she believes that she's actually in it, *now*. She looks towards the barn doors and sees the crack that tells her that they're slightly ajar. Slowly they creak on their hinges as something begins to emerge from inside. She starts to turn and run but her feet slide over the greasy cobbles. Then with a final crunch the doors open wide and she hears a voice.

'Did you see that?' It's Grandad. 'Brazen old bugger! Like he damn well owns the place.'

Grandad leaves the barn door open as he crosses to her. 'Look at the state of you then, white as a sheet.'

Beth looks at him and realises that she's started to shake.

He puts a leathery hand on her shoulder.

'Bless, you're absolutely freezing. What you doing out here?'

'I'm, err. Fresh air…' is all she can say.

'Come on inside, I'll do us some eggs.' He propels her gently to the closed kitchen door and she stands aside to let him open it. Instantly the buzzing is there. To Beth, it seems to fill the air.

'Bloody hell, this stuff's supposed to kill the beggars, not feed 'em up!' Grandad snaps the yellow tape, now alive with flies, from the hearth and marches outside with it. Up by the ceiling the bluebottle now swings by a single thread and beats against the glass.

Beth sees Dad's newspaper, still on the table, and takes it, rolling it into a baton. She grabs a chair, scraping it across the floor and crashing it up against the wall. In one movement she's up on the chair and swinging the paper hard. The swaddled bluebottle splats on the window, leaving a purple bruise on the glass. Grandad's back in, muttering about the flypaper.

'Must've lost its strength.'

She drops down and replaces the chair. 'I'll clean all this up, Grandad.'

'Will you? There's a girl. I'm too old you see and I daren't ask your mum.' He winks conspiratorially at her, sharing the joke.

'Where's the cleaning stuff?' she asks.

'Pantry. You dig it out and I'll get the eggs on.'

The pantry is more of an outhouse, leaning drunkenly against the side of the farm. She walks there on autopilot, a feeling of fear filling her chest, rising like bile. The flies and the bluebottle were dead. The paper didn't fail.

The sun is starting to warm the fields in the distance but the yard smells cold and damp, like wet soil. She feels a sharp point of pain in her thumb and swiftly brings it up to her face.

There is a small button of bright red blood there; where Grandma pricked her so many years ago. This doesn't make sense, Beth thinks. I'm bleeding. Standing still and wiping the blood into the palm of her hand, she is aware that her hunger pangs have grown in intensity. She winces slightly at the pain and then pushes at the pantry door.

The door squeaks open and she flicks a light on, banishing the gloom. There is a cardboard box with a dustpan and brush sticking out of its top and she bends to retrieve them. Dragging the box from under a shelf, she stops and recoils. There, hidden behind it, is a mousetrap. In it, head at an obscene angle, is the long dead, desiccated body of a mouse. It has the spike from the trap jutting through its neck.

Then the feeling starts. She wants it to stop but there's nothing she can do. Beth seems to swell with heat, feeling faint with it. She tries shaking her head, putting her hands over her ears – nothing works. There is a *dragging*, somewhere low, beneath her belly. A loosening. The mouse skeleton lifts its head slowly, bones clicking as they snap. The spike holds it fast. Beth clamps her eyes shut but that makes things worse,

40

seeming to amplify them. Now there's a squealing; high pitched and pitiful. She feels a warm and shaming flood between her thighs. Mary's voice floats through her head, 'when the blood comes…'

She knows what she will see before she opens her eyes and this makes her want to clamp them tighter. But somehow she forces them open and looks down.

The mouse has thickened, fleshed out. Crimson blood spills from its broken neck as it twitches against the spike. Its cries are getting louder. Its back legs scramble frantically to gain some purchase on the floor and its tail swivels crazily from side to side. The heat in her head is cooling and there is a tang of blood on her tongue. Without thinking further she reaches down and prises the trap open.

With a tearing of flesh the mouse is free, although its head is still set grotesquely against its body. It scurries away, out of the pantry door and across the yard. As Beth watches it go, and with a final click, its head straightens and in a second it has disappeared behind the barn.

Now she retches, only there's nothing in her stomach to bring up. She sits back, weakness flooding through her and spits uselessly on the floor. She peers at the spreading patch of blood in her lap. Oh God, she thinks, I've done what Mary did. That mouse came back to life – I know it was me, I did it!

She sits, breathing slowly through her nostrils until her heart is back under control. Only it isn't. Not really. She's terrified. She gathers the brush and pan and kicks the empty trap back under the shelf.

Back in the kitchen the sun has clawed its way through the

windows and suffused the room with a warm glow. Dust dances in its shafts and the air is a fragrant mix of sweet polish and honeyed eggs, thick with melted butter. Her stomach lurches again. The smell has brought Mum down.

'God, are you alright?' she asks as she enters and sees Beth standing in the doorway, legs clamped together.

'Yeah, fine.' Beth's abrupt, not wanting to stay in there a moment longer.

'Your eggs are ready,' Grandad sings from the hearth.

'Not hungry, Grandad. Going for a shower.'

'Beth?' Mum asks.

'I'll have some later, okay?'

Beth slips past her mum and runs upstairs to her room. She can hear their muffled voices as she grabs her towel and slips quickly across the landing into the bathroom. She kicks her pyjama bottoms off and fills the sink with steaming water. Scrabbling through the contents of the cabinet reveals that at least one decision has been taken for her. Plug or towel – no contest, Mum only has tampons. Sienna would be thrilled.

She plunges the pyjamas in and out of the water, the heat stinging her hands as the sink foams red. The pain is a welcome distraction from what happened in the pantry. This was what Mary had foretold. With the blood comes the 'gift.' Only Beth doesn't want the gift, thanks all the same. Jesus, what the actual fuck, she thinks harshly. The bluebottle, the flies, are all of these down to her too?

There is a mounting sense of panic gripping her and her breaths start to come in small gulps. She sits on the edge of the bath, dripping pink water on the tiled floor, her mind racing; can I control it? Can I cause it to stop? Can I tell anyone? Right, like anyone who is actually sane, would listen for a single second longer, after she utters the words 'dead things.' They'd have her committed. Maybe Sienna?

Thinking about her best friend seems to help. It's normal. It's real and she needs real right now. Maybe today will prove to be a one-off? The day she started her period, triggering this, this... *horror*?

She rinses the sink out and wrings as much water from her pyjamas as she can. Then she gets in the shower and scrubs the drying blood from her legs. The cramping has calmed down a bit and so has the flowing from her body. She begins to hatch a plan, of sorts. Stay indoors, at least until they leave for holiday, a mere three days from now. Stay away from... stuff. Anything that might trigger another... she struggles to find the word; incident? Incident will do for now.

CHAPTER 7

The noise in the kitchen dies as she walks in. Dad's preparing lunch as Grandad tries to keep up with Max's explanation of Clash of Clans. They hunch over Max's iPhone.

'Who are those little fat fellers on the pigs?'

'Hog riders, Grandad. And, what you do is… aw piss…'

'Don't swear, Max!' Dad calls over his shoulder.

'Signal's gone again!' Max howls.

All the time Beth stares at her mum, who now lifts her head from a book.

'Good shower?' she asks neutrally.

'Yeah. Thanks.'

'Marvellous, isn't it? What you can do on these things.' Grandad tries to calm Max.

'My old man wouldn't even have one in the house. And in those days, they were fixed to the wall! He used to say, "if I want to talk to someone, I'll go out and find them." Different when I took over, like. Your Grandma was never off the bloody thing.'

Max sniggers. He loves it when Grandad swears.

'People would call all the time you see? For advice and that. She was well thought of…'

He trails off and Dad turns to look at him. A sad smile breaks across Grandad's face.

'When's lunch ready?' Beth asks.

'One,' Dad replies.

'What is it?' asks Max.

'Seafood linguine.'

'Pasta and prawns then,' adds Grandad.

'Great. I'm starving,' and Beth realises that this is true. She is starving.

Eve looks at her, sensing something. 'Fancy another run?' she asks.

'Erm, not today Mum…' Beth looks up at the ceiling and sees that Grandad has hung some fresh flypaper. 'I'll just have a stroll…'

As Beth steps into the yard, she can feel someone following her. It's Eve.

'Everything alright?' she asks.

'Oh. Yes. I've got my period.'

Eve seems to melt a little. She takes Beth into a strong embrace. 'Oh, my little girl…'

'I'm okay, Mum…' Apart from the death thing.

'What have you used?' Eve breaks the hug and puts Beth at arm's length, keeping hold of her shoulders.

'Found some of your stuff, in the cabinet.'

Eve nods sagely. 'Oh, well, well, well.' She puffs out her cheeks and sighs. 'We'll get you your own from town.'

'Thanks.'

'Still going for that stroll?'

Beth nods and Eve links her as they start off up the path. Mother and daughter, bonded by blood.

~·~

Beth doesn't know why, other than feeling inexorably drawn

there, but she starts to steer her mother up the hill leading to Craig Gwaed.

'Not been up here for a while,' Eve comments. 'Years…'

With lead in her legs Beth, steps past the silver birches. The rock seems to literally vibrate in the air and she finds herself bending to embrace it. Eve is talking behind her, something about hawks, but the words fade away.

Beth begins to hear what she believes is her blood, roaring through her veins. She lays her face against the warm stone and can feel a current running through her, into the rock. It seems to loop back into her and she can feel her pulse racing. It's as if the rock has traced every last drop of iron in her blood and magnetised her, pinning her to its face.

Images flit through her mind. Images from her dream. The night. The barn. The shadows. The baby. Then an awful image, with blinding clarity; that baby, coil around its neck, lying on top of the rock itself. Wailing and kicking.

Beth jumps back from the rock as if stung. The connection is broken and the images stop. She sits heavily on the grass. Eve's face pops into view, concerned.

'Beth?'

Beth gasps. 'Just a cramp, y'know?'

Eve helps her up, looking around. 'Always given me the creeps, this place.'

Beth doesn't trust herself to speak.

Eve continues. 'Your gran insisted on dragging me up here. Used to dig my heels in, drove her round the bend.'

Beth manages a wan smile. 'Let's go.'

'Course,' says Eve. 'I've got painkillers if you want?'

'No, I'm okay, Mum, promise.' You don't have pills for

what I need…

They step back into the kitchen just as an angry Max stomps past Beth on his way up the stairs.

'Get a better signal if I hang out of my window…' he is shouting.

Dad opens his mouth to speak, but swallows his unspoken words back down. Grandad is reddening, he finds Max's 'moods' frustrating, sometimes accusing him of being spoiled. Eve intervenes.

'Go after him, Beth, please?'

Beth's grateful for the chance to escape and trots up after Max.

She swings through Max's door and finds him sitting on top of his wardrobe, lifting the phone to the ceiling.

'Max, come down.'

'Can't. I'm stuck.'

'Seriously,' she whispers, under her breath. 'Hand me your phone.'

'Piss off.'

'Suit yourself.'

And she turns to leave him there, that forbidden word' twat' on the tip of her tongue. Then she sees a glass bowl, turned upside down on Max's windowsill. The sharp sun glances off it, obscuring whatever is inside, so she goes closer.

It's a butterfly. Dazzling. Beautiful. And dead.

'Max, you absolute twat! You've killed this!'

'Don't call me twat! Gonna tell Mum…'

'Yeah? I'll tell her you killed a butterfly…'

God, she thinks, I'm squabbling like a nine-year-old. She

turns to Max, but he springs lightly and expertly from the wardrobe, bounces off his bed and is through the door without a backwards look.

She goes over to the window. The butterfly lies still; opalescent wings brilliant green against darkest black. The surface of the bowl is hot to her touch as she slowly lifts it away. She extends her fingers until they brush the silken wings.

There is no air in the room. Just the heat from the closed window. With one fingernail Beth tries to coax the butterfly into action. Nothing. Now something different fills her. Not any fear, but a slight disappointment. Dead and rotten mice; yes. Flies and disgusting bluebottles; not a problem, she thinks. Beautiful butterfly? No.

She unlatches the window, which eases open with a sigh of hot air. What little breeze outside faintly disturbs the wings of the butterfly. Suddenly she feels immensely sad. Does she have a gift but no power to control it? What use is that? Her eyes feel hot, like she's about to cry.

She dabs at her eyes with her sleeve and turns from the window. Then she feels it. And hears it. A buzzing at first, so that she thinks she's hearing an insect. But this is inside her head. She turns in the doorway just in time to see the butterfly lift crazily from the sill and stagger out of the open window. For a second it plummets down but then weaves triumphantly back into view and swiftly disappears into a green and black dot against a blazingly blue sky.

So, I *can* do both, Beth thinks.

And closing the door behind her, she walks away, her dreadful secret swallowed back down.

CHAPTER 8

O f course, over the next two days, Beth almost convinces herself that she's imagined it all. Is this what periods *do* to you? 'Goin' doolally,' Grandad would say... of himself.

Eve has tried to get her running again but she's played the period card. Beth can see this upsets her mum, but she doesn't care. She *has* to stay indoors – away from... *things.* But then, just staying away from bad things doesn't mean they are going to stop occurring.

Beth is the only one to actually see it happen. The day before they are due to leave for the Maldives, she leans on her windowsill feeling the sun on her face. She sees Grandad crossing the yard, leaning heavily on his stick, Rags trotting in front of him. Something moves in the corner of her vision and she glances quickly enough to see a shadow being thrown against the far wall of the barn. She squints against the glare to make it out and then wishes she hadn't. It's pig-shaped. Big pig-shaped. But Grandad doesn't have a pig anymore. She throws the window open and shouts down.

'Grandad!'

He turns to look up, and in doing so seems to misplace his stick, which is going forward for him to lean on. It slips off a cobble and he goes down, trying to regain his lost balance. His right leg twists horribly beneath him, at the ankle, and he howls with the pain. Rags starts barking. The pig-shadow has gone.

She's off the bed and downstairs quickly, passing Mum on

the landing.

'Well…' Eve says sarcastically, '*you've* found your feet…'

'It's Grandad!' Beth tells her, watching the shock register on her smug features.

Grandad's foot is facing the wrong way and he is as pale as the moon. Rags whimpers, not knowing what to do. The ambulance takes thirty minutes. *Thirty* minutes! They give him oxygen and lift him gently into its cool interior. Dad and Max have gone fishing and so Mum tries in vain to call him on his mobile.

'Jesus Christ!' she cries. 'Fucking signal!'

She never swears.

'Come on,' she orders Beth, 'jump in the car.'

'What? Why?' Beth realises that she's been searching the farm for shadows.

'The hospital. We're following the ambulance.'

The hospital. In Bangor. All of an hour away and full of death.

'I… I can't.' Beth mutters pathetically.

'What?'

'I'll stay here. Dad has to know…'

The ambulance is pulling away and so Eve has no choice. She stares at Beth for a beat then runs to her Jeep, slams the door and screeches out of the yard.

As the sound of the engines dwindles, a hush falls over the yard. She can't even hear the birds. It's windless and hot.

Beth looks all around her. Grandad's stick lies where he dropped it and so she stoops to pick it up. She takes a second to feel the smooth, knotty head. He'll be okay, Beth tells herself. I'd just have got in the way, Mum can cope. She rises and looks up. There, at the corner of the barn, is the huge sow.

Its ears cast unfathomable shadows over its eyes. It does not move. But, Beth does, slowly, one foot at a time, the stick held out before her. The kitchen door is just feet away and still wide open where Mum left it. The sow just stares, its bulky head turning inch by inch to watch her go, until she can feel the shadow of the kitchen on her shoulder. Then, in a sudden burst of speed, she's inside and bolting the door.

Breathing hard she goes over to the window to peer back out. She sees the barn, but no sow. No pig of any description. Equally, she thinks, no pig could live to be that age! Okay, it didn't *look* dead, but then, neither did the mouse – not after she'd finished with it.

But it's just *so* huge. Surely I'd have felt something if I'd done it? Beth argues with herself. Yeah, that's right, it must be someone else's pig. It must have got loose from the neighbouring farm. She should tell Grandad. When he gets back. She runs upstairs and jumps onto her bed, drawing her knees up to her chin and hugging them.

She is still like this an hour later when Dad and Max arrive.

~·~

It turns out that Grandad has broken his ankle and Beth is summoned to a family meeting. Mum breaks the disastrous news.

'We're staying here. For the summer.'

Beth feels sick. 'Mum, we can't!'

'Is this a "we can't" like the "I can't" go to hospital?'

'I'm sorry…' If only her mum knew how sorry. 'This is different.'

'I hate flying anyway,' Max pipes up.

'Shut up, Max,' Beth snaps.

'Don't snap at your brother,' Mum again.

'Yeah, Beth,' Max taunts.

'Dad…?' she is about to beg.

'We've already decided, Beth,' Mum speaks for Dad. Until he speaks for himself.

'Your mother's right. The Maldives can wait.'

'I thought they were drowning?' Max adds, stupidly.

'My dad needs us. It's final.' Mum's last words. Or they would have been if Beth had left it alone.

'But he's in hospital, they'll look after him there.'

Eve seizes the chance. 'Ah great, is this what we've got to look forward to?'

Joe casts a nervy glance in her direction, as if to say, 'not now…'

'We'd better watch ourselves when we're older Joe. Turn an ankle, bit of a sprain, and our daughter will have us sectioned.'

'No, I didn't mean…'

Dad speaks. 'Look, Beth, this is difficult, but we just can't leave now. Your grandad means the world to you…'

'I'm not saying he doesn't.'

'Well then,' Mum adds, 'what's one little holiday hey? After all the places we've been. All the places I've taken you to?'

Beth starts at the 'I've' and checks her dad's reaction. He looks into his lap.

'Mum, I know all that…'

'What is it, Beth?' her mum asks, gently.

Beth feels an absurd Sixth Sense moment coming; 'I see dead things…' But of course doesn't say it. With Beth it'd have to be, 'I bring back animals, flies are my speciality.'

Instead, she mutters. 'Nothing. It's nothing. When will he be out?'

Dad's relief fills the room. 'When they get the cast on. Few days with rest.'

Mum's not finished. 'We should visit…'

Beth nods mutely. This is unavoidable. Right now, everything seems unavoidable.

~·~

God how she hates hospitals. Bangor is huge with endless, empty, sunlit corridors. Where do they keep all the sick people? Grandad's ward however, is full of old men, hollow cheeked, waiting to die. One lies in an adult nappy and is moaning, slack-jawed, caught up in some terrible dream. The ward stinks of piss and disinfectant.

'Hi Grandad,' Beth feels ashamed at leaving him and her mum alone in the yard now.

'Don't mind moaning Maurice over there. Should be in renal they reckon, but they don't have the beds.'

Eve has gone for coffee and Max is flicking through a gaming magazine.

'I hate hospitals too,' Grandad smiles at her. 'Full of farty old men like me.'

'You're not farty.'

'How would you know?' He sees her look. 'Oh, I'm not

53

having a go. No, I wouldn't visit me either, given the choice.'

'They give me the creeps.'

'Ah, that'll be the cheery disposition of the inmates. That and the death.' But he's still smiling and she smiles back.

'Grandad, does the farm next door have a big sow... y'know, a pig?'

'The Joneses?'

'They're actually called Jones?'

'Sweetheart, in Wales you can't spit in the street without hitting a Jones.'

She smiles again. He's really trying to put me at ease, Beth thinks.

'No they don't. Not last time I looked that is. Why?'

'Nothing.' Everything actually.

'I'll tell your mam not to bring you again. Miserable place.'

Her mum arrives with a scolding coffee she has to leave behind when time is up. They drive back to the farm in near silence, field after field flashing past the car windows. Endless green flecked with white sheep and then the sea, opal blue and still as a mirror.

All this beauty she thinks, and all this death. Where do I fit in? What's in my future? Who can I tell, who will listen and understand? Beth closes her eyes to it all and plugs in her iPhone, letting Dad's latest playlist start and Pip Millett's glorious voice flood into her head...

CHAPTER 9

It seems weird getting texts from her friends. As the days go by she feels more and more sucked into life here and messages from Sienna may as well be from outer space.

'*OMG. Crying face. Pile of poo*,' she texts when Beth tells her about the Maldives. '*Ur life is over for summer*,' Sienna adds thoughtfully. Then she sends a red stiletto and a cocktail, as if they have anything to do with what Beth is feeling about what her life is right now. Deep, cold, outer space.

They have developed a rhythm since Grandad returned. Mum runs. Beth doesn't. Dad commutes back and forth to work in Manchester. Max runs wild.

Grandad sits by the kitchen hearth, in his favourite chair, which Dad has dragged from the living room. It's like Grandad, saggy and comfortable; worn and frayed. His hand still opens and closes over the stick, settling into the grooves worn there and fitting so well that his fingers actually become the stick, like marbling.

Eve says he must exercise or he'll 'slip downhill.' She marches him around the kitchen whilst he swears under his breath, mostly in Welsh, which only Eve understands and scolds him for it.

Max has four dead butterflies under his bowl but they're none of Beth's business and she stays out of his room. Soon summer will be over but no one is talking about it, least of all Mum. Sienna's having an end of summer gathering at hers and Beth is counting the minutes...

Then the day Max goes missing arrives.

She's sitting with Grandad. On a stool at the foot of his chair.

'This heatwave's going to break soon,' he tells her. 'Not been this hot since seventy-six.'

'Eighteen-seventy-six, Grandad?'

'Cheeky mare. See that old biscuit tin. Top shelf, above the fire?'

She nods.

'Fetch it down.'

He flips the lid and dozens of old photos spill out. Vivid reds and blues. Grainy black and whites. Curled and musty. He rustles through them, chatting as he does.

'You know what this farm's called?

'Yeah, Craig Gwead'

'Know what it means?'

Boy, does she know. 'Duh, Blood Rock.'

'Duh yourself, missy. Mary's favourite spot. Ahh, here we go…'

He hands her an ancient looking black and white picture of a couple standing stiffly outside the front door. The door no one ever uses. They are scowling.

'My nan and grandad,' Grandad explains. 'Only ever picture of them. On their wedding day.'

'They don't look very happy.'

'Oh, you didn't dare smile in them days, exposure on the camera took too long, you'd end up gritting your teeth and looking like barmpots. Been in the family generations, this place. Hah, right…' He has found another picture.

'Nineteen seventy-six. The year your mam was born. I had

56

an old Leica then.'

'Is that a car?'

'Would you tease a feeble old man?'

'No,' she answers truthfully. 'Anyway, you're not feeble.'

He winks at her. 'It was a camera. Here, look.'

He hands her two faded colour pictures. In one Grandma sits in this very chair, her hands folded underneath her massive, swollen belly.

'That's your grandma, expecting with your mam.'

She smiles. Her grandma looks happy. Swollen and happy.

'The next's of her and her own mam. Day the baby Eve was born.'

She slides this next picture over and the breath halts in Beth's throat. There's her grandma again, only this time she's standing in the yard. She dwarfs the smaller woman at her side, who stares malevolently at the camera. The traditional Welsh bonnet you see on fudge boxes doesn't soften the hardness in her face. In the background, in the shade of a wall and half hidden, is a huge pig.

'Hotter than hell that day. Your mam was born into a furnace.'

'Whose is the pig?' she manages to ask.

'One of ours. We always had pigs. Dunno which one that was though... your nan took care of them. Your great-gran hated having her photo taken, can you tell?'

He laughs at the memory. 'This is one of her smiling...' he jokes. 'Used to actually leave the room if I so much as took the camera out of its case.'

But he's cut short as her mum blusters in.

'Max should have been back hours ago. Go and fetch him

will you, Beth?'

'I don't know where he is.'

'By the stream he said. He's taken a jar and a net.'

Beth's annoyed. And a little scared. 'What's wrong with his bedroom and Clash of Clans?'

'Confiscated,' Mum adds briskly. 'Off you go.'

'Phone him.'

'Tried. Straight to messages.'

'Text him then, better chance of getting through.'

Mum draws a deep breath. 'Just go, Beth. Now.'

Beth angrily tosses the pictures into the open biscuit tin and stomps out, imagining the swapped looks between Mum and Grandad. And not caring.

~·~

The stream is about fifteen minutes away and the day is boiling hot. Again. God, she's being haunted by pigs! She's fuming; literally. The gate snaps behind her as she leaves the lane.

The stream runs in a tight little gully, dipping out of the treeline of Gwilym's Wood. Part of the wood belongs to Grandad. It grows thick and lush on the crown of the nearest and highest hill to the farm. Under the shade of the trees the stream swells into pools every now and then. You can catch trout there, or, in Max's case, probably nothing.

By the time she reaches the treeline she's sweating and regrets stomping out like that, without changing into shorts. Her joggers feel glued to her thighs and her T-shirt has stuck to her. She's also not bothered to tie her hair back and it hangs lank and lifeless around her neck, like an unwanted scarf.

She stoops at the side of the stream and dips her hands into its cooling waters, scooping some over her face and down her top. She realises that she looks stupid, half wet like this, as if she's sweated the lot, and so she sticks her whole head under, taking the water into her mouth and spitting it out when she rises. Now she's properly wet and doesn't give a toss.

She looks up at the treetops. There's not a breath of wind to stir them. They seem unnaturally still, like they're guarding the wood, saying, 'don't go in…' There's only the gurgle of the stream to break the quiet. She scans the cloudless skyline for movement and sees a hawk, wings a blur as it hovers over a field, just yards away. Another life about to be snuffed out, she thinks. She turns from the stream and enters the wood.

Away from the sun, her wet clothes feel cold against her skin and she regrets not wearing a bra. Bloody Max. She marches upstream as the hill rises beneath her feet. It's so quiet here, deathly quiet. She's about to lose all patience and shout out for him when she sees an upturned glass jar, lying on the bank.

Feet away from it, there's a net; discarded. She increases her pace now, hearing the rush of water as the hill grows steeper and the stream races past. She knows there are pools over the top of the next rise. Pools deep enough to swim in, deep enough to drown in…

She's just about to break into a run when she sees two bare feet sticking out of the ferns. They shift slightly and Max slips into view. He sees her and immediately sticks a finger to his lips.

'Shhh.'

'What?' she mouths, silently.

Max shakes his head, as if even looking is a bad idea; but she ignores him and takes another step.

He waves his hands at her, motioning her to lay low. She's almost too angry to play silly games but he looks genuinely spooked. So, down she goes, crawling on all fours to peek through the ferns into the glade that shelters the pools.

There's Trev, flat on his stomach, sleeves rolled up and sticking his arm into the closest pool. He is perfectly still, facing away from them. Then, in an instant, he flicks his arm out of the water and something silver flies over his shoulder onto the bank.

It's a small trout, bouncing off the grass in an effort to get back into the water. She looks around and sees about five or six similar sized fish. These aren't bouncing. Trev is over to the live fish – quick as a fox – smashing it over its head with a small rock he has in his other hand. The fish shudders and is still. Trev is still hunkered over the trout and hasn't looked up once. She pushes at Max's shoulder, wanting to get away. Desperate to get away.

'Don't go on my account...'

Trev's voice makes her jump.

'The kid's been watching me half an hour now. S'that right Maxie?'

Max nods. She realises they look stupid hiding in the ferns and she gets up. Max stands by her side, closely.

Trev looks at them, still squatting. 'You're wet.'

Too late she crosses her arms, covering her chest.

'This my Grandad's stream,' says Max, belligerently.

'Land's his,' replies Trev. 'But water comes from up there.'

He nods behind him, up the hill. 'Fish are just visiting…'

'They were…' She's surprised to hear that her own voice is steady. 'Until you fished them out.'

'Do you see any gear?' he asks, gesturing around. 'Them fish just threw themselves out. I did them a favour, stopped 'em from drowning. Don't like to see creatures suffering.'

'You tickled them out,' Max won't give up.

'I wouldn't know about that…' Trev's cocky now, enjoying himself. 'Although it has been said that I'm a wicked tickler… by those who know…'

His look goes straight through her. Through her defensive arms, through her wet top.

'You like a bit of tickling?' he asks her. 'I had a thought last year you might've been ready…'

She casts a glance down at Max and then back at Trev. She wants to say, 'not in front of my brother' but doesn't know exactly what she's scared of. It's broad daylight and Trev works for Grandad. But he has this sick, glassy look in his eyes and she can feel her cheeks burn. She's ashamed that he has frightened her and feels the need to fight back.

'Those trout are too small.'

'Oh, expert are you?' Trev takes a step forward, over the dead fish. Then another step, wiping his wet hand on his trousers. She feels something moving in her chest. A surge of blood. Anger and fear in equal measure. She instinctively places an arm around Max's shoulders.

'No, but I could ask Grandad, see what he says…'

Trev smirks at her, still walking slowly towards them. There's a pounding at her temples but she doesn't want to run. Not with Max.

'I heard he did his ankle. Not moving so well…' Trev's close now.

Right, she thinks, do something! Run, scream. Just. Do. Something.

She bunches her free hand into a fist, nails digging into her palm. She can smell Trev; sweat, oil and beer…

She hears the first splash before she sees anything. So does Trev and he slowly turns his head to see. Another splash. She doesn't take her eyes off him but Max shifts from under her arm.

'Wow!' he exclaims.

'Bugger…!' Trev drops away from them, back to the pool. Her gaze follows his broad back and then she looks beyond him to the pool's edge. Just in time to see the three remaining fish bouncing, almost together, up into arcs that quickly take them back into the water with three triumphant splashes.

Trev arrives at the bank, only to watch them swim safely away. He twists his upper body around to look at them, his forehead creasing, making a monobrow.

She realises that she hasn't been breathing for what seems minutes now and gulps some air in. The roar of blood in her head eases.

'You're a shit poacher!' Max gloats.

Trev is dumbstruck. Struggling to make sense of what he's seen.

'You're right,' she says, 'they're not suffering now. No need for Grandad to know.'

She can see the anger building up inside him and feels the fear returning. But then, just as suddenly as he swells with rage, he deflates. The switch is amazing.

'Yeah, didn't I tell you? Magic fingers…' His smile is awful but she understands, they can go.

She turns quickly and drags a grinning Max with her. They scoop up his net and jar and walk swiftly from the woods.

'Trev's a retard,' Max decides.

'No he's not,' she says. 'Don't let him fool you and don't use that word.'

'Should we tell anyone?' he asks.

She thinks of the dead fish, springing back into the water. 'Nah, what's the point? The fish have gone, he'd just deny it?'

'He should have killed them properly. Like I said, retard.'

This time she lets the word slide, grateful that Max will forget what he has just witnessed. She doesn't want complications, she has enough in her head to keep her busy. Trev worries her though. He's not thick but now she's convinced that he is really, actually, dangerous.

~·~

Sometime into the night she slips into a dream. She's in bed and can see moonlight seep across the ceiling. She hears her door open and turns to look. Trev's there, shirt off and sweaty from working in the yard. He stands in the doorway, filling it.

'You're wet,' he says.

She feels a shift in her chest, a tightening at the base of her throat. She slides the covers from her bed and holds out her hand. Beckoning. He lumbers forward, fumbling with his belt. She feels her dry lips part.

Then there's a tap at her window. A single tap. She turns to

63

look but sees no shadow cast against the curtains. She looks back but Trev has gone. Another tap. Harder. Then scratching. She kneels to open the curtains but they seem to peel apart as she reaches for them. Grandma Mary smiles at her. Mary taps on the window again, her finger bony and white. She slowly tilts her head, 'let me in' she seems to say, but no words come from her lifeless lips.

'Breathe,' Beth thinks. 'Breathe.' She wants to move but can't. She needs to wee really badly. Grandma scratches. She tries to shout but is hoarse with terror. Her body convulses with the wasted effort. Grandma smiles again and then speaks with a voice that isn't hers.

'I'm lonely Beth, bring me back?'

She pisses herself. And wakes up.

CHAPTER 10

'Mum, I want to go with Dad.'

'Have you put a wash on?' her mum enquires. Beth ignores the question.

'To Manchester. I can stay with Sienna when he's at work, come back at the weekend?'

'I hope you used conditioner.'

'Mum, listen!'

'No, Beth. You're too young to stay on your own and Sienna's too…' she trails off.

'Sienna's too what!?' Beth asks, getting angry.

'Too… I don't know! She gets too much of her own way.'

'What's that supposed to mean?'

'Too much freedom.'

'Jesus!'

'Please, don't let's argue?'

'Mum, I *need* to get away.'

'Why?'

'I just do.'

'"Just" isn't good enough.'

'Stop treating me like I'm twelve.'

'Then stop acting like it.'

'Why are you being such a bitch?' Beth can't believe she actually said it.

'Beth!?' Mum's face flushes scarlet. 'Apologise!'

'No!'

'Is this about a boy? Is that it?'

'Yeah, like you'd ever let me *near* anything in trousers!'

She's aware that this has got completely over the top. Quickly, out of nothing. Well, not nothing.

'Whoa, when have we *ever* stopped you?'

Beth interrupts her. 'There's no boy. I want to see my friends, okay?'

'Why don't you run with me anymore?'

'Don't feel like it.'

'Are you punishing me?'

She mumbles. 'No.'

They both take a breath. She can see how much she's hurt her mum, made her angry. But Eve's made *her* angry too. Now she can't back down.

Eve has walked to lean over the sink, her spine clearly visible under her running top as she breathes.

'I want you here. With your family.'

'Dad's family too. In case you'd forgotten.'

'What?'

'The way you treat him, like he's nothing, like it's all you…'

She has no idea where these words come from, but they feel right. In this moment, they feel dead right.

'You know what, Beth? If you were twelve I could send you to your room, ground you. But you're fifteen for Christ's sake!'

'Yeah Mum, like you've ever known what it's like to be fifteen!'

She knows she's losing so she's out through the door, vaulting a side gate into a field and wading through knee high grass, still dewy from the night. Beth expects to hear Mum's voice calling after her, but there's nothing. She thinks of her mum crying over her daughter's show of spite, sobbing.

Part of her wants to turn back and hug Eve, saying sorry. Over and over. But another part of her drives the anger on, a kind of hatred boiling in her stomach. It bubbles and rises until she has to spit.

She doesn't stop marching until she reaches Porthmadog High Street. The late summer day has brought crowds onto the street and she can smell fish and chips, sun tan lotion, hot tarmac and petrol fumes.

She slips between families; garish clothes, skin burned pink, yappy dogs. She makes for the harbour, passing topless, tattooed men swigging strong lager and dropping crabbing lines into the water. She's vaguely aware of a bustling behind her, a feeling of being overtaken. There's a hand clamped on her shoulder and she's spun around. Face to face with Susie and three of her mates.

'Slow down, princess. What's the hurry?'

Susie wears skin-tight marbled jeans and a black crop top; hair stretched back from her forehead and piled into a ridiculous fountain. Her belly button is pierced, loops dangle from her ears.

'Get off me.' Beth feels emboldened by being in public.

Susie tightens her grip, oblivious to the people around her.

'You stay away from Trev, right?'

The dream flashes back into her mind and Beth knows that she has guilt written all over her face.

'I know you fancy him. So much as look at him again and I will fuck you up proper.'

Her face is inches from Susie's. She sees herself gouging at Susie's prefect eyes with her nails. Biting at her ears, snapping those loops from the lobes. Slashing and slashing.

'Got it, skinny bint?'

'Yes,' Beth says.

Susie relaxes her grip and Beth shakes herself loose. People's faces are a blur as she crosses the Cob road bridge, past the Ffestiniog Railway Station, over the narrow gauge tracks and down the rocky sidings onto the sand.

She snatches at her shoes, taking them off and strides, barefoot over the mud towards Ballast Island. The island is a small, neglected mound of discarded rocks, ballast from many of the old ships that used to clutter the harbour. A small yacht lies there, long since abandoned and wreathed in seaweed. The open cabin is a dark mouth, sand banked up at its entrance.

The rank mud starts to squeeze obscenely between her toes, sucking her ankle-deep in places. Each footstep squelches, loosening the stench of mud-gas; eggy and foul.

She pulls herself free and heads across the sea grass to where the sun has dried the sand into a hard crust. This is like another world. A world of her own making, where she should be queen, but she's not. In fact she has no control at all. The opposite.

She reaches the middle of the bay and looks back. The sky is immense. It dwarves the distant Snowdon, making the mountain peaks look like so many ragged teeth. The sea has withdrawn so far she can't even see it. Just a hint of its roar on the breeze, the smell of its salt.

Out here it's just her. Her and her awful fucking curse of a gift. She lies in the sand, lets it blow softly into her eyes and hair, feels it filling her ears; wanting it to cover her over until only a shape remains. She lies here for what seems like hours but can only be minutes. And then she opens her mouth and howls until she is snotty and her breath is jagged. She is lost.

CHAPTER 11

She has lain here for so long that she can smell the heat coming off her skin and hair. She feels the wind shift up a notch and senses that the tide has turned. Perhaps I should lie here until the sea washes over me and claims me too, she thinks.

'Don't wallow,' Mum would say, sometimes after Beth had lost a race. Fine for her, she never lost. There are times when it's more than okay to wallow. I've got plenty to wallow about, she thinks. I deserve it, I've earned it.

Her lips are parched and crusty. She really should move.

There's a weird popping noise at her feet and she sits up stiffly. There's a black shell sticking up out of the sand, a metre away. It looks like a clam, quite big. It's open.

Just as she staggers to her feet, another shell pops up out of the crust, gaping. Then another, and another. They keep coming. Pop, pop, pop. She steps cautiously over and bends to pick one out. They are clam shells. Inside there is a dried, shrivelled, long dead clam, like a piece of old orange peel. As she turns the shell over in her hand the clam starts to thicken and to moisten. The smell returns and salty water starts to spill through her fingers as the clam comes alive. She should be horrified but she's not. It's a clam, she reasons, what can it do to me?

She tosses it back on to the sand and starts to walk away. Pop, pop, pop goes the sound behind her as she walks for home and the beach gives up its dead as an offering to her gift.

~·~

Back on the high street she searches for signs of Susie and her scrunchy gang. The shadows are longer now and the crowds have thinned. They would be easy to spot. Next time she won't be as scared. Next time I'll smack her in her perfect face, she thinks maliciously. Maybe. A car horn sounds and her dad pulls up alongside her.

'Want a lift?' He smiles.

They drive out past the old abandoned cinema, windows boarded, paint peeling. A relic of happier times. She remembers its mildewed seats, chocolate covered raisins, Harry Potter. Innocent times she can never get back.

'You're quiet?' Dad prompts.

'Had a row with Mum.'

He breathes deeply.

'I wanted to come home with you.'

'Ahhh...' He reaches for the window button and warm air fills the car. 'Well, you know...'

'It doesn't matter, Dad. It's done.'

They drive through Tremadoc's small square and turn towards Beddgelert. The river estuary glows in the late afternoon sun.

She feels sorry for her dad, stuck in the middle. 'How's work?'

'Erm, work's okay...' He lowers the window further. 'Max behaving?'

'Yeah, s'pose...' She looks at his profile. He looks back, smiling sheepishly.

'Got the new Grimes' album,' he announces proudly.

'Dad, you're too old for Grimes.'

'It's in the glove box.'

Her dad's car is old enough to have a CD player. He is stubbornly proud of it and refuses to upgrade, despite what Mum says to him.

'The what??'

'That thing in front of you. Holds stuff.'

'The cupboard-thing?'

'If you like. Correct name – glove box.'

'You don't own any gloves.'

'Beside the point. One day I might. And on that day I'll be sure to put them in the cupboard-thing. If only to validate it.'

There's relief on his face, as if he's avoided something. She's seen it before when he's dodged a row with Mum. It's obviously not something he's passed down to her. Grimes swamps the rest of the journey.

They bump down the farm lane and pull up in a cloud of dust outside the barn. Dad gets out first.

'Be nice.' It's not an order, more of a request.

'Thanks for the lift.'

Mum is at the door.

'You didn't take your phone.' To Beth.

'Hi honey, I'm home,' Dad trills.

They kiss and Beth tries to walk past her.

'Your phone, Beth?'

'Sorry,' she mumbles, I've been out raising clams.

'It's okay,' her mum adds. 'I was worried, that's all.'

She has the phone in her hand and Beth takes it, giving Eve a weak smile. It's all she can manage.

'Beth was asking about my work...' Dad looks at Mum

72

pointedly. Beth sees her mum give a little start before she looks back at him.

'Oh,' Eve says, 'and how was work?'

'Okay.' He shrugs and looks pointedly back at her. But Mum's adding nothing and it's all a bit too weird for Beth.

'I stink, I'm going for a bath,' she announces.

'Damn right, had to have the windows down all the way from town.'

She gives her Dad a sarky smile and sets off to run the bath. When the taps are gushing loudly she slips out of the bathroom door and creeps to the top of the stairs. She can just about hear them, in the kitchen. They are speaking in urgent, hushed tones, so that she can only hear the very peaks of their sentences.

'...tell her!' Dad.

'...weren't here today. never, never... good time.' Mum.

'...too late...' Dad

'...to me... settle it.' Mum.

'...the boss.' Dad.

She can fill the last one in as she's heard it so many times. 'You're the boss,' Dad will always say. It drives her mad.

She hears the first footstep on the stairs and dashes into the bathroom, shutting the door behind her. So they're plotting, they have a secret, it involves her and she's clearly not going to be happy. No news there then, she thinks. Bring it on.

She's stinging from the hot bath as she wraps a towel around her dripping hair. She's used some of her mum's Bath Bombs and smells vaguely of patchouli oil. She stares at her reflection, sliding her lips over her teeth, hiding them. Then she blazes a smile at herself. It's strange, she thinks, but at full smile, I don't look that bad. It's the in-between stage that gives things away. She should either full-on flash her teeth or keep them shut away. Sulky Beth or loony Beth. Great choice.

Sulky Beth makes her way downstairs and finds her parents sitting, side by side at the kitchen table. Like a small committee. Like they've decided something.

Mum speaks first. 'We want to talk to you.'

She looks at her dad, who looks back queasily.

'Sit down,' he says. She does.

'Grandad's going to need more help than we thought at first,' he adds. 'Much more.'

A sense of dread balls inside her stomach. Dad carries on and Mum just looks evenly at her, a hand placed carelessly on Dad's shoulder.

'So I've decided to take a sabbatical from work,' Dad says.

She feels herself blinking rapidly.

Mum speaks. 'It's when you take time off…'

'I know what a sabbatical is,' Beth has almost snapped.

'So this way I can be here more often,' Dad tries to make this sound like this is actually his idea.

'Right,' Beth says.

'So we will all be staying here. At the farm. For a while.'

'It's nearly September…' She's trying not to think the unthinkable.

'Yes…' says Dad. 'It is…'

'School?' she adds.

'There's a school here,' Dad tries to swallow the sentence but it's out.

'No,' she's shaking her head.

'I thought…' Dad's pale.

'*You* thought?' Her anger's rising, 'what about *her?*'

Beth stares accusingly at her mum, who flushes furiously.

'Don't talk to your mother like that.' Dad's trying to be harsh.

'Don't tell me she had nothing to do with this!'

Her mum sucks in air. 'Beth, your Grandad. *My* father, is an old man. He's hurt himself, he's vulnerable, he's trying to run this farm like he was forty years old and he isn't. He needs us.'

'I'm doing my GSCEs.'

'And the school has a great reputation,' her mum has taken over now. No more pretending Dad's actually in charge.

'I'd have to learn Welsh.'

'I can help with that.'

'All my friends…'

'You'll make more.'

She feels exhausted, the fight draining from her. She needs to get away, take this in. Re-group.

'Grandad is going to need full time care,' her dad's back on the scene now.

'We owe it to him. Until we can, you know… sort something else out.'

'Sort what out?' she asks.

Her mum glances into her lap for a moment. 'Proper care for him. Permanent care.'

'A home?' Beth asks incredulously.

'Maybe,' Mum adds. 'In time.'

'When?' she demands.

'I don't know yet,' Mum looks genuinely pained.

'Does Max know?' Yeah, imagine that.

'No, we're telling you first.'

'Does Grandad know?'

Eve nods.

'Oh, so you're telling me second then?'

No answer.

'Is that it, can I go?'

Eve nods again and Beth rises from the table and retreats to her room. Actually not her room at all. Her mum's room. Beth didn't want to cry in front of them but now she does. She cries until she's sick of crying. She cries herself to a deep and dreamless sleep.

CHAPTER 12

Sienna is devastated. She texts a single word. *Fuck.*
Obviously there are not enough emojis in the world to
summarise the way she feels. She calls instead.

'Babe!'

'Hi, Sienna.'

'I'm coming to get you. Stay put.'

'Sienna…'

'It's all fixed. Parents have spoken, I'm on my way.'

Sienna spits words like bullets. Blunt, to the point. There's
a knock on Beth's door and Eve slides in.

'Sienna's coming,' she says.

'I know.'

'She's staying the night. Thought it'd be nice for you.'

'You hate her.'

'No I don't.'

Beth lets this go. Her mum slides back out. Then she does
get an emoji off Sienna. It's a cocktail glass.

~·~

Outside the heat has built as she sits at the top of the lane
waiting for Sienna to arrive. Since seeing Trev by the stream
she's taken to wearing her sports bra every time she leaves the
house. She's got a loose, faded tie-dye T-shirt over it and
white shorts. She's still roasting.

The air is thick and chewy. It's over two hours from

Manchester so she's got a bit of a wait. From here Beth can look down the valley to the sea. It shimmers elusively. Growing out of it like towering columns of cotton wool are colossal storm clouds. They have great sagging bellies that are the colour of lead. They look angry.

Grandad had said that summer was about to burst, she remembers. I know how it feels.

She was wrong thinking Max would be on her side. He's made up to be living on the farm, he hated his old school anyway. Grandad has stayed out of her way. She can see him now hobbling around the yard, pointlessly poking his stick at stuff he can't reach, Rags shadowing his every move. She can't imagine him in a home. But then again, she can't imagine her being here for another day, let alone months stretching into years.

What, she thinks. – what if what I do to dead things only happens here? I know it's stupid and weird, but isn't everything about me now? Can I tell Sienna? Only if I want to see it tweeted and face-booked to death. She'd want examples. She'd want to see it in action. She'd want to film it. No way. Beth shuts down that particular line of torment and enquiry.

Eve walks half way up the lane and shouts to ask if she wants sun cream and a drink. Beth raises her hand with the bottle of water she's brought, shaking her head. Her mum wants words but she doesn't have any. Not right now.

It's so hot the cows in a nearby field have lumbered under the shade of the trees. Sheep lie, panting. Even the birds fly through the thickening air as if they're flying through soup. Sweat trickles down from her forehead. Her water is warm.

The clouds on the horizon swell and bloom with darkening rain. You can almost feel the air crackle.

A blindingly white Range Rover races down the lanes towards the farm. Black windows and spinning, glistening wheels. It's by her side before she's had the chance to jump down from the wall. A black window slips down with a hiss, revealing a strikingly glamorous woman with a face tanned the colour of copper, scarlet lips and a sweep of black hair. She leans forward from inside the air-conditioned gloom. Mirrored Miu Mius show Beth back her sun-reddened cheeks. This is Trish, Sienna's mum.

'Baby Beth. Poor baby.'

'Trish, leave her alone.' Sienna drops down from the other side of the car. She only ever calls her mum Trish.

'I'll pick you up tomorrow, Sienna. Seven-ish okay?'

'You not staying to say hello?' Beth asks.

'I don't do farms, Beth.'

The window sighs shut and the Range Rover effortlessly whistles away down the road.

'She's off to Abersoch,' Sienna explains. 'Wilmslow-by-the-sea.'

Sienna hugs her hard. She smells of something sweet and expensive. She's dressed down for the country, black leggings sticking out of tight cut–off Levi shorts. Cherry-Red eighteen eye Doc Martens, a tight black All Saints top that shows off her chest and tortoiseshell Clubmaster Ray Bans. Purple lips, foundation and glossy red hair flecked with honey coloured highlights. She looks about twenty.

Sienna zips open a bejewelled rucksack she's carrying. It holds a half bottle of Belvedere. The vodka clinks against two chunky shot glasses as Sienna rummages around before producing a single lime and a penknife.

'We need ice,' she proclaims.

'Mum will ask why.'

'Then we'll cut her out and go straight into town.'

'Looks like it might rain,' Beth protests feebly.

'Hasn't rained in a month, why start now.' This isn't a question.

There's no arguing with Sienna.

'I'm here to cheer you up, so shut it and get a move on.'

Beth tags along beside her as they set off for Porthmadog. Her phone twitches in her pocket. Text from Mum.

Where U going?

To town with Sienna.

OK.

'That your mum?' asks Sienna.

'Yeah.'

'Cow.'

Beth doesn't contradict her.

'This is all I could smuggle, but I've got a mate's ID.'

Beth checks the ID. It's Alice's provisional driving licence. Alice is Sienna's go-to girl back home.

'Alice gave you her ID?'

'I didn't say she gave it to me, just said that I'd got it.'

And Sienna's glorious smile says that everything will be okay. Better than okay. And Beth believes her.

There's an Off Licence on the corner of the high street and Sienna emerges swinging a carrier bag.

'Woman in there's never heard of Triple Sec!' Sienna's

scandalised. 'We've got to go to Tesco's for ice, come on.'

As they turn to head away, Beth sees Susie and Trev waiting to cross the road and go into the shop. Trev smirks, eyes on stalks, and Susie scowls.

'Jesus, who are they?' Sienna's gawping and Beth tries to hurry her along.

'That guy works for Grandad.' Beth would never say 'guy' if she wasn't with Sienna. 'And that's his girlfriend.'

She realises she's being economical with the truth but doesn't want a scene.

'He's almost cute…'

'Sienna!' Beth's appalled.

'In a Channing Tatum kind of way,' Sienna adds.

She has Sienna's elbow now and they're off down the street.

'His girlfriend looks like someone stuck a lemon in Miley Cyrus's mouth. I mean, a *whole* one.'

'She doesn't like me. Come *on!*'

'Really? Why?'

'She thinks I like her boyfriend. He's a perv and he's dangerous.'

'All pervs are dangerous,' Sienna replies. 'Comes with the territory…'

'Not like this one, okay?' Beth tries to shut her friend down, but doesn't need to. Sienna being Sienna, she's moved on.

Looking at her Docs, Sienna announces, 'I'm breaking these in. Feet are killing me, can we get a taxi back?'

'No Sienna, we can't, they need a week's notice. There's a bus…'

'*Bus?*' She's genuinely affronted.

'Big orange things, carry people..?'

'Okay, but no selfies right? No one must ever know.' Deadly serious.

Despite herself, Beth laughs. She realises that she hasn't laughed in a while. Things are already a little bit better.

The bus swings out of town as they gingerly pass the bag of ice between themselves, until their fingers become too cold. Sienna has bought two garish picnic Margarita glasses and a box of Atlantic sea salt too.

'Where can we go to neck this lot?' she asks.

Beth's not too worried, she's seen Sienna drink before. It's all bravado, immediately before she throws up and crashes. Beth decides not to venture too far away from the farm though; I carried her down Deansgate once, she remembers.

'We could go into the woods, behind the farm. There's a stream there, and a pool, keep the drink cold?'

'No clubs? You know, places of entertainment?'

'British Legion?' Beth offers.

'I'll pass. Woods it is.'

As the bus drops them off Beth can hear the first distant rumble of thunder. The black clouds are close now, low, crowding the sky, oppressive.

'Actually, buses aren't bad,' Sienna declares. 'If you like melting into your own thong.'

On the way up into the woods Beth sniffs the air.

'What is it?' asks Sienna.

'Rain. I can smell the rain.'

'Don't go all Bear Grylls on me girl. Sooner we get you back to Manchester, the better.'

But Beth can smell the rain. Minutes away. The incoming

storm is breathing cool air at them from down the valley, a warning. She urges Sienna on, under the cover of the trees, past its pine gateway. The wood envelops them quickly and completely. There are still brilliant shafts of sunlight piercing the leafy canopy above them, seeming to point the way uphill, to the pool.

'I like it here,' Sienna approves.

They find a rock for Sienna to sit on by the water – no grass stains, thank you very much. She proceeds to mix them what she calls 'guerrilla Margaritas.'

Beth watches, amused, as Sienna tips salt onto her bag before running the lime over the rims of the plastic glasses and dipping them into the small piles. Trust Sienna to find Triple Sec after all.

'Cheers to Tesco!' she calls, handing Beth a huge cocktail.

'Sienna, this is pure alcohol…'

'And your problem is?'

Beth thinks about this for a second. I have many problems, sharing them is another question. 'Cheers,' she says back and takes a sip. It's potentially lethal.

As they drink Beth can see the pinpricks of sunlight in the canopy slowly disappearing, one by one, as if someone was going round flicking off switches. The storm must be gathering over the woods.

'I'm going to dump Olly,' Sienna offers.

'Oh, I thought you were with Freddy?'

'I was. Don't you look on Insta anymore?'

'Not if I can help it. Reminds me that I once had a life.'

'Anyway, he's too needy. Wants sex, like, all the time.'

Beth looks down, not wanting to catch Sienna's eye,

knowing what it will bring.

Sienna ploughs on. 'I mean, it was great to start with. Olly's hench, second row for the first fifteen,' she drains her glass, Beth's is still half full.

'But now he's like, "Hi babe, I'm here, let's do it…" I'm not asking for flowers or any of that shit, but, y'know…' She starts to make herself another drink, fishing the carrier bag from the water.

'Anyway, he's in Abersoch, waiting for me.'

'And so what, you're going to dump him *after* you've like, you know, *been* to Abersoch?'

'What, and have him grope me for the rest of the week? Christ no, I'll do it now, let Trish sort it out.'

Sienna gets her phone out and swipes it, beginning to text. 'He's always had a thing for her anyway, who knows what will happen?'

'You're kidding, right?'

Sienna looks up from texting, genuinely perplexed. 'What? No. You know what Trish is like.'

Beth shakes her head and is about to complain about the lack of fairness in dumping anyone by text when there's a massive clap of thunder above them that shakes the ground. Even Sienna jumps out of her complacency.

'Jesus Christ!' she shouts.

Big fat raindrops start to fall. Most of them hit the canopy, the start of a steady drumming. Some come through, splatting into the stream. One lands in Beth's drink with a neat 'plink' sound. At least that'll dilute it, she thinks. Soon they can barely hear each other over the riot of the raindrops tipping from the sky like they will never stop.

'Oh, this is actually cool,' Sienna turns her face to the rain, mouth open, laughing. Beth copies her, allowing her half full glass to spill over onto the grass.

'Rain stopped play with the Margaritas,' Sienna calls. 'Washing all the salt away… and the ice has melted.' She reaches for the Belvedere and pours them two generous shots.

'Down it, down it!' Sienna's hair is sticking to her face, the blonde streaks making it look like someone's cracked an egg over her head. Beth downs the vodka, which burns her throat, leaving a sticky aftertaste.

'Come with me to Abersoch.' Sienna is serious. 'You can have Olly on the rebound if Trish hasn't got in first.'

'What, so he can grope *me*?'

Sienna shrugs. 'Unless you've had a better offer here?'

Ah, Beth think, here it comes.

'I mean, there's got to be someone special around? Hasn't there?'

'No Sienna, there hasn't.'

'Back home?'

'No.'

'Ever…?'

The clincher. 'Never.'

Sienna pours two more shots. 'Don't believe you.'

'Not asking you to.'

'Well, actually, you are,' Sienna persists.

'Okay. I am.'

'Okay. I do. Cheers.'

Sienna smiles, letting her off the hook. For now. Sienna pulls at her top which has stuck firmly to her chest, leaving little to the imagination. Beth thinks of finding Trev tickling trout – you're wet. She shudders.

'You cold?' Sienna asks.

'No.'

'Well I am officially piss wet through. Might as well have jumped in that stream…'

Beth can almost see the thought forming in her friend's head.

'In fact…'

'Not a chance,' Beth's serious.

There's a sudden flash that lights up the entire glade, casting instant and perfect shadows. The thunder is a beat behind it. They both scream, slopping the vodka.

'Oh, come on!' Sienna jumps to her feet. 'When are we ever going to have the chance to swim, naked, in a thunderstorm?'

'Who said anything about being naked?'

But Sienna is already stripping off, dancing on one foot as she grapples with the Docs. She stops to down her shot and tosses the glass carelessly on the ground. The dancing resumes until she topples backwards, giggling.

'Oops grass stain alert!' she laughs.

'You're pissed,' Beth says.

'Never! Get your skinny arse in that pool or I'll drag you in!'

Beth shakes her head, but sits and starts to peel off her trainers. There's another almighty bang above them. For a second they are flash-lit, stark against the gathering gloom. Beth sees how tiny they are here, under the trees. How vulnerable.

Sienna is down to her matching black bra and thong. Her

freckly body is pale in the half light, glossy with rain. You can't see Sienna's ribs. Beth can clearly count hers.

Beth can feel a slow building of unease. The vodka is kicking in, she can sense it, filling her bloodstream. She tries to rationalise things. You're about to get naked with your best friend in a stream, in a storm, full of vodka and in a place where Trev scared you half to death only hours ago. What's to be anxious about?

She hears a splash and a scream. Sienna is rib-deep in the pool, her chest just under the water.

'Oh my frigging God!' she cries. There's another flash and this time Beth counts a full second before hearing the tremendous clap. Swiftly she pulls off her pants and sports bra. The water is cold. As cold as that time with her mum. This thought hits her suddenly and she feels a kind of shame. Not shame at being naked outdoors. A different kind of shame, about her mother.

The clouds have now shut out all the light and it's practically dark in the pool. Sienna has swum out into the middle of the water and her hair, now a dark mop, seems to float, disembodied, on the surface. Beth swims out to her and when she's in close, Sienna spits a stream of water in her face.

'Ha! Minging or what?' she laughs.

'You think?' Beth gathers a mouthful of water and spits it back at her. The rain hammers down on the pool's surface. Another flash, another clap. A feeling in Beth's chest that isn't the cold.

'Ow, ow, ow.' Sienna's grimacing, tipping her head back, water spilling into her open mouth. 'Got cramp…'

Beth dips her toes, feeling for the bottom of the pool. She

can't find it.

'Beth…' Sienna's barely on the surface now and it all happens quickly. Sienna grabs at Beth, nails scraping down her arm, a gurgling noise coming from somewhere in her throat.

Beth instinctively kicks back and away. If she gets hold of me we're both dead, she thinks. Sienna goes under. Beth takes a huge breath and follows her. In the murk of the dark pool she can't see her friend. Then there's another brilliant flash and there she is feet away, clawing at the water, eyes open in terror.

Beth forgets what her mum has told her about staying clear and kicks down after her friend. A frantic hand grips her foot, then another clamps itself onto her calf. Beth swims up again, trying to lift her leg with her, straining against the weight. She feels the pressure of the water, the need to breathe again. Her runner's lungs resist.

She pulls and swims, fingers searching for the moment when she can breach the surface. She feels Sienna's strength draining and her grip slipping.

Her head erupts into the air, which she gulps in. There's a roaring in her ears. She strikes out with both arms, heavily, through the water. On tiptoe, she feels the pool's floor. She brings her knee up, dragging Sienna with it. Her seaweed hair emerges and Beth quickly grabs her under both arms, lifting her clear.

They stumble, nakedly entwined, onto the grass bank. Beth's breath scorches her chest. Sienna throws up, great gouts of water hitting the ground. Beth's head is singing, yet she can still hear something else. Something under the drumming rain. Something she doesn't like. A rustling, a snapping of twigs. She stands. If it's Trev, she's prepared to fight. But it isn't Trev.

There, in a corner of the glade, something is disturbing the ground. The earth is splitting; soil is slowly tippling out of a grassy wound. There is a sound like Velcro being pulled apart, an unsticking of things. A shape begins to emerge, hunched, almost crouching. It grows, becoming spiky in places, things sticking out of it, and all the time, that sucking Velcro sound.

Beth is frozen. The shape unsnaps itself from the ground. It has legs. It is huge, as high as her shoulders. She can hear a low, insistent growl. She peers into the darkness and then shockingly, a flash of lightning brings the horror into full focus. The image is burned into her brain.

She is looking at an enormous dog. Its teeth are bared under still-forming gums. Tendons are still worming over exposed bones. Guts gleam between ghost white ribs. Its breath is captured in a cloud by the flash. In that flash, in that moment, they have seen each other. Now, in the dark, it's all in her head. The absolute horror. She waits as she hears the dog pant and growl. She catches the stench coming off it, waves of sodden, rotting fur.

'Beth..?' She can hear Sienna behind her, coughing.

'Stay there,' Beth tells her, never taking her eyes off the shape of the dog.

Then, slowly, it shakes its head, turns its great body and lopes off, through the ferns and over a hill.

'What the fuck was that?' Another cough.

'Nothing. Just a dog.' She hears the words as if spoken by someone else.

'You've only gone and saved my life.'

'Yeah, I have, haven't I?'

'Oh God, does this mean I'm forever in your debt and will have to rear your babies and all that shit?'

'No, Sienna, it does not.'

'Jesus, I'm shivering.'

Beth goes to wrap her soaking clothes around her, for what good they will do. Her skin is clammy and when Beth touches her, Sienna hugs her fiercely. They rock together as the rain still clatters down. Beth has to gently push her away, and, on doing so, sees that Sienna is crying.

'Hey, it's okay…'

'No it's not. I don't cry in the same way I don't do buses.'

'Well now you've done both.'

Sienna snivels a bit, wipes her nose. 'If that Trev turned up now, he'd think he'd won the lottery. Either that or think we're lesbians. Actually the lottery thing still applies.'

Sienna detaches herself and scoops up the Belvedere, taking a long glug of it.

'Don't you think you've had enough?' Beth asks.

'Screw that, I just watched my life flash by and it didn't take long. I've got some living to do.'

They both put on soaking clothes, but Sienna baulks at the Docs.

'My feet are swollen. Can't get them on.' She cocks her head like a small, pathetic puppy. 'Piggyback?'

'Forget it. You owe me as it is, remember? Babies and stuff?'

Beth walks over to where the dog had stood as Sienna grumbles about how mean she is. Beth looks down into what looks like a shallow grave, interlaced with tree roots. Worms twist and squirm in the soil. There are places where the roots have recently snapped, exposing their pale shoots.

Sienna is alongside her, peering over her shoulder.

'Give me the vodka.' Beth tells her and takes a gulp of it herself. 'I feel like I need it.'

CHAPTER 13

By the time they stumble into the yard most of the vodka has gone. Sienna is telling Beth just how *muuuuuch* she loves her, *rilly, rilly* loves her. Beth's head is spinning from the drink. Every time she stops to think though, the image of the dog's skin crawling with the muscles that were forming under it snaps back into her thoughts, and she reaches for the bottle.

It's only when they begin to push at the kitchen door that Beth realises she hasn't got her phone on her. I must have left it up at the pool, she half remembers, I could cry, Mum will go mad…

She doesn't have long to wait, because Eve practically snatches the door out of her hand and they fall into the kitchen.

'Where the hell have you been!?' her mum demands.

Everyone's there. Grandad watches sadly from his chair. Dad scowls from the kitchen table and even Max has managed to sneak down to the bottom stair; Beth can see him squirming to get a better look through the crack of light that is spilling from the kitchen.

'Had an accident,' she manages, working hard to get the words out right.

'I love your Beth,' slurs Sienna.

'She does…' Beth tells her mum, feeling herself grin to help reassure Eve that they're both okay and if she would just let them go to bed…

'You're drunk!' Mum seems disgusted.

'No…' But Beth feels her stomach lurch, the smell of the dog in her nostrils, the worms, the insects…

She throws up over her mum's bare feet. She can hear the sick splatter on the tile flagged floor. She can hear Max scramble up the stairs, even *he* knows when to get out of the way. Managing to stagger over to the sink she is sick again. And again. Eve holds her hair out of the way. Somewhere there is running water and she is handed a glass. It comes straight back up. Her belly seems out of control as it tries to heave and she jerks along with it, hitting her head on the taps.

'You go up,' she hears her mum say to Dad. 'Put Sienna to bed, keep an eye on her.'

'I been sick, me…' Sienna adds, helpfully.

Eventually it's just Beth and Eve. She is helped upstairs feeling like she's been emptied a thousand times over. She flops on the bed but the ceiling dances and spins crazily and she has to dry heave by the side of the bed. Eve wipes the wet hair from her clammy forehead.

'You're a stupid, stupid girl…'

Beth knows she is and she's sorry. The words are only in her head, where they spin along with the rest of her world. Images of dead mice, flies, the dog. The baby dream is there, Grandma at her window. Bring us back, they all say, bring us back. They spin and hover until a blackness sweeps over her and washes them all away.

~·~

The morning goes by in a painful blur. Her head is crammed with a ridiculous amount of pain and all she wants to do is lie in the dark. But of course, there are arguments to be had.

Sienna and Beth sit there, taking it all, because what else can they do? Yes, we know how bad it was. Yes, we know how worried they all were. Yes, we could have died. Yes, yes, yes.

Just when she thinks the ordeal is going to make her sick again, the door bursts open and Trish stands there. The morning sun makes a halo around her head and for a moment Beth thinks she's hallucinating.

'What the fuck, Sienna?' Trish asks. Which isn't really a proper question. The swearing brings a dark cloud over her mum's face. Trish is wearing the tightest T-shirt Beth has ever seen with a massive picture of a piñata donkey on it. The words under it say, 'I'd smash that.'

Her toned and tanned legs stick out of a mini skirt, tight as cling film, and end in leopard pattern wellies. This is Trish 'doing' farms. Beth giggles despite herself. Trish slowly removes her mirrored Miu Mius.

'Eva phoned me…'

'Eve,' her mum corrects.

'Said you'd been a bit of a car crash.'

'I didn't actually say…'

'And here you are, looking like trash. Both of you.'

Sienna speaks first. 'Are you wearing my T-shirt?'

'I like donkeys…' Trish offers.

Sienna goes to open her mouth but Trish isn't finished. 'Oh, and as for that *boy* of yours… what's he called?'

'Olly.'

'Darling if I'd wanted a lap dog I'd have bought myself a fucking poodle.'

'I think…' Eve interrupts. 'Trisha is it?'

'Close.'

'That you should just take Sienna home. Better all round.'

The two women eye each other warily. If there was a fight right now, Beth is really not sure where her money would go.

'C'mon baby,' Trish nods towards the car outside.

'Beth's coming to live with us,' Sienna blurts out.

She's not sure who snorts the loudest, Trish or her mum. Dad rises from the table and leaves the room. Grandad slowly taps his stick on the floor. Click, click, click it goes, ticking through the silence that follows.

'That's not going to happen,' Eve speaks slowly.

Trish snaps her sunglasses back in place and turns, quite elegantly, on rubber heels. She swishes back to the car as Sienna sheepishly rises to follow. Beth and Sienna have a huge hug and Sienna whispers in her ear.

'I'll send you some money, you can get a train.' And then. 'That T-shirt's waaay too tight, right?'

Sienna snivels a bit but then squares her shoulders as she exits the door.

'Bye Eve, thanks for having me.'

Eve flicks a look at Grandad, but he's contemplating his knuckles as he works his fingers into the grooves on his stick.

Trish actually manages to make the Range Rover's tyres squeal as she swings it out of the yard. The heavy rain has filled the ground with muddy puddles and they explode under the car's tyres as it plunges up the drive. Eve sits and runs her fingers through her hair, then covers her eyes as she cradles her head, elbows on the table.

'I could, you know?' Beth speaks through the pain hammering at her temples.

'You could *what?*' Eve replies.

'Live at Sienna's'

'Oh, and throw up your entire body weight in vodka every night?'

'That was a one-off.'

'And who'd be there, mopping your brow and holding back your hair? Hmm, *Trish*? I don't think so.'

'Mum, you don't know what it's like. Here, for me…'

'It's the same it was for me, when I was a girl.'

'Oh, I doubt *that.*'

'Because you're more special, is that it?'

'No Mum… well, not special, just – *different.*'

'So, my home isn't good enough for you?'

Grandad speaks for the first time. 'Eve, let the girl speak.'

They both look at him but he doesn't return their gaze. He just turns the stick around in his hands.

Beth struggles for the words. 'Things are difficult for me. I need to get away, not forever, just a bit. Back to normal…'

'Welcome to *life* Beth. This is normal.' And Eve gets up from the table and leaves.

Grandad speaks again, and this time there's a tough edge to his words. 'How are things difficult, Beth?'

She thinks of her Grandma, at the window. 'Believe me, they just are, Grandad.'

CHAPTER 14

Beth stands and waits for Max to catch up. The high school is a few yards away, across a bridged stream and at the end of a short drive. Eve wanted to drop them at the gate but Beth had said no. She can feel peoples' eyes on her and she can hear the murmur of words spoken in Welsh. Her uniform is hideous and itchy. She's insisted on wearing her pleated skirt long, almost to her knees. Her hair is tied back into a ponytail. She looks and feels about twelve.

'Come on, Max.'

The school buildings look cobbled together; afterthoughts down the years. They walk into a small courtyard where someone has graffitied onto one of the outbuildings. There is a picture of the high street, years ago, almost in darkness. People have been painted in, along the edges; black, shadowy people, like ghosts crowding to get in the picture at all.

'Hey, goofy!'

She's not been called goofy since Year One and instinctively covers her mouth with her hand. Max is standing by her side and looks back at the owner of the voice. But she doesn't need to look back because she knows who it is.

'Talkin' to you. Goofy,' Susie calls again.

'Come on, Max,' she talks softly, starting to lead him across the courtyard to what looks like the entrance.

'Think you're too good for us eh? Titless tart with your fake Welsh family.'

Beth feels her face burn with the humiliation. And the

anger. They're almost at the door when she feels the first tug at her shoulder. She shakes it off but gets ready for the next one, testing the weight of her schoolbag in her fist. Then a boy emerges from the door in front of her and everything changes.

'Susie, stop being a twat.' Welsh accent.

'Do one, Will,' Susie replies.

He looks at Beth and then down at Max. He's tall, maybe six one and has broad shoulders, filling out his school blazer. He has a shock of black hair and a lot of perfect teeth. Oh, and chocolate buttons for eyes. It's weird that these parts of his face are what hit her first, not the whole face.

'I mean it, Susie.'

Now she turns to look at her would-be torturers. Susie is very angry, but the two girls with her look like they're about to melt. If they fluttered their eyelashes any more, Beth swears they'd take off. The fight's over. Susie flashes one last glare to the boy and winks at Beth.

'See you around.'

They flounce across the yard. Beth turns back to the boy.

'My sister.'

'Your *what*?!' She's stunned. She sees Susie as having been manufactured, not reared by actual humans.

'I'm her big brother.' He grins and shrugs his shoulders, blazer straining over his biceps.

She begins to walk past him, no way is she getting into this.

'But *I'm* nice!' he appeals. 'Honest.'

'What do you want?' Beth asks, hard, making for the door.

'Grand slam for Wales? Audi R8 would be nice? See, I'm easy to please.'

He reaches out for the door and holds it open. 'A smile?'

Well he's not getting one, she thinks. Not from this girl. She sweeps through with Max and seconds later they are being welcomed by a Mrs Williams – Ellis, the Head of Year. Beth's not really taking it in. It's like the dead stuff is normal and this is all a mistake.

Her form aren't that bad. A few smile at her when she sits, near the back. Names are swapped, they all say Hi. Her teacher is Mr Thomas and he's tiny. He has tiny, dancer's feet and he flits between the aisles as if oiled and on wheels. He's okay too.

At lunch, she's followed out by a round, bubbly, open faced girl called Kate. Kate stands like a perfectly balanced pile of pebbles. Beth gets the feeling Mr Thomas has asked Kate to check that she is okay.

'You livin' at the Williams' farm?'

'Yeah.'

'This must be a right pain for you.'

'It is.'

'Your grandad called Christmas?'

'Yeah.'

'Ever call him Santa? You must've done..?'

'Never.'

'God, I'd do it all the time. You know, if he was mine, like.'

Max comes running over.

'This your brother?'

'This is Max.'

'Alright, Max?'

'Who are you?' Max is blunt.

Beth is about to do the 'he's not rude, it's just his way'

speech when Kate butts in.

'He's special needs, right?'

'Screw you,' says Max.

Beth turns to Kate to apologise, but Kate gets in first.

'I'm not fussed, me. Don't care. There's loads of not-rights in Port.'

'We don't say "not-right…"'

'Oh I don't mean anything by it,' Kate adds, 'I get it, it's just the way things are…'

And she's off without a dent in her smile. No harm done.

'Max,' Beth says wearily, 'if we're going to try and fit in here, we've got to, like, speak nicely to people…'

'Screw you,' says Max. 'Where's my sandwich?'

She hands it to him, out of her bag, and he runs off across the sports-field, shirt coming undone and flapping behind him. She watches him go and blinks back the tears forming at the corners of her eyes. She looks at her own sandwich, wrapped in tinfoil by her mum. There are two healthy muesli bars alongside it. Chocolate, Mum, she thinks. Why couldn't it have been chocolate, just this once?

She finds Max under a bush in the far corner of the field. They can literally see Snowdon in the distance. She scans the horizon. There's Cnicht too, like the sneeze. Max is licking the crumbs from his tinfoil. She offers him both the muesli bars and he takes them quickly, peeling one and jamming it into his mouth. He stuffs the other into his blazer pocket. She sits next to him.

'I hate it here,' he spits, through a mouthful of grains.

'Thought you were excited? You hated your old school remember?'

100

'Hate all schools now.'

'Everyone needs schools.'

'I don't.'

She sighs and starts on her sandwich. Chicken, cucumber and lettuce. No butter. She and Max chew in silence until they hear the bell go. Then, just as silently, they walk back across the field. At one point she can feel his fingers reaching for hers. When she looks down, he quickly snatches them away and they walk on, their separate shadows stretching across the grass in front of them as the school looms.

~·~

The afternoon sucks. Beth now sees her GCSEs as this unscalable mountain and feels sick just thinking about it. Does her mum have some left-over guilt at having abandoned Wales in the first place? At having left her parents? Don't all children do that, eventually?

And here I am, she thinks, paying for it with every second I stay in this place. The beauty she sees all around her; the woods, mountains, rivers, the sea – all the things she used to love – they all count for nothing now. They suffocate her.

She's waiting by the small bridge at the entrance, looking down at the weeds swaying in the stream's currents. Max is late. Then she sees him, walking towards her and talking furiously with a small girl. He points to Beth and the girl looks up from their conversation. She beams a beautiful smile at her, all freckles and braces.

'I'm Sadie and I'm Max's new best friend!'

'Are you?'

'She is!' Max beams at Beth too.

'Nice to meet you, Sadie. Let's go Max.'

'Can I go to Sadie's for tea?'

'Maybe not today, eh?

'Why not?'

'Just because, okay..?'

'You scared of that girl?' Max accuses.

'Which girl?'

'Her,' Max says, pointing past Beth's shoulder.

She turns to see Susie and her mates on the other side of the road.

'Mum says I should tell if anyone bullies me.' Max's world is so black and white.

Beth takes his hand but he pulls away.

'Come on, Mum's waiting round the corner.' Beth has begged not to be picked up outside school.

'Are we gonna run away every time we see her?' asks Max.

'She's an evil witch,' Sadie offers.

Then Eve walks around the corner. Susie sees her and starts to cross the road, mates in tow. Beth feels faint.

'Hi Maxie, got a new friend?' Eve is oblivious.

'I said we'd come to you, remember?' Beth doesn't like the tightness in her throat.

Eve ignores her. 'God, I remember the times I've stood out here…'

'You Beth's Mum?' Susie is right next to them.

'Yes.' Eve looks directly at Susie and frowns.

'Eve, yeah?' There is a horrible cockiness to her.

'Are you Karen's daughter?' Eve asks.

Susie looks from Eve to Beth, shakes her head disdainfully and walks briskly away, her posse gathering around her, whispering questions.

'She's an evil witch,' Sadie offers again.

'Is she really?' Eve asks lightly.

'Can I go to Sadie's for tea?' Max tries again.

'Not today,' Eve replies breezily. 'We'll fix it for another time, okay?'

But Beth isn't listening any longer. She strides to where her mum has parked the car, swallowing down the rage she feels building inside her. Eve arrives and she and Max get in without a word.

~·~

Half way through the drive home, Eve starts quietly.

'You'd tell me if there was anything wrong at school, wouldn't you?'

Beth catches Max looking at her. He looks away.

'There's nothing *right* at school.'

'You know what I mean, Beth. I need you to look after Max.'

'Don't need her.' Max is sulking.

'God's sake, Mum, I can't even look after myself.'

'What's that supposed to mean?'

'My GCSEs are going to be horrible.'

'No they won't, not if you work hard.'

'And then my life will be horrible. Oh, wait a minute, it already is.'

'You need to grow up Beth. Life is tough.'

'Whatever,' Beth says softly. Something Sienna would say.

'What was that?' Mum has heard.

'Nothing,' she replies.

Eve's silent for the rest of the journey, but, on a bend, she misses a gear change. The engine revs loudly and the gears crunch. Beth knows her mum is as mad as hell. Makes two of us, she thinks.

~·~

The car is barely still before Beth's away and into the kitchen. Joe has his laptop out on the table and Grandad is in his chair. His leg and cast are up on a stool by the hearth. Joe shuts the laptop down suddenly and sits back, hands behind his head, blowing out of his cheeks with frustration. Beth knows it's because he's lost the signal, again.

'Get yourself down the library, Joseph,' Grandad always gets grumpy when anyone points out anything that might make living in his farm in any way inconvenient. Or rubbish. That's why he's used Dad's full name. Dad doesn't deserve this and neither do I, Beth thinks. She looks at Grandad as she throws her bag onto the table. Normally Grandad makes her feel warm, but not now. The warmth is turning to real heat. She resents him. Eve is in behind them with Max.

'What's to eat?' Max is straight over to the fridge.

Mum looks to Dad. 'You said you'd start dinner?'

'Oh, yeah. Sorry if my afternoon disappeared up its own arse, looking for a signal.'

'Don't start, Joe. I've just had an earful from madam.'

Beth's anger goes up a notch. 'No one asked you to pick us

104

up. In fact I'm pretty sure I said not to.'

'And we all dance to your tune, eh Beth?' Mum has no gears to crunch now.

'No! No one's listening to me! I *need* to get out of here. It's poison for me.'

'It was good enough for your grandma and me all these years. And for your mum.' No sing-song from Grandad now.

'I'm not you, Grandad.'

'Don't speak to your grandfather like that!' Mum is very still.

Beth swallows her words but there's a sense of boiling inside her and she can't help what happens next.

'I hate it here. I feel trapped. It's not *my* home, it's yours. You can't force us to be Welsh just because you gave all this up and now you're guilty.'

'You'd better stop right there,' Mum's head is down, not looking at her. Beth needs her to listen and so goes over, closing the gap between them. A bizarre part of her realises that she's as tall as her mum.

'We're not Welsh, Mum. There's only you. Me and Max were brought up in Manchester. Dad's from Manchester. We don't belong here and you're keeping us… like prisoners.'

Eve looks at her daughter now. She's scarlet.

'You are a selfish, *selfish* little cow.'

'Eve!?' Her dad stands. Beth finds herself blinking back more tears.

'We are here to look after *our* family! Not just mine, *ours*, and if you had one decent, selfless bone in your body you'd see that,' Eve is blazing.

'Okay, right.' Beth knows exactly what she's about to say.

'So what was all that shit about sticking around until you can shove Grandad in a home?'

Beth can almost feel the air leave the room. Then her mum slaps her, hard across her cheek.

'Jesus, Eve!' shouts Dad.

'Oh my God, I am so sorry…' Mum's hand has flown to her mouth.

Beth's cheek stings and the tears are out now, whether she wants to cry or not.

'Beth, please?' Mum reaches out for her.

'Get off me!' Beth shoves her hand away and sprints from the room.

She slams the bedroom door behind her and sticks a chair against the door. She's spinning with anger and hurt and all she can see are her mum's medals and cups. She jumps onto the bed so that she can reach the shelves and then, next thing, she's clawing at them, sending them crashing across the room. The cups are tinny and hollow and they make a terrible noise bouncing off the walls.

She's not quite sure how long the rage takes, but, when she catches her breath, the shelves are empty and she sits heavily on the bed. Her mum's past glories lie shattered around her and she's glad, because right now, they mean nothing to her. Beth feels alive with hatred.

CHAPTER 15

The day slides into night without Beth noticing. She looks at all the mess. She texts Sienna – *Call Childline*, is Sienna's texted reply. Beth's not even sure Childline exists any more. She reaches out and picks up a single, dented trophy. The plaque on its plinth has cracked and she has to push the parts together to read it.

'*Eve Williams, Cheshire County 1500 metre Champion, 1990.*' How ironic, she thinks, the same age as I am now. Different people though, eh Mum?

She tosses it back onto the bed just as there's a knock at the door. May as well face her, Beth thinks. She drags the chair away and turns the handle, leaving it open as she sits back down, leaning against the headboard to put some distance between them. Only, it's not her mum. Grandad stands there in the doorway, swaying a little, leaning on his stick and breathing a bit heavily.

'Can I come in?'

'Yeah, course.'

He hobbles over to the bed and sits on the end, cradling his stick in his lap. He sees the broken trophy and examines it, squinting.

'Nineteen-ninety! A lifetime ago.'

His gaze takes in the rest of the room. 'Did you know you were born in this room?'

She is genuinely surprised. 'No…'

'On that bed.'

She almost jumps off.

'Ah, it's okay, we changed the mattress. Bit of blood and that, y'know…'

He puts the trophy down, gently.

'I knew I'd been born in Wales, thought it was in the hospital.'

'Your mum lived in Manchester then of course, just came here for a rest.'

She realises that this is going to be one of 'those' chats with adults. Where they tell you stuff you should have known all your life.

'Stayed a whole month. Joe popped down when he could. She hated being 'fat' as she called it. I still say you couldn't tell from the back. Drove her round the bend. I'd tell her, "what, you'd rather I called you a whale?" Made her worse. Made Joe laugh mind you. She was booked in at Bangor, had her mind set on you being Welsh. But she was so slight, see? So tiny. People would look at her and say, "no way is *any* baby coming out of *that* woman".'

He smiles at the memory.

'Immovable object, irresistible force and all that. She was still running, right up to the end.'

'The end?'

'Wrong choice of word that. The beginning, in your case. She was late see, with you. Well into the second week. Midwife said it was normal, with first kids. She was to take it easy, do things lightly. Not words you'd naturally associate with your mam eh?'

She almost smiles. He catches Beth's look and smiles for her.

'Anyhow, labour started and she still had her trainers on. No time for the ambulance, not from Bangor. Mary delivered you, on this bed. Six pounds dead on. Any bigger and you'd still be in there!'

'Did you see?'

Grandad blinks once.

'Lord, no! Think your mam wanted her dad seeing her starkers? I was chucked out before the trainers came off. Heard it all though, through the door. Choice language to say the least, a lot of it aimed at your dad. He probably heard it in Manchester. Then a real hush. Could hear myself breathing… then you started squealing, door bursts open and I almost fell in!'

Now Beth does smile at him.

'Caught red-handed, I was. Mary pushed me out of the way, gone to get a bowl or something, blood all over her, and there you were, in your mam's arms. Perfect.'

He stops talking and looks at her, eyes shining wet, set deep in wrinkly sacks.

'I'm sorry about what I said. The home stuff.' She means it.

'Don't be. I'm a burden, care home's the best place for me, tottering around this place like I can still run it. A bloody nuisance.'

'You're not.'

'Your grandma had it right. Out like a light, no pain, no lingering…'

'But then you don't get to say goodbye?'

'*You* don't; those who stay behind. Us oldies though, we need to get our goodbyes in early, 'cos you never know the day.'

'Why are you saying this?'

He sighs, 'don't be too hard on your mam, she loves this place, it's in her blood. And 'cos you were born here, it's in yours too.'

Beth's about to point out that Eve left first chance she got, to go to Uni, but it feels mean so she keeps her mouth shut. About that anyway.

'So Mum had no pain relief?'

He shakes his head. 'Brave woman…'

Beth sees what he wants her to think, how her mum suffered to bring her into the world. He's right, she's seen childbirth on television. It hurts. Mum said it herself, Beth thinks; I am stupid, selfish…

'Ever seen One Born Every Minute, Grandad?'

He shakes his head. 'I'm a Strictly man myself, always been partial to a bit of singing and dancing.'

There's a thought growing in her mind.

'It's about babies. In hospitals.'

He nods.

'And all the stuff they have to do to keep the mums and babies safe. All the drugs and that…'

'I had a bottle of rum on hand. Drank most of it myself.'

'It must've been really dangerous, delivering me, in here?'

'Mary was a dab hand at all that. She'd be out in all weathers, dragging the new-born lambs out of half frozen sheep up on the hills. She was the talk of the valley, never lost a single one.'

Beth feels herself begin to harden.

'A lamb's not a child.'

'No… true…'

'I was a first child, late birth, there could have been complications?'

He shrugs and looks away.

'If you know you're about to give birth, and you're miles away from a hospital, you *don't* go out for a jog.'

She watches him sit a little straighter, more alert.

'Your mam had Mary here…'

'And no drugs, no instruments…'

Now the thought is getting clearer.

'Mum wanted a run, so she had one, simple as that. She put herself and me in danger. It was a stupid, selfish thing to do.'

'I didn't come here to upset you.'

'You haven't.'

She looks around at all the scattered trophies. 'You don't get all this if you don't put yourself first.'

Grandad rises awkwardly off the bed.

'Look, I'll leave you to it. It's getting late and I've kept you talking, muddled you up.'

He limps over to her and bends to plant a soft kiss on her forehead. She reaches up and hugs him. He smells of soap and warm wool.

'I'm not muddled, Grandad.' She can see he's stuck now, this isn't what he wanted, but it's too late. He ruffles her hair and totters out, closing the door gently behind him.

~·~

Come the morning, her dad runs them to school. Mum is nowhere to be seen. No one talks. Susie's brother, whose name has gone completely out of her head, is talking to a

111

bunch of other lads by the bridge. She ushers Max past them and heads for the courtyard, only to hear him trotting up alongside her.

'So you're *that* Bethan?'

'What?'

'Susie told me. I tried to remember if we ever met as kids, but Suze says no.'

'I think *I'd* have remembered seeing your sister.'

'To be fair, she stopped pulling legs off spiders when she was eight.'

'Look, err…'

'Oh my God, you've forgotten my name.'

He seems really cross.

'You never told me it.'

'It's Will.' Those teeth again, she remembers *them*.

'Don't suppose that happens to you a lot?'

'What?' he asks.

'People forgetting your name?'

'Never. Small town, everyone knows everyone else.'

'Well, people don't know me.'

And she picks up the pace, reaching the front doors and leaving him behind. Sadie waits for Max inside and they take off together, whispering. How does Max do it, she thinks? The most socially disastrous person in the family and he has a friend in just a few hours.

~·~

Because no-one was talking, Beth had forgotten to ask her dad to park around the corner and she now sees him sitting

112

in the car, a few metres away. She also sees Trev jogging into view from across the road. He sees her too and stops, taking his time to lean casually against a low garden wall. He shoves his hands into his pockets. Susie brushes past her, deliberately clipping her with an elbow.

'Alright, skank?'

Susie's over the road to Trev and snogs him deeply. He fishes something out of his pocket and tosses it to her. She catches whatever it is and gives a little squeal of delight. Linking his arm, she drags him off, but not before he has cast a last glance in Beth's direction.

Max runs past Beth and straight up to the car as her dad gets out to greet him. Dad opens a door for Max to get in and then looks to Beth as she arrives. He's about to speak when he notices something over her shoulder that draws his attention. Next thing she knows, Will breezes past her and shakes her dad's hand.

'Mr Gray. I'm Will Hughes, your wife and my mum were best mates at school.'

'Oh right, pleased to meet you, Will.' Dad smiles and Will turns to her.

'Been chatting with Beth, trying to help her settle in.'

'That's good of you, Will, thanks.'

She's gobsmacked at his cheek. Words fail her.

'Anything I can do to help, just let me know, alright, Beth?'

Beth gawps.

'See you tomorrow!' he says jauntily and jogs off down the road.

'What a nice lad,' Joe offers. 'Should I be looking for a new stick?'

Ha, ha, she thinks.

'His sister's an evil witch.' Max calls from inside the car.

'S'that right, Maxie?' Joe replies. 'Fancy that, a wicked sister…'

This is unfair, especially from Dad and it hurts her. They have another miserable drive home. Almost.

At the top of the drive she can bear it no longer.

'How long do we keep this up?'

'What?' asks her dad.

'Being picked up, silent lifts home?'

'As long as it takes for me and your mum to trust you.'

'*Trust* me? Trust me to do what?'

'Get on a bus. And not one that takes you to Manchester.'

'You're kidding right?'

'No.'

She breathes deeply.

'Your mum has tidied your room.'

Oh. Right, Beth reasons. So she's seen her precious trophies. Of course. And if I can do *that*, I can run away.

'It's not my room.'

They stop in the yard and Beth gets out before he can answer.

She gets into her running stuff and fills a water bottle in the bathroom. All the trophies have been moved out of the bedroom. There's nothing of her mum left in there. What did she think when she saw it? What can Beth say to her now? If her mum had come straight upstairs after their row Beth would have had loads to say but now she has this hollow pit where her feelings should be.

She straps her iPhone to her sleeve and plugs the

headphones in. This is going to be a long run. When she comes back she might be ready to talk to her mum. The word 'mum' is beginning to grate with her; perhaps, she thinks, I should take Sienna's stance and start using 'Eve?'

She ties her hair back and checks herself in the mirror. There's still a small redness around her cheekbone where Eve hit her, like she's used too much blusher. Like I've *ever* used blusher, she thinks. Looking out of the bedroom window she sees that her mum's jeep still isn't around and so slips lightly down the stairs and makes for the kitchen door. She's almost through it too.

'Beth?'

She stops in the doorway to see Grandad hobble up. He holds out his fist and opens it. The St Christopher lies coiled in his palm, shining brightly.

'Managed to fix it. Good as new.'

She takes it and tries to fasten it behind her neck.

'C'm here…' he says and she turns so he can do it for her.

The medallion lies a few inches beneath her throat, not quite long enough to tuck into her running top. As he fiddles with the clasp she picks it up. Now it's clean she can see all the times it's been banged or scratched. It's that bright it almost glows. It's beautiful.

'There, that'll keep you safe.'

'Thank you.'

But then she hears the diesel of the jeep at the top of the drive. She starts to run, not looking back at Grandad although she can sense his sadness. Eve sees her and stops the jeep so that Beth has to run past her to get up the lane. Eve opens her door and stands on the frame, talking to Beth over the roof.

'Beth, wait.'

Beth puts her head down.

'Beth, please, I'll come with you..?'

Beth powers past the car and can feel the slope on the lane pulling at her calves. She taps her iPhone and the sound of Foals fills her ears. Then she's at the top of the lane and still breathing through her nose. She turns away from the farm, hitting her rhythm, arms like pistons and the medallion slapping her, keeping time. Beth feels like she can run forever.

~·~

After four or five kilometres she realises that she hasn't broken her stride. She also realises that she's heading for the pool she swam in with her mum. There's a public footpath to her left, going up and away from the river. She takes it, having to dig in on the incline and feeling the burn course through her thighs at each step. Head down, she is steadily killing this run. The medallion swings from her neck and it glitters in the early evening light that blinks through the trees towering over her.

Suddenly she breaks out of the cover and the path evens out onto a flat grassy hill. She knows she should be breathing hard by now, but she's not. The sun is on her and she can see for miles. She stops running and switches her music off, yanking the earphones out and letting them dangle at her waist.

She can hear the river, crashing through the gorge below with all the power of the recent rains. It's like she can *feel* the water's power. All that anger, all that pain of the last few weeks flows through her like the river, roaring through her veins. There's a burning in her throat and she looks down. The medallion is like a molten eye in the middle of her chest and she lifts it up. It feels hot in her palm. Really hot.

Under the river's noise she can hear a car. Someone's revving through the gears and the engine is screaming with the effort. A tyre squeals. She looks down at the road and can see the bend where she and her mum climbed over the wall.

Something catches her eye, coming through the trees and along the road, away to her right. She squints and can just make out a figure, running. It's her mum, flickering in and out of her vision as she passes underneath the trunks of the pines lining the wall.

There's another squeal to Beth's left as the car gets closer, but she can't tell exactly where it's coming from. Eve must have run like the wind to get here so quickly, Beth thinks – she must have let me win that sprint down the lane. Condescending cow. And now what? Beth thinks; she's running to catch me, confident that I would come here, of all places? Proving that she's faster, cleverer?

Eve runs clear of the trees and stops at the bend. Eve looks over the wall they climbed then stoops, hands on her hips. She looks like she's out of breath, like she's got a stitch. Serves her right, Beth mouths the words, how dare she slap me?

And then, of course – then to actually think Beth would come here for sentimental reasons, when it was a mistake. Beth just ran and didn't think; nothing to do with her mum. But then again, she considers, Eve thinks everything is to do with her, 'cos that's the way she is…

Beth feels something tickling her top lip and instinctively licks it. Metallic. She touches it and her fingertips come away red. She realises that she's still clutching the medallion tightly. Beth looks down. Her mum seems to stagger a bit, taking a step forward, hands still on her knees.

Beth's lips are wet and the back of her hand smears with blood when she wipes them. Eve tries to stand and then, with a burst of noise, a car appears from nowhere, back end sliding, tyres smoking. There's a hollow whump as the car sweeps Eve off her feet and Beth sees her mum twist in the air before clipping the wall behind her and disappearing. The car's gone just as suddenly as it had appeared and Beth's left staring at nothing. Just a road.

The word Mum is stuck in her throat and she lets go of the medallion. She clutches at her iPhone to detach it from her sleeve. It won't come out and she's grabbing at it, trying to make a sound from a useless mouth that won't work.

There's something to Beth's left, level with her. A blur of colour against the trees. She's gasping for breath as she looks around. There's a man standing there; no, a boy, she can't tell. He's covered in mud. He stares at her soundlessly. He looks calm, not comprehending. The way he stands, the way he looks, not moving; bizarrely, there's a beauty about him. He looks back at the road and Beth follows his gaze, expecting to see her mum climbing back over the wall. She gets her phone free and suddenly her voice croaks back into life.

'Mum! Mum!' She turns to look at the boy. 'Help me!'

There's no one there. The field is empty. She gets her legs working and begins running downhill, gathering pace, trying to punch in 999.

She crashes through some small gorse bushes, ignoring the snags on her bare arms, and vaults the low wall onto the road, sprinting across it, almost flinging herself over the opposite wall, where her mum disappeared. Beth hopes to see her clinging to one of the trees they climbed through, face looking up at her, asking for help. But there's only the raging river. The pool has gone and thick foamy water crashes through it, muddy and impenetrable. Endless, unforgiving water.

CHAPTER 16

The pain is a dead weight under her ribs. She can't comfort Dad, she can't comfort Max. Grandad shuffles around, dry and lifeless, like one of the many leaves swirling around the yard now that autumn is here. Her dreams are terrible and vivid, a kaleidoscope of ghouls. Eve was found three days later by some poor local man, fishing with his young son, some four miles downriver.

She knows everyone blames her. She blames herself. Her mum wouldn't have been running after her if she hadn't been such a spoilt brat. I drew her up there, by the river, Beth thinks. I caused her death and I can bring all the vile things in the world back to life, but not her.

Now she stands, head down, staring at the soil as it thumps onto her mum's coffin and surprised to see that someone has placed a handful of soil in her own hand. She lets it go, hoping that the sound it makes will wake her mum up. Her eyes are hot from the tears and her throat aches from the sobbing. The murmuring of the vicar washes over her.

'Ashes to ashes, dust to dust…'

But they're not though are they, she thinks? Not to me. Ashes to flesh, dust to blood. Maybe she could start up her own alternative services for pets of the bereaved. Instead of burying them, they would rise up in a grotesque kind of play-zoo. A petting farm for the undead.

She looks around, past the bowed heads of Dad, Grandad and Max, who clings to his dad like he was afraid of falling in the grave. Dad's parents have come, Grannie Annie and Grandad Rob. They flank Joe, occasionally reaching out and touching him on his shoulder. She sees Susie at the back, looking coldly at her. She is standing between Trev and some woman. Will hovers behind them. Trev catches her eye then looks away. Why are they even here?

Sienna's come, of course. And Trish, impossibly stylish in something diaphanous, black and floaty. They can't stay and she doesn't want them to. The fight has been sucked out of her, life has been sucked out of her.

The murmuring has finished and people start to drift away. She stands on the edge of the grave, rooted. Grandma Mary's grave sits alongside Mum's. Here lies Mary, here lies Eve... The woman with Susie leaves her and walks over. She's been crying.

'I'm Karen, I went to school with Eve.'

'Susie's Mum.'

'Yeah, that's right. Look, I'm so sorry, I'm... we were going to meet up, your mum and me. Have a coffee. Anyway, now that you're staying...'

She's pretty. Beth can see where Susie got her fairy princess looks from.

'You're pretty,' Beth tells her.

'Oh. Okay, thanks.'

They stare at each other for a moment.

'If there's anything we can do for you? My Susie's your age, she could help you settle in?'

'She's done loads, thanks.'

'Oh, has she? Great. Well... offer's still there...'

Karen leaves, picking her way across the soil-strewn grass

with care. As Beth watches her go she sees someone move out from behind a tree at the graveyard's wall. It's the boy she saw in the field. When Mum died. Even though she can't properly make out his face, Beth can tell he's looking straight at her. She feels a touch on her arm and turns to find her dad there.

'Come on, Beth.'

'I am, just want to...'

She turns back but the boy has gone. She gets a glimpse of his shape as he slips away through the trees, hands deep into his pockets.

'What?' Dad asks.

'Nothing.'

'What did Karen want?'

'To help. Do you know her?'

'From our wedding, y'know... and after, a bit... '

He trails off and cups her elbow gently. She lets him lead her away, not allowing herself a final look into the grave. There are two men leaning casually against the lych-gate, cigarettes palmed against the breeze. They each have a shovel by their side. Just another job for them, Beth thinks, envying them their detachment.

They have a wake at the farmhouse where lots of local people cluck away and drink tea. It's like someone let all the chickens loose in the kitchen and it's all meaningless. People smile emptily, like they've been let off the grieving hook. Look, they seem to be saying, we're drinking tea, eating cake – life goes on. In a way they're right. She's standing in the same kitchen, drinking the same tea.

Some of Mum and Dad's friends have come from Manchester but they stick together, in corners. Mum's gym bunny empire has sent some Armani – clad acolyte to pay their respects. She's like a supermodel, sleek, toned and staring vacantly at the road back to the M56. She's also conspicuous by being the tallest person in the room. Her skin is the colour of strong coffee. Beth watches as the woman slowly shifts her languid gaze from the windows and holds Beth with a surprisingly steely look.

The woman glides through the crowded room and the guests simply part and fold back behind her, as if she had just zipped them open and shut again. She has luxuriant hair, crimped and flattened against a marble – perfect skin. She towers over Beth and offers a poised and immaculately manicured hand. Beth takes it and, for a split second, feels a slight jolt from their contact. She checks the woman's features for some sort of acknowledgement and finds herself staring at perfect eyes, the colour of conkers.

'I'm sorry, static from my car,' the woman purrs. 'Hi, Bethan. I'm Octavia Joseph. But please, you must call me Octavia.'

The accent is cut glass with a hint of something else… is that French? Beth thinks. The woman takes Beth's hesitation as shyness.

'Octavia, I know. Sounds like a yoghurt. My father's a Shakespearian scholar, things could have been soooo much worse.'

She smiles, exposing dazzlingly white teeth.

'I'm the Managing Director of your mother's company and I appreciate that this is the worst day of your life, the saddest and bleakest of times. I'm sorry we are meeting like this but, please, take my word on how important your mother has been to us as a company. And to me, as an individual. These times will pass.'

Beth swallows.

'I'd like to come and visit you some other time, when things are cooler?'

Beth nods, there's something about Octavia that makes the request impossible to turn down. Then, with another flash of that smile, she has parted the crowd again, her imperious head weaving away from Beth.

Beth hasn't said a single word. As Octavia has to duck through the doorway to leave, Beth sees Karen enter the room, almost apologetically and on her own. She goes over to Joe and touches his shoulder, kissing him on the cheek. They hug and Beth sees her dad's shoulders start to shake.

Beth drifts through all the people like she's not there. Apart from Octavia, they don't see me, she thinks, they avoid my gaze. She finds Max on the stairs and sits with him. The vicar comes over, delicately balancing one of Grandma's best china cups on its saucer. Beth takes a deep breath.

He stands over them and his face breaks into a wide smile, exposing startling teeth. His bottom row are as uneven and stained as the stones woozily leaning to in his graveyard but the top row are bright and identical, like new piano keys. For a small man, his voice is very deep and very Welsh.

'How are you, children?'

She speaks for them both. 'We're okay thank you.'

'You did very well during the service.'

She expects him to hand them a badge each.

'You should take comfort that God has taken Eve into his kingdom.'

'With Grandma?' asks Max, and his face is full of hope. Beth feels that this is somehow wrong.

'Of course. They are free from mortal pain now.'

She feels her colour rise. 'Are they actually, though?'

The vicar blinks once. The smile freezes on his face.

'The promise of eternal life...' he starts.

She interrupts. 'No one should be able to promise eternal life. It's not fair.'

His smile slowly slides shut across those teeth. Beth quickly thinks, and I think *I* have problems.

'Dear child, we all, in this room, have God on our side. And with God on our side, who can defeat us?'

She keeps the anger from her voice. 'Those with God on *their* side?'

His mouth twitches.

'Or does God bat for both sides? In that case, it'd be a draw?'

He sucks on his teeth, like he's trying to keep them from falling out. 'This has been a trying day for you both. Loss is difficult to bear...'

'Then why inflict it on us?'

He blinks, once.

'My church is always open. If you feel you want to talk? One day?'

She feels Max's hand stealing into hers and simply stares at the vicar, a bursting dam of words threatening to spill out.

'I'm afraid I've let my tea go cold...' He turns sharply and wanders back into the huddled throng.

She squeezes Max's hand and pulls him up as she rises to ascend the stairs. They lie on Mum's bed and cling on to each other like they're drowning. Underneath them, teacups chime and voices whisper, people hissing with a sibilance of sorries. Max falls asleep like that, but Beth doesn't. She stares at the ceiling, wishing it would crash down on her and take her out, away from all the pain.

~·~

Sometime after dark, Joe comes in and bends over Max, lifting him gently from the bed. Beth can smell whisky and cigarettes. She watches him stagger a little as he shuffles through the door then she turns her head to the window and waits for the sun to come up.

CHAPTER 17

Today is a school day, but not for Beth. A watery sunlight picks out the cobbles in the yard as she laces her running shoes. It's so early she can see her breath rise in a cloud. She doesn't need music to drive her on. It's a distraction. She needs to feel every step, smell every smell. She sets off at a ten k pace. She's in no hurry.

In places, the trees have shed their leaves into a carpet of red and gold. She feels the wind pick up and can hear the branches above her begin to rattle with its breath. She turns up that same path without thinking, the one that takes her up to the field where she saw her mum die. The St Christopher slaps on her chest. She's never taken it off since Grandad gave it to her. Patron saint of travellers. She's decided she's not religious, she's seen too much, made too much happen. She believes in the certainty of death but not the finality of it. A medallion's not going to make any difference, but it feels like it belongs around her neck.

As she reaches the top of the hill she sees him straight away. He's standing where he stood that day. She stops running, keeping a distance between them.

'I knew you'd come here. Eventually.' His Welsh accent is soft, hardly there.

'Who are you?'

'I live over there.' With a nod, he gestures over his shoulder, towards the woods.

He starts walking over to her and now she notices his

clothes. He wears ripped jeans, but, really ripped, by being old. He has a baggy T-shirt, black with the phases of the moon all over it. One moon wears a smiley face. He is slim with wide shoulders. His clothes look too big, but somehow they flow and he moves easily within them. He has covered the grass between them in one fluid movement and she is now looking straight into his eyes. Green eyes, long lashes. Long nose, full mouth, high cheekbones and he grins, showing pearly teeth.

'I'm glad you came back.' He sweeps a lock of messy, straw-coloured hair off his forehead, but it just falls back.

'You didn't tell me who you are.'

'I'm Rhys.'

'You were here, weren't you?'

'Yes.'

'You saw what happened.'

'I saw you.'

He hasn't stopped looking at her. Has he even blinked?

'I'm sorry,' he says, 'but you mustn't blame yourself.'

'What?'

'Hating her for that second. Didn't cause anything. Didn't make her die.'

'What?'

'You're too thin,' he speaks calmly.

She's flushing red, can feel it creeping up from her neck. He notices it too. He looks at her neck.

'This is nice...' He reaches out and takes the medallion in his hand. For a split second his fingers brush her sweaty skin. She feels a sharp, short shock and steps back.

'I'm sorry...' He looks genuinely hurt, not understanding.

His brows knit and his eyes seem to darken. 'I didn't mean to upset you.'

'Are you local?' It seems such a stupid question but she asks it anyway.

He nods slowly. 'Yeah. Used to be.'

'You don't go to school?'

'Not anymore.'

They look at each other.

'What did you mean, about my mum?'

'You do, don't you? Blame yourself?'

'She was following me…'

'Were you driving that car?'

Is he serious? 'What is this, Year Ten psychology?'

'You're angry, it's twisting you up.'

'You don't know me.'

'Better than you think.'

'Yeah well, bye, whatever your name is…'

'Rhys.'

She begins to jog off, and yes, she is angry.

'See you around,' he calls. It's not a question.

Typically arrogant boy. He's ruined her moment, the time she planned to spend at this spot; remembering.

She pushes herself on the run back and arrives at the top of the farm lane breathing hard through her mouth. Hands on knees, she looks down into the yard, expecting to see it empty. But it isn't, there's a police car there. Oh God no, what now, she thinks? Grandad?

She skids to a halt as a male police officer emerges from the farmhouse, bare headed, ruddy faced, chubby. Grandad stands behind the man, leaning on the door frame for support.

'You been out running?' the officer asks.

'Yes.'

'PC Hughes…'

'What is it? Is it Dad?' There is alarm in her cracked voice.

'No, no. We're okay…' Grandad answers, clearly not okay at all.

'I'm sorry about your mam,' Hughes looks genuinely concerned. 'Was just telling Christmas here we found the car. Burnt out, some joyrider's idea of a laugh probably. No prints, no ID. Sorry.'

'Thank you,' seems the right thing to say.

Hughes smiles weakly and opens the car door, stopping to look back at Grandad.

'You might think about keeping your sheep in for a while.'

Grandad nods.

Hughes looks at her. 'Not the best time to ask, but, on your runs, seen anything unusual? Big?'

'Big what?'

'Dog probably. Powerful. Had a few sheep recently turn up, throats out. Rams too, put up a fight…'

The lightning flash in her head. The unsticking sound. The sight she will never forget.

'No.'

'Well if you do – stay away. And call us. Okay?'

'Okay.'

'Condolences again. Bye now.'

His car pulls away and she goes to Grandad. He reaches out and envelops her in his wiry, strong arms.

'He shouldn't be bothering you with all that.'

'It's okay, Grandad.'

'Your dad's made dinner.'

'Has he?'

'Well, was me actually…'

'I'll be down in a bit.'

'You've got to eat, Beth.'

'Yeah, course.'

But she doesn't go down and she doesn't eat. She stays in her room. No one comes. She sleeps. And dreams.

CHAPTER 18

The next day and she is running again. The dreams were vile and she feels exhausted. It only takes a quarter of a mile before she feels her pulse racing. Too fast. She pushes on, up the same path. If he's there she will just turn around and run back.

She breaks out of the canopy of thinning branches and sees the ram. It's lying in the middle of the field. She comes to a halt – straining to hear anything, looking around wildly. There's just birdsong and a slight breeze. She looks back down the tunnel of trees she's just emerged from. It seems sinister now. Gloomier, more dangerous.

She walks over to the ram slowly. Bone glistens white where its neck has been ripped open. Its beautifully horned head lies in a pool of its own blood, eyes unseeing, teeth bared. It is so beautiful she simply stares. Have I done this, she thinks? Is this my fault too?

She hears something; wind rushing? But she can't feel it on her hot, wet skin. She looks to see if the trees are moving, but all is still, apart from in her head. In her head, the wind growls. That increasingly familiar sensation – her stomach folds in on itself.

She hears a coughing sound, a gurgling. The ram is starting to struggle on the ground, kicking out feebly. Its blood is flowing again, still oozing from the open wound. The neck is fixing, like a zipper. Eyes wide in terror, the ram staggers to its feet. And then an awful bleating noise comes from its mouth. The sound isn't right, nothing about this is right. Her mouth suddenly fills with blood and she has to spit.

The ram shifts its slitty gaze from her to the tree-lined tunnel. Then it's off, up the hill, moving swiftly. She looks back at the tunnel, wiping blood from her lips. She sees something shift between the trees. Something big. She has a choice, follow the ram across open ground or make for the wood. There are about three hundred metres between her and the first trees and she's across them in seconds, knees pumping, elbows grazing her ribs. Terrified.

She slaps branches out of her way as the wood swallows her. Not daring to look back, her mind racing along with her feet – jumping over low, fallen logs. She can't trip now. Don't run straight. Weave, dodge. Round the next tree, quickly now, quickly. She sees a wide trunk looming – get behind it, put it between you and whatever's there. She's rounding it now, but it moves, or something moves out from behind it and she can't stop.

She slams into something hard and she's down, the breath being knocked completely out of her. On her back, trying to twist up, defend herself…

'Jesus, girl, where you going?'

He's standing over her, same winking moon T-shirt. She's bounced off him like she would that tree.

'Being chased…' It's all she can say through ragged breaths.

He looks behind her at the wood and the field beyond.

'Well, whoever it was, you burned them.'

'Not a "who"…'

'That old ram!? Surprised it's still got the legs…'

Her breath is returning but she's still on her back and he's still looming over her. He holds out his hand. He has a wrist full of festival bands. She ignores his hand and hauls herself up.

'That was my fault, sorry. Didn't see you coming so fast.' Flecks of amber spark in his cool, green eyes.

'I brought you this,' he says, shrugging off a backpack and dumping it on the ground between them, unzipping it. He takes out a plastic box and flips the lid open to reveal the contents; rice, mushrooms, grains of various colours. He has a plastic picnic spoon in his other hand.

'Sit down and eat this.' Not harsh. More matter of fact.

'What do you think you're doing?'

'Feeding you. I can count your ribs.'

She crosses her arms. 'You've got no right…'

'This is going to sound weird, but, I think I have.'

He holds out the box again.

'And you've cut your mouth by the looks of it. Must've been the branches.'

He drops the spoon in the rice and, before she can stop him, reaches out and wipes the blood from the corner of her mouth. It's like a charge. She's tingling where his hand has been.

'Please eat it. I've been at it all morning.'

'At what?'

'Picking the mushrooms, getting the other stuff, boiling the bloody rice.'

He's smiling, not angry. 'Come on, what's the worst can happen?'

'With mushrooms? You're kidding, right?'

'Fair point. I know what I'm doing, been collecting this

134

stuff all my life. Watch.'

He takes a spoonful of the rice, chews, swallows, wipes the spoon on his moon T-shirt and offers her the lot again.

'Not dead, see?'

'Not yet,' she says.

'Okay. Sit down, give it, say, fifteen minutes. If I'm not writhing on the ground in agony, you'll have some?'

She looks past him to the field. It's empty. For now. She sits and takes the box from him.

'You've still got fourteen minutes, fifty five seconds.'

I am hungry, she thinks. The rice tastes good. Earthy. She doesn't tell him this.

He watches her eat and they sit in silence until she has finished the whole box. Suddenly he groans, pitching forwards off the log he's been sitting on, retching and clutching his stomach.

'You okay?' She drops the empty box on the grass. His groans get louder as he curls up into a ball of pain.

'Rhys?'

Just as suddenly he stops and looks up at her from the floor, grinning.

'See, you do remember my name.'

'You absolute twat!'

'That's not nice.' He wags a finger at her. 'After I've fed you...'

'You're not funny,' she's furious.

'And you're not hungry anymore?'

'I'm going.' She stands, feeling the lactic acid ache from not stretching.

'I'm on my own here...'

'What's that supposed to mean?'

'I live on my own.'

'Where?'

He nods at the woods behind them. 'Up there.'

'How old are you?'

'Older than you.'

'Where are your parents?'

'Dad's dead. Mum went off with some other feller. Took me, but I didn't like him. Or her. So I came back home.'

'She hasn't come to get you?'

'He keeps her high all day long. She doesn't know I'm here and probably couldn't care less.'

He's speaking simply, like none of this matters. Hiding things, like Beth herself does.

'Want to see my house?'

'No.'

'Okay. Be here tomorrow?'

'No.'

'That's okay too.'

'I know it is… Don't need you to tell me…'

He blinks back, unmoved. She feels bad. 'Thanks for the food.'

'No worries.' He picks the box and spoon up and stuffs them back into his backpack. She gets a glimpse of fur.

'What's in that?'

'Rabbits. Dinner. If a chicken was a rabbit, they'd taste like chicken.'

She sees more fur, an ear.

'Join me if you want?'

'You wouldn't want me around at dinner time…' Unless

136

you want to have to catch it all over again, she thinks.

'You a messy eater or what?'

'Something like that.'

'I don't exactly live in a palace, bit of mess'd make no difference.'

She stares at the rabbits, waiting. Nothing happens. She looks at Rhys and he smiles back, guileless.

'There's no rush, I'm sticking around...'

'How far is it?' she hears herself ask.

CHAPTER 19

They walk on uphill, Rhys leading the way, picking through brambles and dying ferns. It's cool under the trees and she's not dressed for walking. The chilly air is beginning to get under her skin. Rhys talks.

'Step with me. Avoid the traps that way.'

'Doesn't it bother you, killing animals?'

A shrug. 'I need to eat.'

'How did you learn that stuff?'

'Dad used to poach a bit. Nothing serious.'

Eventually a path of sorts emerges. Then a couple of tracks that could have been a rough road at some time. They have been walking for around fifteen minutes when she can make out slithers of white amongst the dense trees ahead. They step out into a clearing and the house is there.

'You live *here*?'

'Yep.'

It's falling down, Beth thinks. Well it would be if the vines and bushes weren't holding it up. Scabby, whitewashed walls. The roof sags alarmingly, tiles drooping towards the gutters. Grimy windows are shaped by blistered, flaking once-green frames. It's cabin-in-the-woods scary. Fairy-tale scary. She shivers.

'You cold?'

'Err, yeah…'

'Come in.'

She looks at the open door. 'Not sure that's going to help.'

'Less of the cheek.' He sets off towards the door. 'I'll light a fire, give you something to wear.'

He's through the door, into darkness. Beth hesitates. This is stupid. She's just buried her mum. Here's a stranger inviting her into his remote home and freaking her out with what he seems to know about her...

'Freaking you out eh?' His face appears in the dark doorway. 'Don't blame you.'

'No.'

'Safe, I promise. I will never hurt you.'

His words drop like stones, full of real intent. She steps towards the house.

She was right. Inside, if anything, it's colder. Faded, patterned walls sprout blooms of damp. Here and there brown stained rectangles show where pictures once hung. A weak flame stutters in an old tiled hearth. Rhys stoops to toss splinters of wood into the grate. His jeans part from his T-shirt, exposing the knuckles of his spine, lined faintly with wisps of pale hair. She looks away.

'This is... nice...'

'It was. Once.'

'You're alone here?'

'Yeah.'

'Aren't you scared?'

'No.'

The fire crackles into life and Rhys stands back, pleased. He reaches over to a wide, sagging sofa that has been pulled away from the wall to sit in front of the hearth. From its depths he fishes a plain grey zip top.

'Put this on.'

She takes it from him and sniffs it.

'Oi, I'm clean!'

She pulls it on and zips it up.

'Want the tour?'

'You want me to go upstairs with you?'

'Err, we could just do downstairs. Do a twirl.'

'A what?'

'Twirl. Like this.' He spins on his toes, perfectly balanced. She copies him.

'There, that's downstairs done.'

'You must have a kitchen.'

'There's no pleasing you, is there?'

She starts to unzip the top. 'Look, this was a mistake…'

'You and me. One day we will be together. But not yet. We're not ready.'

Beth is stunned. There's nothing on his face that betrays what he has just said. He may as well have commented on the weather. She feels her face burn.

'You're blushing. Makes your eyes bluer.'

'If I wanted to leave now, would you stop me?'

'No. You can even keep the top.'

'How can you say those things?'

Another shrug. 'One second they're in my head, the next they're out of my mouth. Doesn't say I don't mean them though.'

'What do you expect me to do?'

'I expect you to look in the kitchen, since you asked.'

'I don't even fancy you.'

'Not about fancying. This is deeper. You'll see.'

He mock bows, showing her the way to the kitchen.

'Why do you keep touching your nose?'

She jerks her hand away from her nose. 'I don't.'

'D'you get teased about it?'

'What?'

'Your mouth…'

'Why would I?' Now she feels her fingers touching her nose.

''Cos it's unique. People don't like that, want everyone to be the same, they feel safer that way.'

'Sometimes…'

'So you hide it with your hand?'

She doesn't answer.

'Or that way you smile.'

'Have you been stalking me?'

'I'm observant.'

'Nosy.'

'If you like.'

'Your kitchen's minging.'

And it is. Pans and grimy plates sit in a scummy sink full of water. A single fluorescent tube hangs from marbled ceiling tiles. The floor feels spongy under her feet and the smell of damp is keener here than in the lounge.

'Haven't had a chance to get the place up and running properly since I got back.'

'How long have you been away?'

'Dunno. Years.'

'Are you *happy* living like this?'

'Define happy.'

She slides her gaze from the blackened hob of the sad looking cooker to find him looking intently at her.

'Happy's something I just lost,' she says.

'With your mum?'

'Yes. And before that…'

His eyes never seem to leave her. Like a game she used to play when she was younger, trying to catch herself looking back at her reflection in a mirror. No matter how quickly she tried, her own eyes never seemed to have moved. She moves back into the lounge. His words follow her.

'I'm happy now I'm back here. I'm happy that I've found you.'

'You don't know me.'

Silently, he is standing before her again.

'Yeah I do.'

His gaze is unnerving. She looks down to a place where his throat meets clearly defined chest bones. There is a small pulsing there. She realises it's his heartbeat. Steady, rhythmic. His life, beating through him.

Her eyes begin to sting with tears and she can feel huge sobs begin to well up in her chest. Within seconds she is a snotty wreck, legs tucked under her chest, curling up on the saggy sofa. She's cried over her mum before but this is different. She's lost control and wails, past caring.

Rhys sits softly beside her and takes her hand in both of his. That surge again, like being plugged in. Slowly he pulls her towards him and she sinks onto his shoulder. He smells of wood smoke and soil. She sobs until she's still. It's only then that she can hear him whispering.

'It's okay, you and me, against the world… it's okay…'

CHAPTER 20

First day back at school and she's being treated like a leper. It's like her grief might be catching. Max is angry. Mum would joke that you wouldn't like to see him when he's angry, calling him her mini-hulk. Beth sees him at break, tearing off across the sports' field. He even runs angry.

Max isn't at the gate at the end of the day. God, he must have been kept behind, Beth thinks. She starts back into school, frustrated and angry herself now. A small knot of boys race past her and out of the gates. They chant as they go, 'fight, fight, fight...' She watches as they turn right out of the school, towards the monument. There is a memorial garden sitting above the school, lined with the names of the local dead from the two world wars. She avoids it like the plague, figuring that she has enough dead things in her life.

She can see the rugby pitch as she enters the yard. The rugby team are playing and she can see Will, ball under his arm, ploughing through the opposition like they were simply skittles. He straight-arms a player, sending the lad's head snapping back. There's a savage beauty about it all.

Beth has almost reached the main door when it hits her. She runs back out of school, panic mounting.

There are curved steps leading up to the monument and she can hear a frantic chorus of male shouts all blending into one long howl of rage and hate.

About twenty boys form a ring around two small figures writhing on the ground. Max is one of them.

His shirt has been wrenched from his trousers and his blazer lies in a heap on top of his bag. He has blood coming from his nose and mouth and his hair sticks on end where the other boy must have grabbed it. Both are punching haphazardly at each other, arms swinging, eyes clenched shut.

Then Max starts screaming. Not with pain, but anger. It sends a chill through her as she tries to push through the circle of boys. Max breaks free of the other boy's attempts to hold him down and begins pummelling him in the face and shoulders. There is a frightening intensity to Max's fury and the other boy curls into a ball, trying to protect himself from the onslaught.

'Max!' she shouts. 'Max, stop it!'

Suddenly she is roughly shoved aside. Within a second Max is grabbed by his collar and flung off the boy and onto the ground. Max doesn't realise the size of this new attacker and launches himself at the newcomer, snarling. Before Max can land one single blow, Trev slaps him hard across his face, sending him sprawling. The blow has stunned Max and he tries to get to his feet dizzily.

'Get up arsewipe!' Trev looks ready to hit him again.

'Leave him alone!' She rushes between them.

A vein pulses at Trev's temple. He's red-faced and breathing hard. Then Beth feels the wind being knocked out of her as someone piles in from behind. She hits the ground, feeling gravel gouge at her hands. Someone pulls at her hair, forcing her head backwards. It's as if they mean to pull the hair from her scalp.

She reaches behind her, fingers searching for a purchase on whoever's holding her so tightly. She feels flesh and digs her nails in. Susie yelps and lets go.

Beth jumps up and twists round but Susie's at her again, too quick for her. Beth staggers back, hitting the plinth of the monument and going down, Susie tumbling on top of her. Susie hits her hard, a cracking sound coming from her cheekbone. Beth literally, for one split–second, sees a single silver star. Her vision blurs and she tries to cover her face but Susie's pinning her arms by her side. Another crack. Beth stops struggling. The pain is sharp and already she can feel her eye closing.

There's something wet on her cheek. Susie has spat on her and is wiping her lips as she rises. The ring of boys are slinking away, cradling the boy who was fighting with Max.

Susie hisses at her. 'Think I'd cut you some slack just 'cos your mam's dead?'

Beth's skirt has ridden up in the fight and she tries to smooth it down, catching Trev's dark look as she does this. Susie takes him by the hand and they catch up with the gaggle of boys. Somewhere Beth hears the word 'brother'. Of course, Max was fighting Trev's brother.

She sits up and looks over to Max. He's wiping the blood from his nose onto his jumper sleeve.

'I was winning,' he says, 'til you messed it all up…'

~·~

They walk home in silence, stopping by a stream near the farm where she bends to the water and washes the stray blood from Max's face.

'Don't tell Dad,' he asks.

'*Why* Trev's brother?'

'He said something bad about Mum.'

'What?'

'A nasty word. I *had* to fight him. He's scum.'

She smooths his hair down. Remarkably, he looks untouched.

'You look fine,' she tells him.

'You look like shit.'

As they try to breeze in, acting as if nothing has happened, she can feel her hands start to shake. Adrenalin is kicking in. Grandad sits by the hearth, Rags at his feet. Dad flicks them a look from the cooker, where he is frying onions and garlic.

'How was your day?'

'Crap,' says Max, pounding his way upstairs.

'Max! Don't say 'crap!'' Dad says, too late.

'How about you… Jesus!' He has seen her eye.

'Netball. I caught an elbow.' She holds tightly to her bag in an effort to steady her hands. Her right knee begins to twitch. She doesn't trust herself to speak clearly, teeth beginning to chatter. 'Shower…' she adds, following Max.

She stands forever under the cleansing water, the heat making her face pulse with pain. The mirror sends back her image. Left eye, red and swollen; puffy and slitted. She touches her nose. It's true, doing this does cover her mouth. She's still shaking but the adrenalin's long since drained from her system. Anger has taken its place. Despite the shower she can still smell Susie's candy-scented perfume stench on her. Sickly-sweet.

Dad has cooked pasta but she hardly touches it, fending off his questions about school.

146

'Did anyone say anything about your mum?'

She can feel Grandad's eyes on her and shakes her head.

'Karen's been in touch. Something about her daughter being around for you. That kind of thing.'

Beth puts her half loaded fork down.

'Kind of her, yeah?' Her dad's monotone tells her he's just going through the gears of being alive. She doesn't answer.

'Do you see much of this Susie?' he persists.

Max keeps his eyes on his plate. Grandad keeps his eyes on her. The air in the kitchen is thick. It seems to hum with her mum's absence. She wants to scream. She wants to cry. She wants to run out. She picks her fork up instead. The food tastes like plastic.

'Bits...' she mumbles through the pasta.

Her dad seems happy with this. He plays with his own food. She grips the table to stop the tremors. She can feel her life opening up beneath her like a huge, empty chasm. For a second she feels that this is real and that all of them are going to be tipped headlong into it. She needs to talk and can only think of one person who will want to listen.

'Thanks, Dad. I'm going for a walk.'

Can Grandad see the fear and anger in her?

'Take Rags.' It isn't a request.

'No, I don't know how far...'

'Take him. He needs the exercise.' Grandad is insistent enough to use moral blackmail.

Rags' ears have pricked up at the mention of his name and, with a nod from Grandad, he's on his feet, tail wagging.

There's a real bite in the autumn evening so she takes a zip top over her T-shirt and joggers. She tucks the St Christopher into her top as she slips the latch on the kitchen door. There's a yellow smudge of late afternoon light on the horizon. She steps out.

'Got your phone?' Dad asks.

'Yeah,' she says from the open door. 'Bye.'

'Go on boy…' But Rags needs no prompting off Grandad and he's in front of her, skipping sideways, claws skittering across the cobbles.

They leave the warm glow of the farmhouse windows behind as they walk up the drive. Now she can shake out that anger, gritting her teeth against it, gulping in the cold air. Rags bounds alongside her, head pulled from one side to another by invisible threads, scenting things only he can scent.

They soon reach the tunnelled path, inky black. Having Rags keeps the fear at bay, at least some of it. It's only when they find themselves looking down on that awful bend in the road beneath them does Beth realise she has no real idea how to find Rhys' house.

What little light there was has now been leeched from the sky, leaving it bruised blue. She scans the woods for a sign of the entrance, feeling stupid now, and angrier than ever. She strides out for the nearest tree; maybe once I'm inside I can find the trail, she thinks. She steps over a fallen log and into the cover of the first trees, only to hear a whimpering from behind her.

Rags has stopped dead and dropped to his haunches. His whimper turns into a low growl, ears flattening against his head.

'Come on, Rags.'

The growl intensifies and Rags shuffles backwards.

'It's just a wood, you stupid dog!'

Rags has turned to stone, not moving a muscle.

'Go home!' she orders him. The growl just gets lower.

She turns and leaves him behind, pushing the dread she feels to the back of her mind. Her pace increases until she's batting random branches out of her face, frustration driving her on. It gets darker with every step she makes until she knows that she is absolutely lost. She cries out with anguish, lifting her head to the fractured pieces of sky she can see through the canopy. She gets nothing back. Then a sucking, wet sound; at her feet.

There's something pressing through her running trainers like she's stepped in something soft, something squelchy. She flicks on her phone's torch and points it at the ground. Dozens of worms squirm over her feet and she yelps with shock, flicking them off, doing a weird dance. Under the worms, small skeletons reveal themselves; bones stitching together, flanks fleshing out, fattening. Mice, squirrels, birds; all writhing to the surface of the soil stretching their undead limbs.

She starts to run, her torchlight zigzagging crazily across the wood as she blunders through it. There's a constant crunching under her feet but she doesn't stop to see if it's caused by twigs or bones. She runs until she can feel the ground sloping away from her. This gets steeper and she has to slow, picking her feet over bracken and fallen branches. The canopy above her starts to break up, offering glimpses of sky.

Then, a few feet away, she can see a strip of something pale, leading the way out of the trees. She reaches it and feels it softly give way with each step. It's sand. I must have found a beach, she thinks. She stops to catch her breath. Behind her, in the impenetrable darkness, she can hear terrible scuffling and squeaks.

She jogs down the sandy path and what's left of any light in the sky spills in pale shafts before her. She stops to switch her phone off, saving the battery and that's when she hears voices and tinny music.

The path opens out onto a broad stretch of sand spreading in both directions. To her right the beach ends in the high wall of a dark hill. It looks like a dead end. To her left, around three to four hundred metres away, there is a large campfire, surrounded by several silhouettes.

She can hear the clatter of Welsh voices, laughter. All male. She can hear some techno rattling through a small wireless speaker. She looks behind her into the wood and then back at the fire. No choice really, she thinks, I'll stick to the woods' edge. They probably won't see her.

But, of course, they do.

She hasn't moved for more than half the distance before one of the silhouettes takes a large swig from the can they are holding and turns to throw it into the trees.

'Hey, Trev…'

There's no way into the woods from where she's standing and this bunch are between her and the sea. She looks back at the other end of the beach. She's no sprinter, but if she had a twenty metre start?

'Hello, lovely, what you doing out this late?' Trev looks

unsteady on his feet. His mates whistle at what he's called her.

'Not all wet again, are you?'

A wave of humiliation and fear threatens to wash through her. She tries to control her thoughts, I won't let this happen.

'Piss off, Trev.'

She gets a chorus of ooooos.

'Now, that's not nice. You want I should walk you home?'

'Ho, wait 'til Susie hears about this...' One of the silhouettes speaks.

Trev talks without raising his voice or looking at them, 'like any of you little shits is going to breathe a word...'

There's nervous laughter. Trev tosses his beer away, not caring where it lands. She starts to step sideways, away from the fire. Someone has killed the music. Trev's face comes from out of the shadows, he has that same look as the day by the pool.

'They won't. But I will.' She tries to keep the panic out of her voice. He's too drunk to chase. If she can just get a few more feet between them...

'No, you won't,' he smiles a horrible smile.

She instinctively dips into her knees, ready to propel herself sideways and away. But she's forgotten how quick he is, she's forgotten those rabbits freshly sprung from his traps. He has a steely grip on her shoulder, forcing her face around and up to his. There's something rank under the beer on his breath; weed. He's too close...

She spits full in his face, lashing out with her right foot, aiming for his knee. The kick just bounces off, sending a bolt of pain through her foot. His grip tightens, fingers digging into her shoulder, making her yelp with pain.

'You dirty little bitch,' he's hissing.

Despite the dryness in her throat, she tries to hawk up some more spit. Then he hits her and her head explodes.

She's lying on the sand, feels it between her fingers as she tries to claw her way upright. Can't stay down here…

Trev's face looms over her. 'But that's okay, I like dirty girls…' He has her by the armpit and picks her up effortlessly.

'Trev?' Another silhouette speaks.

'I've told you, keep it shut…'

'There's someone coming…'

She can still see through her one good eye as the other is beginning to shut completely. A figure is walking calmly towards them, from the woods where she emerged only seconds earlier. They walk loosely, easily. No rush.

'The fuck d'you want?' Trev still has hold of her.

The stranger walks into the light from the spluttering fire and offers her a hand.

'Here,' Rhys speaks softly.

'Hey, she's with mates here. Do one.' Trev tenses his hold.

'I don't think so. Come on Beth.'

Trev laughs and lets go of her. He stands squarely above Rhys and then shoves him hard in his chest, sending him back a pace or two. Trev's mates emerge from the shadows and begin to crowd in, surrounding Rhys.

Rhys speaks calmly. 'Don't make me hurt you…'

The smacking sound as Trev hits Rhys full in the face is awful. Rhys doesn't flinch, his head has only twitched at the blow. It's like he's simply absorbed it. A look of dumb perplexion crosses Trev's features. He draws back his ham of a fist again.

Rhys' punch is a blur and Trev's head snaps back on his shoulders, spittle flying from his open mouth. His knees go and he folds into the ground, fists still raised, eyes vacant. It is so quick and so final that no one moves. Rhys drops his guard and looks around the ring of Trev's mates. They seem confused, they shift on their feet, some still holding beer cans.

'We're going now.' It's as if Rhys is talking to a class of ten year olds. He takes her hand and leads her out of the circle and back to the path from the woods. He doesn't talk until they are wrapped in the blackness of the trees.

'You shouldn't be out on your own like this.'

'I was looking for you.'

'Well, you found me.'

He stoops to gather some dark leaves and begins to roll them under his fingers, pulping them.

'Here, hold this to your eye.'

She does and they sting like mad.

'What is this stuff?'

'Dunno, I only know it helps.'

'You could have been hurt then. There were loads of them.'

'But only one who counted.'

'Thank you.'

'Is it like that at school?' he asks.

'Sometimes.'

She watches him swallow down whatever he was going to say next.

'How come Trev didn't hurt you?' She can't even see a mark.

'He did. It's all about not showing it.'

She touches her cheek. 'Oh, okay…'

They walk on in silence until they reach the lane at the top of the farm. The lights still glow in the windows. Rags is there and trots to meet her, tail wagging. He stops short of Rhys though, ears flattening.

'Your dog doesn't like me.'

'What can I say, he's a stupid dog.'

'I'll watch you go in.'

'No, I'm, fine now.'

'I'll still watch.'

She searches his eyes for some emotion, but finds none. It's unnerving and she thinks Trev has hurt him more than he wants to let on.

'Go on, they'll be missing you.'

She reaches for his hand and places the sodden leaves in his palm. As he looks down at them she quickly tips onto her toes and kisses him on the cheek.

'Thank you. For today.'

She's back on her heels and Rhys is looking down into her eyes. Did he even register the kiss?

He flashes a quick, awkward smile. This disappears just as swiftly as he turns away, walking off down the road.

She hadn't planned the kiss, probably even surprised herself and now wishes she hadn't done it. She stands there on the lane wanting to shrink into the ground and have it swallow her up. Then there's Rags, nudging at her ankles, bringing her back to reality. Or at least, to her version of reality. He'd said he'd watch me go and now I've spoiled it, she thinks. Well, wasn't *that* inevitable?

She watches as Rhys' shape bleeds into the dark then turns away and heads for the lights. The cosy glow suddenly drives tears into her eyes. Her mum won't be there. A wave of bottomless sorrow makes her heave. She touches her swollen eye. It's sore but she can just see out of it. Rhys' herbs or whatever have worked, kind of.

She's often wondered what happens to people when they get as low as it's possible to be. Those people who kill themselves. What pulls some of them back from the brink? Is it that they recognise there are people who care for them? Is it the little things like that clump of leaves? When Trev hit her she now knows that she was in fear for her life. And fought for it. She fought for whatever the future has in store for her. For whatever's next.

CHAPTER 21

Dad has asked if he can come and watch her play netball. Beth doesn't think he's buying her black eye story, so she's told him she's quit, it's too violent. The first few days at school have been eerily quiet, no sign of Susie. It's almost like a taste of what it would be like if she never existed.

Beth keeps a close eye on Max and she insists they walk home, or get the bus. It's getting darker with every day though and the clocks go back soon. She doesn't fancy the walk in the dark. Max has told her about the school gossip from the lads; someone battered Trev. No one ever batters Trev.

She hasn't run for a while now, hasn't seen Rhys. She guesses she's too embarrassed and he's obviously keeping his distance. There have been times walking home, when she's felt as if they've been followed. It's got to be Trev, but he's never shown himself.

Today though, Susie is back and Trev's here, lounging in his usual spot opposite the school. Beth's trying to ignore him, thinking about taking the bus for a change.

Max and his sidekick, Sadie, trot out and say their goodbyes. Susie's behind them. She's taken to rolling her walk like she's some kind of cut-price Kardashian on a shopping trip. It's ridiculous and makes Beth hate her even more. Then several things happen almost at once.

Trev stands to attention, slouch gone, and she assumes it's because of Susie. Susie spots this and follows Trev's line of vision. They're both looking off down the road, towards town. Beth turns to see what's grabbed their attention to find herself looking at Rhys, walking slowly across the railway lines.

A car arrives and then pulls up at the kerb, in front of Trev. Beth can see the driver; it's Karen. Karen lets her window down and waves at her. Beth waves back and then looks over to Rhys. He's concentrating on Beth, smiling slowly.

Susie's crossing the road to her mum's car but she can't take her eyes off Rhys. Trev's gone purple, literally the colour of a rotten plum. Susie bends to speak to Karen through the open window, blocking her mum out.

'Hi, how's school?' Rhys is smiling, almost lazily. It's like nothing's happened. Rhys stands in front of her and Max, hands in the pockets of his ripped jeans. He wears a fading black cord jacket over a plain white T.

'Okay...' Goddammit, she thinks, I'm touching my nose again.

'Who's this?' Rhys asks.

'I'm Max.'

'Hi Max.'

'Did you batter Trev?'

'No.' That lazy smile again.

'Yeah, you did.'

Rhys shrugs.

'Who are you?' Max won't let go.

'Friend of Beth's'

Beth hears a car rev and watches as Susie steps away from Karen's car window, which is sliding up. Karen looks straight ahead as she pulls the car into a U-turn and sweeps past them.

She looks angry, but then again, Susie does that to people. It's not Karen's fault her daughter's a bitch. Beth waves at the departing car and draws Rhys' attention to it, all in the same beat.

The casual look on his face changes and lines appear where before he was loose.

'You okay?' Beth asks.

'Yeah, I'm, err, yeah. Fine.' He watches the car disappear. 'Who was that?'

'Susie's Mum.'

'Who's Susie?'

'*She* is,' states Max, pointing across the road where Susie and Trev stand side by side. Trev tries to take Susie by the arm but she shrugs him off, eyes on Rhys.

'Do you know her?' Beth asks. Rhys is still acting weird. 'Karen. Susie. Either of them?'

'Never seen that one before. The woman in the car, I dunno...'

'She used to teach here.'

The lines on Rhys' face deepen. Beth starts to wonder why he has turned up now.

'Have you been following us? All week?'

'Yeah.'

'Why?'

'Make sure you're alright.'

'Go and fight him, now,' Max is looking up at Rhys in awe.

'No.'

'You scared?'

'No.'

Rhys looks across the road and Trev seems to wither under

his gaze. Suddenly Susie strides away and Trev trips after her without a backward glance.

'I'll walk you both home.' Rhys watches them go.

'You don't have to,' Beth tells him.

'I want to.' He turns his green eyes back on her.

'Are you two kissing?' Max asks.

'Does it look like it?' Rhys replies.

Max thinks through his answer. 'Nah.'

'Well then...' And Rhys begins the walk home. Beth pushes Max out in front of them.

'Your eye's healing well,' Rhys comments.

'Yeah, thanks.'

'So, that Susie, is she with the big lad?'

Beth nods. 'They're made for each other.'

'Are they?' He's deadpan.

'God, yes... both bullies.'

'So you think like attracts like?' he asks.

'Dunno. S'pose so in their case.'

'She was staring at me.'

As if I hadn't noticed, Beth thinks.

'Has she hurt you too?' he asks.

'What will you do, knock *her* out?' He looks as though he might.

'I could talk to her.'

'I think she'd like that.'

'Do you?'

'You're being weird today,' as Beth speaks, she realises how stupid this sounds.

'Define weird.' He knits his brows.

'Me,' Beth answers honestly.

'You? Weird? No.'

'She so is,' from Max, over his shoulder.

'Shut up and stop listening.' She thinks about making him walk further ahead.

'Want to go to Criccieth?' Rhys' smile is back, warmer now.

'Criccieth? What's there?'

'Castle. Ice cream. Fossils.'

'Wow.'

'Is that sarcasm? That's very good, *very* funny,' he teases her and Beth realises that she likes it. Kind of.

'Do you drive?' She tries to mask what she feels.

'Err, no. I don't think so...'

'Err, either you know or you don't.'

'I had lessons, while back... never got round to passing.'

'So what, we walk?'

'Walk there, bus back?'

Criccieth is a good six or seven miles away. 'Do you run?' She thinks he looks like a runner.

'Only when I have to.'

She hasn't been to Criccieth for ages. Was it always raining there, or is that her memory playing tricks?

'That'd be nice. Like a date?'

He smiles again. 'Just like a date. I'll pay.'

'No you won't! I owe you for saving my life.'

'Bit of an exaggeration?'

'I don't think so.' She's serious.

'If I'd known, I'd have hit him harder.'

'I should have gone to the police.'

'Your word against his... and his mates.'

'*You* were there…?'

'I avoid the police. Technically speaking, I have run away…'

'So where's all your money coming from then?'

'Here and there. I manage.'

His look tells her she's getting no more. 'We could go on Saturday?'

'Okay.'

'A date then?' he asks.

'A date.'

'Can I come?' asks Max.

'We'll buy you a postcard,' Beth tells him.

'It's just over there.' Max points over to the north.

'Save on a stamp then,' Rhys adds.

They walk on in silence and she starts to feel guilty that she's going to have a day out, supposedly enjoying herself, whilst she's leaving a house of misery behind. She snatches a look at Rhys, loping along by her side and he's done that eye/mirror trick.

'You need a break,' he says, simply.

He's not wrong.

CHAPTER 22

Saturday is crisp and bright, like Saturdays should be. From her window she can see the early sun drawing steam off the grass. She rests her forehead on the glass and feels the chill. She'll need more layers. She slips into her Levi's, ever-present sports bra and goes for a T-shirt Mum bought her last birthday.

It has a picture of a carrot on it and the word 'potato' underneath. She doesn't know why, but she remembers Mum finding it hilarious, saying it just about summed Beth up. She swallows down the lump in her throat and covers the T-shirt up with a grey Adidas hoodie. Hiding who I really am, does that sum me up, she thinks?

A last check in the mirror before she goes gives her another dilemma; hair up or down? Up makes her mouth huge, down almost hides it. Down it is. She checks her phone for messages. None, not even Sienna knows what to say right now.

Seeing the three males in the kitchen brings it home that she's the only female here. Dad's scanning his Saturday Guardian, sports' page first as Max and Grandad eat a fry-up.

'There's some in the pan for you, love.' Grandad smiles at her.

Dad's phone trills with a text and Max is lightning-quick in snatching it up before Dad can put his paper down.

'Karen,' says Max.

Dad reaches for his phone, idly looking at the text before

placing it, face down on the table.

'I'll get something on the way, thanks, Grandad.' Beth scans Joe's face for an emotion.

'Damn right you will girl.' Grandad rises from the table to slice two book-sized pieces from the loaf in front of him. As she slips her blue trainers on, he crams the contents of the pan between the slices. Bacon, a sausage, an egg... black pudding.

'Yuck, no black pudding, thanks?'

'Bit of blood never did anyone any harm, build you up.'

Beth doesn't argue that she's trying to cut the blood out of her diet.

'Who's your friend?' asks Dad as she takes the doorstep butty off Grandad.

'He battered Trev but hasn't kissed her yet,' Max explains.

'What?' Dad now looks up from his sports.

Grandad is even more intrigued. 'I'd heard Trev had a bit of a smack. Wondered where he'd been.'

'He didn't batter anyone,' she lies, 'he's a friend.'

'From school?'

'No. He's left.'

'Oh. Right,' Dad leaves this hanging, waiting for more. He's not going to get any.

'Dad, he's nice okay? Normal and nice. Trust me.'

'So, not a date then?' He won't let go.

Beth cocks her head at him, a warning look.

'You need friends right now,' Dad says, warning heeded.

'Like Karen?' She can't help it; see if *he* likes the third degree.

'I might go back, to Manchester, in a week or two, pick up

163

some stuff from work… we should all go – half term maybe?'
He's ducked the question.

'Yeah, that'd be good.' She checks her phone, almost late.
'Okay, see you later.'

'Not inviting… errr?'

'Rhys.'

'Not inviting Rhys in?'

'Not today, no. Bye.'

'Don't be late.'

Beth smiles at her Dad and slips out of the door.

Looking up the lane she sees Rhys marching confidently
down it, so she jogs to head him off.

'Hi.'

He's wearing all black. Black skinny jeans, a T-shirt with
the Damien Hirst diamond skull on it and black Converse.
His rucksack is also black. The effect makes his fair hair and
green eyes stand out even more.

'Let's go,' Beth says.

'Your family in?' he asks.

'Yes and no.'

'Eh?'

'Yes they're in, and no, you're not meeting them.'

'Oh, okay.'

'Here have this.' She offers him the black pudding from her
butty.

'Thanks. You look good. Is this like… grunge chic?'

'That's rich. Wannabe Goth.'

'It's Damien Hirst, he pickles dead things.'

'I know.'

'You eating all of that?'

She looks at the size of the sandwich. 'Not sure.'

'You should.'

They set off as she takes her first bite. Rhys pops the black pudding in his mouth, whole. She can smell autumn; woody and fruity. The sky is a flawless blue, turning purple on the horizon as it folds into the sea.

They decide to get the bus to Morfa Bychan and bounce along, the sun now hot through the windows. Rhys pays. Occasionally their thighs bump together.

'I have got my own money you know?' she tells him.

'My treat.'

'I might not want "treating."'

He turns his gaze on her and tilts his head quizzically. She feels mean. He holds out his open palm.

'Three-twenty.'

'What?'

'Your fare.'

She looks, but he's not joking. She prises herself out of the seat and fishes in her tight jean pockets. A ten pound note and some twos and pennies.

'I don't want your shrapnel.'

'My *what?*'

'S'what my dad used to call change, pennies and stuff. Fills up your pockets.'

'This all I've got.'

'You pay for the castle then.'

He turns to look out of the window and they bounce back along. In silence.

They walk along the road leading to Black Rock Sands. He still hasn't said a word, so she's starting to think that he's sulking. Then she realises she has no idea what's going on in his head, because she hardly knows anything about him at all; other than he's weird and he saved her life.

The road gradually gives way to sand and then opens up onto the beach. It's a huge expanse of ribbed sand, the tide way out, a thin strip of deepest green. The sun is a perfect ball of gold hovering over distant Harlech. It's all ridiculously beautiful. Their shadows stretch out before them as they stride along.

'We can walk around the cliffs,' he says, 'with the tide being so far out.'

Okay, small talk will do. For now.

'Yeah, okay.'

Apart from the odd dog walker, they are the only people on the beach. It feels special. The day has turned so calm that the sea is supernaturally still, like glass. They walk right by the water's edge, listening to it barely slap the sand as the tiny waves fold over at their feet.

'It always makes me feel like swimming, when it's like this...' he says.

'We could. Bet you it's no colder than being out here.'

He looks at her like she's mad. Then he stops and kicks his trainers off without touching the laces. He's not wearing socks. He steps confidently into the water, forgetting to roll his trousers up.

'You're right. Just as cold'

'Don't sound so surprised.'

'Come on then...' He's grinning.

166

'Swimming?'

'As if. We can paddle all the way to Criccieth.'

She unties her own trainers, tucks her socks into them, rolls up her jeans and steps in. It's colder than she'd expected but she's determined not to show it. On they go, shoes in hand.

Ahead of them, beyond the cliffs that give Black Rock Sands its name, the sun has picked out the castle at Criccieth. It's going to take them another hour at least. She looks back. The nearest dog-walker is now a tiny dot on the horizon. They're as good as alone on a three mile stretch of sand and rock. Just the rhythmic splash of their bare feet and the occasional screeching of a gull.

She ditches the small talk. 'I don't know anything about you.'

'Yeah you do. Mum's an alky, Dad's dead, stepdad's a dick.'

'Okay, but that's not about you... now?'

'True.'

'So? What d'you do all day?' she persists.

'I get by.'

'Where d'you get your money?'

Rhys looks at her, serious. 'You think I steal it?'

'God, no!'

He looks away, not convinced.

'Really, I don't,' she adds.

They spend a few minutes not talking. Splash, splash, splash. The rocks at the foot of the cliffs are closer now and she can pick out the Welsh flag hanging limply from the top of Criccieth castle.

'I sell what I kill. Restaurants, bars, they'll all take rabbits

167

and fish for cash. Other stuff, I catch. I never steal them though.'

'Okay. That's cool.'

'So now you know more.'

'You seem to know a lot about me. That stuff you said about me and my mum.'

'Intuition. I felt it.'

'That's weird. Isn't it?'

'Yeah, s'pose. Anyway, you never hated her.' He is so certain.

'I was angry.'

'That's different.'

They round the headland between the two beaches and Black Rock's sand gives way to pebbles and rocks that the sea has washed into giant shelves.

'Where did you go? When my mum died? I saw you and then you'd gone.'

'You want to go through all that? Now?'

She's not sure. 'Yeah.'

'I honestly don't know. I mean, I went back to the house, but, not like, straight away.'

'You'd just seen my mum get run over. You watched me screaming.'

'I didn't know what to do. I was scared.'

She checks him for any sign that this might be the truth. Rhys looks properly spooked.

'I have… I had these blackouts. When I was a kid. Low blood pressure. I hadn't had one for ages. Until that day. Usually I just come to where I fell, but sometimes I'd moved. It's scary. It's like my body's woken up without telling my brain. I wouldn't have been any real help, sorry.'

'So why are you doing all this for me now?' she asks.

'All what?'

'I dunno. Everything…'

'Because I can. Because I've got nothing else to do.'

'Oh right, thanks.'

'Sorry, that came out wrong. Because I want to.'

They seem to be eating up the space between themselves and the castle.

'All that stuff about us being together?'

'Did that freak you out?'

'A bit.' More than a bit, actually, she thinks.

'My mum always used to say I was too serious. I think about things a lot.'

'Do you miss her?' she asks, because, how couldn't he?

'Sometimes.'

'Your dad?'

'Always.' He's staring out to sea.

'I'm sorry.'

'Don't be. Look.'

Rhys points out to the water. There, about fifteen or so metres away, a seal has bobbed up to look at them. Its head is the only thing to put a ripple in the vast, motionless water. They stop to stare back. Rhys waves at it and for a split second, she almost expects it to wave back.

'They don't usually come in that close.'

'It's beautiful.' She means it. The seal doesn't move an inch, it seems to hover on the surface. Rhys talks without taking his eyes off the seal.

'I get a bit hazy sometimes. About what's happened. It was

a nightmare at school.'

'The blackouts?'

'S'pose, yeah.'

'That must be horrible.'

Rhys doesn't answer. Instead he knits his brows and turns from the seal to peer along what remains of the shoreline between them and the castle. Then suddenly he sets off and, after a beat, she trails in his wake.

She tries to see what has pricked him into action, but all she can see are the rocks, all shapes and sizes. But of course, not everything on the shoreline is a rock... Now she dreads every step.

Rhys reaches it seconds before she does. The baby seal is a misshapen mess of yellowy fur. Rhys squats and lowers a hand onto the lifeless body. She swallows hard, waiting for that feeling.

'We shouldn't touch it.'

'I don't think it's been dead long... that must be its mum.'

She looks out and sees that the seal has followed them.

'Really, Rhys, it could have all sorts...'

He ignores her and digs his fingers under the sand, under the baby's body. He lifts it clear from the beach. Gently.

Oh God, please not now, she thinks. Not this time.

Rhys stands with the seal in his arms and walks slowly into the water, beyond his knees. Struggling to get her breathing under control she watches as he bends and lowers the body into the sea. He stands and dips his hands back into the water, pushing. Then he's upright, wiping his hands on his jeans.

She feels nothing. Then she looks past Rhys in time to see

the mother seal dip beneath the surface. The tiny wake it has caused widens slowly and then washes silently past Rhys, who is still thigh deep in the water. He turns and wades back out.

'Not sure why I did that.'

'It was beautiful,' she speaks from a sense of relief.

'Was it? The next tide will probably just wash it back up.'

'It might not.' She tries to concentrate but doesn't know what to concentrate on. She scans the water, willing herself to see through it. She closes her eyes and tries to picture the baby seal, but no pictures come.

This is ironic she thinks, most of the time I'm blocking pictures from my head, making them go away. So she stops and imagines the unfolding of a picture this time. Corner by corner, fold by fold the baby seal comes back into her head. But the only image she has is of it lying dead on the shore. Then she remembers the butterfly. She remembers its beauty, its stillness. The sea remains a mirror to the endless sky.

'I'm soaked,' Rhys announces. 'You okay?'

'Yes. Well, I'm sad.'

Rhys sits to slip his trainers back over his bare and sandy feet. He stands, water forming a pool from his sodden jeans.

'You'll catch your death.'

'I'm okay. Don't feel the cold much. Which is probably just as well given how I…'

He stops mid-sentence and looks deeply into her eyes. 'Are you crying?'

'No,' she answers truthfully.

He reaches out and brushes a finger across her cheek. Her face tingles where he has touched it.

'Okay, your eye's leaking then. And it's bloodshot.'

She instinctively rubs at her eye, knuckles coming away wet and pink.

'It must be colder than I thought,' Rhys adds, 'you want my top? It's okay…'

But he has stopped again and he's not looking at her any more. She spins around and there, a hundred metres or so from the shore their seal has surfaced again to stare at them.

'Wait…' Rhys says. 'Watch…'

She does and then a small pale head breaks the surface. The baby seal brushes against its mother for a second and then curls neatly under the water. The mother swiftly follows and only the ripples remain. She feels elated and turns to see Rhys' reaction – just in time to see him crumble and fall hard onto the sand.

'Rhys!'

She's over in a second, kneeling by him, turning him over onto his side, putting him in the recovery position. He's chalk-white, eyes rolled up into his skull. In a dead faint. She looks around frantically. No one. She scrambles for her phone, which, of course, has no signal. She checks the distance between them and the nearest building. She could do it in about five minutes, but that means leaving him lying here. Is the tide coming back in yet?

She needs to drag him up the shore, onto the rocks. She grabs him under his arms and begins to take the strain, her heels slipping in the sand. She can feel tears of frustration choking her. Rhys coughs. A shudder passes through his body, she feels it through her hands. She sits down, raising his head into her lap, keeping it dry. His eyes flutter open.

'Hello,' he says.

'Oh my God, you scared me to death.'

'Told you, I black out. What happened?'

'We were watching the seals…'

'The baby came back…' Rhys is shaking his head.

'She must have two pups,' she offers. Then she realises she still has his head in her lap. He's gazing up at her and the sun slants through his eyes revealing their depths.

'It was the same pup, wasn't it?'

She checks the genuine amazement that has transformed his face. He is grinning ear to ear, scraping the hair from his forehead, eyes alive. 'Wow…'

'You going to get up now?'

'Oh. Right. Sure.' He rises, getting wet sand all over his already soaking trousers.

'You can't wear those jeans all day.'

'Don't have much choice.'

'Criccieth is full of charity shops.'

'Hey, I've got my rep to consider.'

'Trust me, that won't suffer.'

As she starts to walk he bends for a second, hands on his knees, breathing deeply.

'You feel faint?' she asks.

'Nah. I'm good thanks.' He straightens. 'The water must've revived it?'

'Never mind the seal, can you walk?'

'Yeah. Wait.' He shrugs off his backpack and pulls a banana and a couple of apples out. 'Fuel,' he says, tossing her an apple.

'I'm not the one who fainted.'

'Eat it.'

They stand as she takes a bite. His banana is gone in about two bites. Through a mouthful of banana he talks again.

'I was sure it was dead.'

'You were wrong.'

He seems to look through her as he chews, puzzling. Then he dips inside his bag again. This time it's a huge sandwich stuffed with a greyish meat and something green and full of stems. This too is gone in seconds. He hands her a smaller version of his sandwich but she's only half way through the apple.

'Dunno what's wrong with me. Eating for Wales.'

'Feel better though?'

'Loads.'

They set off and she takes a tentative bite from her sandwich. It's gamey and crunchy. The last few yards of the beach are on pebbles that slip over each other, crunching, tipping you sideways. They climb up and walk along the sea wall and she can hear his feet beginning to squelch.

'You sound ridiculous.'

'You reckon?'

'I know.'

He stops and shucks his shoes off again, ties the laces together and flings them over his neck, like a scarf. He sets off, barefoot, making her smile.

'Better?'

'Not really, but you'll do.'

She leads him away from the beach, over the railway that runs through the middle of Criccieth and to a charity shop with telescopes and jigsaws in its window. Inside is like an Aladdin's cave of tat. Boxes of vinyl with middle- aged men on their covers, wearing thick cable-knit cardigans and cradling acoustic guitars. Shelves of ancient family type games. Mousetrap, Cluedo, Bucking Bronco. Rhys is in awe.

'We've shifted into another time zone.'

There's a little old lady sitting by the door who smiles benignly at them as they enter.

Rhys whispers to her, brushing her hair as he does, his breath in her ear.

'I reckon she's for sale too.'

'Shush!'

'Check her out for a ticket or something. Reduced. Closing down, all stock must go?'

'Be quiet.'

They walk past aisles of pastel coloured glass ornaments. The sun struggles to penetrate grime-smeared windows, which back onto the rail lines.

'Oh my God,' Rhys says, 'a typewriter! An *actual* typewriter.'

'What waist are you?'

'Thirty two.'

She looks him up and down.

'Last time I checked.'

In the gloom of the shop she finds a pair of thirty two inch tweedy-looking trousers. She holds them out.

'No,' he says.

'They're the only thirty twos.'

'They're flares.'

'No they're not.'

'If I was an old man, playing golf, smoking a pipe... and colour blind. Then maybe.'

'Try them on.'

He shakes his head.

'You can, I won't watch!' the old lady cackles from her stool by the door.

Beth thrusts them at him, making her eyes wide in mute appeal. He takes them off her, grimacing at how they feel.

'If you don't put them on, she'll never let us out and we'll end up on a shelf, two ninety-nine each.'

He pops the button on his jeans and she looks away, towards the old lady who winks conspiratorially at her. She hears a zip and his wet jeans slop on the floor. The old lady astonishes her by wolf whistling expertly and loudly.

'Forgot to mention. The place is full of mirrors!' she cackles again, slips a cigarette from its packet and totters outside sparking up a lighter.

'Well?' Beth hears Rhys say. She turns and sees that the trousers fit pretty well. And that they are, most decidedly, flares.

'Perfect,' she says, 'come on.'

The old lady takes her three pounds and winks at Rhys, sending him puce.

'I owe you three quid,' he tells her outside.

'My treat.'

'What if I don't want "treating?"' he throws back at her.

'Then it's worth three quid to see a pair of flares on the streets after all this time.'

'You said they weren't flares!'

'I lied.'

They set off for the castle, which for all of its crumbling walls, still dominates the town.

She looks sideways at him, colour still flush in his cheeks, hands stuffed in prickly pockets.

'Do you want to walk a bit behind me, say three or four paces?'

'Funny. You should be on telly.'

'*Telly*??'

'As in telly-vision.'

'Wow, those trousers have seeped into your brain.'

She shakes her head at his look of mock-outrage and they walk on up the hill.

CHAPTER 23

The castle is almost a shell but the views are right across both sides of the bay. Down the south to Barmouth and along the west to Bardsey Island. Ahead of them, somewhere, is Ireland. They lean on the walls and Rhys breaks out two more sandwiches. Beth has paid to get in.

'You a bit of a feeder?' she asks.

'You counting the calories?'

'No,' she says, too quickly.

'I get to wear prickly pants, you get to eat my butty.'

She bites and chews. Minutes seem to pass but she doesn't feel awkward, not talking. She fills her lungs with the sea air, wondering what time it is but not looking. In a strange way she doesn't want it to be later than she thinks it is, she wants the day to last.

'I feel… connected to you,' Rhys says, out of nothing. 'Did from the moment I saw you.'

She looks at him, sandwich paused on its way to her mouth.

'You asked – why was I doing stuff for you.'

'Oh, okay.' She lowers the sandwich.

'I don't *actually* know why. I was never any good with girls. Awkward really. Sometimes I can't believe the stuff comes out of my mouth. About you, you know?'

'Oh…'

'It's like there's this… *need* to protect you. And there are times when I can see through you. I mean, not *literally* in an

178

X-ray kind of way. Not pervy. I sense what you're thinking, how you feel.'

Suddenly she feels vulnerable and exposed.

'I didn't want to say any of this. You must be well freaked out. Again.'

'No. Well, okay then, yes.'

'Should we go?'

'No. Not yet.'

'Sorry.'

'Don't be. I should be flattered. Shouldn't I?'

'It's confusing, isn't it?'

She nods.

'How's the sandwich?' he asks.

She'd forgotten she was holding it. 'Good thanks.'

'Leave room for an ice cream.'

'You'll have to roll me home.'

'We could get the bus?'

She thinks for a moment, the bus would be quicker. She'd be home within the hour.

'No, let's walk.'

~·~

The sun is high on the way back and so warm that she peels off her hoodie. Rhys laughs at the carrot T-shirt until she reminds him of his pants. She has managed a whole ice cream. Even the cone. They both look out to sea as they walk along the beach. There's no sign of any seals.

'How long can you live on your own?' she asks.

'Long as I want?'

'Through winter?'

'S'pose.'

'If I was your mum, I'd come looking for you.'

'But you're not.'

'No.'

The tide has come in quite a way and they can no longer walk around the cliffs separating Criccieth beach from Black Rock. A wind has picked up with the change in tide and there are low clouds on the horizon, like a lace collar. They set off over the headland.

'Where are your friends?'

'I'm not sure,' Rhys replies. 'Moved on I guess, you know, whilst I was away with Mum.'

'All of them?'

'Didn't have many. Not going to either, in these pants.'

'I don't like to think of you, on your own.'

Rhys stops walking. 'I'm not on my own, I've got you.'

'What if we move? Back home, to Manchester?'

'Why would you?'

'This was Mum's home. Not Dad's.'

'I don't think you will.'

He sets off again. She catches him up.

'You might meet a girl?'

He snorts.

'I might meet a boy?'

'You have.'

'I mean… you know what I mean.'

'Like Trev?'

'That's not funny.'

'Sorry.'

He stops again. 'Look, what do you want me to do?' he asks.

'I don't know.'

'Want me to leave you alone?'

'No.'

'You like my sandwiches?'

'Yes…'

'Want your trousers back?'

'No!' She laughs.

He smiles. 'You should laugh more often.'

She stops, hand flittering around her nose. He reaches up and gently draws it away. His touch makes her tingle. He still holds her hand, which is getting warmer by the second. Then he lets it go and lifts his fingers to her face, her cheek. It burns under his touch. She can't bear to look him in the eyes. She looks away, the sea, the grass at their feet, anywhere.

'Your mouth is beautiful.'

'Please don't.'

'Don't what?'

'Patronise me.'

'I'm not.'

His hand falls by his side and she's not sure that's what she wanted.

For an eternity they stand facing each other and she can feel the breeze getting stronger, lifting his hair.

'Come on, there's a bus from Morfa in fifteen minutes, we can make it.'

And they do.

~·~

Rhys walks with her to the top of the farm lane as the sun begins to dip into the trees. The sky is still clear enough to see the first stars. As she glances at the farmhouse she sees the kitchen light go on.

'There you go,' Rhys says, 'home by dark.'

'Thanks.'

'It's okay, I'm not going to ask to come in.'

They stand feet apart for a moment and then go into an awkward, mutual kind of hug. He's warm and smells of the sea. They break and he casually sweeps her hair from across her face, where the wind has blown it.

'Keep smiling,' he says before turning and walking off down the road.

She feels like calling out but doesn't know what to say. Instead it's Rhys who calls, back, over his shoulder.

'And stop laughing at my flares…'

She reaches under her T-shirt and fishes out the St Christopher, twisting the chain through her fingers. The low sun turns the medallion's silvery face orange and it seems to glow in her hand. The patron saint of travellers; safe journeys, safe haven.

Rhys is getting smaller as he walks away, trousers flapping around his ankles. She touches the medallion to her mouth, tasting the tang of silver. It leaves a hot spot where she has brushed it with her lips. She drops it back down inside her top and turns away, down the lane. To home.

Once she's past her dad's cross-examination for the prosecution, she opens her bedroom door and finds that someone has replaced all of her mum's trophies. She also finds that she doesn't mind. It's like her mum's looking down on

her as she draws the duvet up to her chin and falls into a deep
and dreamless sleep.

CHAPTER 24

School and life falls into a pattern. Learning Welsh is like throwing pebbles at a concrete wall, hoping that one day, it will crumble. More often than not Rhys meets her and Max to walk them to the bus. More often than not, Susie follows with her mates.

Trev has started driving a battered old van, more rust than paint. He stays in it outside the school, glowering at everyone. The last day before half term is an out-of-uniform Friday and they all pay a pound each to turn up in whatever they want. Max comes in his uniform, because he can. Beth wears some old jeans, a hoodie and leaves her hair down.

Except her jeans feel a bit tight today, they nip at her tummy. She realises that she hasn't shopped for a while and most of her clothes are for running or training. This has never bothered her before, but now she's started washing her own (and everyone else's) stuff she can see just how little she owns.

Just before setting off for home Beth pops into the girls' toilets. They are vile, so God knows what the boys' are like. As she washes her hands and shakes them dry she hears the door open and someone slip in. It's Susie.

Susie's on her own for once and Beth immediately considers if she can take her. Susie stands a few feet away, arms folded across a fake DKNY T-shirt.

'One of Trev's mates told me about you and him on that beach.'

Gulp.

'He only told me to get in my pants. Or to try. Thought I'd ditch Trev. He was wrong and he won't be telling me any more secrets for a while.'

'Trev attacked me,' Beth decides that truth is the best policy.

'Me and Trev, we're good together, we bring stuff other people couldn't. Especially a freak like you. But he gets muddled now and then.'

'I was going to go to the Police.'

'But you didn't. 'Cos you got someone bigger and stronger than Trev.'

'He's none of those things and he's not mine.'

'Oh right, that's good then, 'cos he's hot. Rhys, isn't it?' Susie can see the surprise in Beth's face. 'Your *special* brother's got a big mouth.'

'Why do you hate us?'

'Apparently we were besties. When we were babies and had no choice. Mam's got pictures and all sorts.'

'So?'

'This place not good enough for you though was it? For your stuck-up *mother*.'

'Is that *it*?'

'Mam's been texting your dad. I check her phone every now and then. Not told *my* dad yet, he's got a bit of a temper, see?'

'It's called being a friend.'

'She's got all the friends she needs.'

'You must be sick if you think…'

'Don't call me sick,' Susie has unfolded her arms. Beth stares at her like she would a mad dog, waiting for the next move. Ready…

'Be best if you fucked off back to Manchester, don't you think?'

Oh my God, am I being run out of town, Beth thinks? She'd almost laugh if she wasn't so scared.

'That's up to Dad.'

'You could stay your whole rotten life, you'd never belong here.' Susie's face is twisted into a mask. Then just as suddenly, she smiles wickedly. 'Tell Rhys I said Hi.'

Susie leaves and Beth finds that her hands have curled into fists. She eases them open, exposing sweaty palms. She thinks of Manchester, seeing Sienna, being in their house, watching Comedy Central on twenty-four hour repeat.

~·~

On the way to the bus station they pass Pike's newsagents. The local newspaper sits outside, a dragon proudly poses on the front page. She has almost walked past when she stops Max and goes back for another look.

She steps inside and pays for the paper, folding it into her school bag and keeping it until they are on the bus, driving through the encroaching darkness. Max thumbs through his phone as she takes it out again and shakes the front page open. And reads.

Porthmadog police have reported a spate of recent attacks on residents and their pets by local wildlife. A spokesman gave us this warnin. 'These attacks are bizarre, animals you wouldn't believe could carry out such aggression are targeting the area's domestic pets, and, in some cases, their owners. There has been nothing too serious to date, but locals should be aware and keep an eye on their pets over night or out walking. Anyone affected by this should seek immediate medical advice on inoculation.'

The dog was my fault – is this, she thinks? She scans the countryside as it slides past. How many *things* are out there, now, because of her? And there's nothing she can do about it. Well, there is. Go back to Manchester, her real home. Stay away from death. Actually, she thinks, that's not so easy – death has a way of creeping up on you.

Grandad has promised not to take up marathons whilst they're away and Dad's packing up the car. She finds him in his and Mum's bedroom, a huge case open on the bed. He's sitting by it, holding something, undecided. He sees Beth come in and offers a weak smile. He's got a woman's scarf in his hand.

'I haven't sorted through your mum's stuff.'

'You shouldn't have to.'

'Karen's offered…'

'I can help,' she says quickly and not meaning it.

'No. It's too soon. There's no rush.'

'Don't take it home, Dad, leave it here?'

'Yeah, you're right. Makes packing easier.'

'When are we leaving?'

'When I've done this…' He waves a hand over the clothes on the bed.

'Can you give me an hour?'

'He'll still be here when you get back.'

'Who will?'

'Your boyfriend.'

'He's not my boyfriend. Don't listen to Max.'

Dad rises and puts the scarf back in a drawer by the bed. She looks at the matching bedside tables. Both have paperbacks on them. On one side there's an Elmore Leonard and on the other is Paula Radcliffe's autobiography. Dad catches her looking.

'Never could get her to like Elmore Leonard…'

Beth doesn't trust herself to speak.

'Go on, off you go. Gives me a chance to feed Max anyway, saves stopping on the way.'

She goes over and gives him a fierce hug and feels him kiss the top of her head. Then she leaves, without another word.

~·~

Of course, as ever with Rhys, she has no idea where she'll find him so all she can do is find his cottage, which should be easier in the daylight. Although now, she's spooked by every stupid animal she sees. Is that one of hers?

Once she's in the woods she can see areas that are beginning to look familiar. They're mostly pine or gnarly old oaks, dry as old bones, some long dead.

She can see a sort of path now, winding through brown, weeping ferns. Except this is taking forever and the morning's dew has soaked her trainers through. Then she finds the rutted path that she knows will lead her to his front door.

She stops, suddenly unsure of what she's going to say. She winds the medallion's chain around her fingers; Hi Rhys, I'm going back to Manchester, yes I know it's only for a week, but the thing is…

Then he's there, having melted out of the trees. And he's wearing the tweed flares.

'Well, seems all I have to do is put these on and you come running?'

'What *are* you doing?'

'I washed them, not so itchy now.'

'That's no excuse.'

'Come on, got a surprise for you.'

He strides off and she follows.

'How did you know I was coming?'

'I didn't. How was your last day at school?'

She thinks of Susie, 'say Hi to Rhys…'

'Dull.'

'Ahhh, *unlike* my house then.'

They reach the clearing and his home. Most of the slates have been set straight and there are pieces of boarding over most of the holes. The windows have been cleaned; well, kind of cleaned.

'Wow.' She's impressed.

'Thought, if you were going to, I dunno, hang out here a bit…?' He trails off.

'You've cleaned?'

'Inside too.'

She steps in after him and immediately smells disinfectant. The house is no more than tidy, but it smells okay.

'Been through the whole place…'

'For me?'

'Yes, well, and for me too, I s'pose. Mostly me.'

There's a small change to his tone. 'Found all sorts of stuff…'

'Look, Rhys. I can't stay.'

'You've not seen the kitchen yet…'

'We're going to Manchester' There, she's said it. Once it's out, what's the big deal?

'When?'

'Now.'

'How long?'

'Week. At first.'

He walks around the sofa, trailing his hand over it. He brings a finger up, examining it.

'See, not a speck of dust.'

'You've worked really hard…'

'So, what you said. On our date. About leaving…'

'I didn't know anything then. Not properly.'

'It was just two weeks ago.' He looks stern and vulnerable at the same time.

'I never wanted to live here. With Mum dying it's…' She doesn't finish. He's looking at her so intently that she feels naked.

'Is that the only reason?'

'What do you mean?'

'Nothing to do with me?'

'No!' The truth, she owes him the truth.

'Listen, you're going to do what you want to do.' He folds his arms.

'I don't feel like I've got a choice.'

'Your dad's making you?'

'No, not really. He's finding it hard, being here. To be honest we'd all find it hard being anywhere.'

He's stopped talking but his eyes follow her as she walks to the kitchen door and peers in.

'Good work.' She gets nothing back so keeps talking. And walking.

'None of this was supposed to happen. Sometimes I can feel life, *my* life, rushing by me. And everything's raw, y'know? It all hurts. Any peace I get from the pain is – it doesn't *last*. I wake up and it hurts. I go to bloody school and it *hurts*. I go to sleep and… God, I get no peace there! And my head's all over the place, I mean scrambled, sometimes I can't catch my breath… Oh God and now I'm going to cry and I don't want to cry. I'm *sick* of crying…'

But she stops speaking because, somehow, Rhys has caught her by the elbow and is kissing her. On her mouth. And her lips burn and her head is spinning and the room is spinning and…

Rhys breaks their kiss and stands back, still holding her by her elbow. His face is inches from hers and her vision is filled with his green eyes. There's a squirming in her stomach, no, lower. Her throat is tight and her mouth hangs open. Her mind races, he's going to kiss me again or am I going to kiss him first? What am I doing? Seriously, what *am* I doing?

'I make things happen.' Her voice is a harsh whisper.

'What things?' His voice is honey.

'Terrible things. Things I can't help. Dead things…'

He cups her chin in his other hand and her whole face is tingling. He lifts her mouth to his and, oh, eyes closed, he tastes sweet. She feels herself respond, feel their lips move together, his hand is sliding over her cheeks, into her hair, the other cupping her back. Blood roars through her head, filling it with sound, making her feel faint, taking the breath from her. She breaks the kiss this time and finds that she's panting. She holds him at arms' length and looks into his startled eyes.

'Whoa,' he says. 'Wow.' He scans her face and she can tell he wants to kiss her again.

'You're bleeding.' He reaches for her nose but she beats him to it.

She wipes blood off her upper lip onto the back of her hand. She feels it starting to drip and watches, horrified as it splashes onto her hoodie. Worse, much worse though, as she stares at the back of her hand. She can see *through* her skin. Blood vessels pump, bones starch white, muscles over muscles. She staggers away from Rhys and feels his arms slide from under her.

'Your lips are weird,' he says.

She sits heavily on the sofa, all energy drained from her.

'Are you fainting?' Rhys sits quickly beside her and she hides her hand behind her back.

'Beth?'

'Leave me alone, Rhys.'

'I'm sorry…'

She feels another surge of blood and reaches to stem it quickly.

'Tissue!'

'Yeah, wait…' He's off to find some.

She checks her hand in time to see the skin thicken, become skin again. But she's shaking all over. Rhys is back, toilet paper in hand.

'It's all I could find…'

She snatches it off him.

'You went white. I watched the blood drain from your

face.' He seems strangely calm but Beth is not.

'I'm a freak. Like Susie said.'

She just registers the shock on his features as she finds the strength to rise from the sofa and begins to run. Out of the door and down the path. Trees blur, the ground rushes past and she runs until all she can feel is her blood coursing through her veins, wiping out all sound, all thought, all pain.

CHAPTER 25

Joe has packed the car and all she has to do is fetch her own bag from the bedroom. They hug Grandad and she automatically gets in the back with Max. It's only when she sees her dad fasten his seatbelt and sit back that she knows he is waiting for her mum to get in – she was always last in the car, always remembering something they'd forgotten. Max is already lost in a game on his phone, so she slips out of her seatbelt and walks around to get in the front.

'Do you mind?' she asks Dad.

He shakes his head and rubs at his eyes. He starts the engine, winds the window down and leans out to Grandad.

'We'll call you later, okay?'

'I'm just grand,' says Grandad, but she sees that he is not.

They always drive home the same way, up past Blaenau and Betws-Y-Coed; through the gorges and mountains their mum loved so much. Today though, their beauty is lost on her, it all seems desolate. She can't drive the image of her hand away. What exactly happened to me, she thinks? She keeps checking her hand, pressing the flesh, pinching it and watching it return to pink.

She knows now that she had wanted Rhys to kiss her. Was the blood and the skin some kind of punishment, for having a second of pleasure in the midst of all this misery? She wonders what the vicar would make of it. Maybe one day I'll ask him, she considers.

She plugs her earphones in but the joy has gone out of

music and she wonders if this will ever return. She listens anyway. It's Half Moon Run, one of her favourites. If she keeps listening will she ruin these songs forever, will they always remind her of this terrible journey? She switches it off and leans her head against the cool window watching as Wales turns into England and England turns into Manchester.

~·~

She's dreading reaching home and here they are, pulling onto the drive. Their home is a detached, double-fronted Victorian, bearded with vines, now turning brown. Her friends love it, calling it the mansion. They joke about servants living in the converted cellar.

She doesn't know how they are going to do this. It's as if the house stands over them, questioning, why aren't you all here? Then the front door opens and Dad's parents step out.

Grannie Annie sweeps Beth and Max up in a swirl of Calvin Klein and a torrent of kind words, washing them inside. Grandad Rob hugs his son, like he's never going to let go. They've been round the house, tidying, cleaning. They've cooked, it smells of lemongrass and coconut. Lights are on everywhere, banishing all shadows. It's a declaration of life. Beth loves them fiercely.

As she climbs the three flights of stairs leading to her attic bedroom her phone buzzes with a call from Sienna. She stops and stares at her name and all the madness it will bring if she answers.

'Hello Sienna…'

Sleepover time at Sienna's. Trish moved to Didsbury off the back of her last divorce. Beth remembers helping her and Sienna move the smaller stuff in Trish's previous Range Rover, stereo banging out 'Hit 'Em Up Style,' by Blu Cantrell. Needless to say this divorce wasn't from Sienna's Dad. He was number one husband and Trish only ever had Sienna, claiming loudly at the housewarming/divorce party that she'd got away with no stretch marks first time around and certainly did not want a second go.

Sienna's house is on Old Broadway and used to be owned by Richard and Judy. Or so Sienna reckons. It's huge and always looks like it's either on the verge of, or has just survived, a party. Anyway, today it is most definitely hosting a party. Sienna says it's a coincidence, Beth arriving. Beth's not sure, she thinks it's for her but doesn't push it. Trish greets Beth warmly. If she remembers her row with Eve at the farm, she doesn't let it show. Trish looks more fabulous than ever, but it's not for Beth's benefit.

'I'm off to dinner,' she reminds Sienna. 'But Sam is on the door...'

Trish always hires private security for her parties and especially for Sienna's parties. Sam is the colour and size of a mahogany wardrobe with tiny ears for handles. He wears all black and an earpiece, like he's protecting the US President and Beth know Sienna's mates will be hitting on him later.

Trish taps her nose as she leaves. 'Sam's my eyes and ears darling.'

'Have fun Trish,' Sienna calls. 'Don't marry anyone.'

'Darling I'm going to the Northern Quarter, not Vegas. Anyway, I'm off men. Might give women a go, what's the worst that can happen?'

The taxi carries her away.

Sienna drags Beth up to her bedroom, which looks like someone has set off a medium sized explosive device in it. She makes Beth try on everything she has brought and declares it all to be tragic.

'We're the same size...' She goes rummaging through a massive walk-in wardrobe. Actually, Beth thinks of the wardrobe, I've lived in smaller rooms. Sienna emerges triumphantly, holding out two tiny dresses. One plunges down to the belly button.

'Sienna. We are *not* the same size. You have a chest, I do not.'

'I've got these moulds somewhere...'

'No.'

Sienna shrugs and hands Beth the other dress. It's bright yellow with what looks like a smile cut into it, just below the breasts. It has a high neck and Beth takes it off her friend like it might bite her. Before she slips it on, Beth checks the label.

'No, Sienna, I can't wear this. It's Versace for God's sake!'

'I'm not *giving* it to you... put it on Beth and stop bleating.'

It barely covers her knickers and Beth tugs at it, trying to make it seem longer.

'You look gorgeous. Want my pulling boots?'

'No, I do not. Anyway, *pulling* boots?'

Sienna flits back into the walk-in and pops back out with thigh-high black shiny boots with stiletto heels.

'Oh, they're ridiculous!'

'You feel naked, right, in that dress?'

'Um, almost…'

'Put these on, they practically meet the hem.'

They do and Sienna propels Beth in front of her full-length mirror. It doesn't look like me, Beth's surprised. I like that, she thinks.

'You look *hot*!' Sienna purrs.

'I can't walk though.'

'You won't need to. I'll stand you in a corner and the lads will suck you up… like pollen!'

Beth cocks her head sideways, appraising her appearance.

'Wear your hair down, it's well sixties.'

And Beth does as she's told, even allowing Sienna to draw around her eyes with Kohl. Beth purses her lips as Sienna paints them red. When Beth opens her eyes again, she has disappeared and someone else stares back at her from the mirror. It's a good feeling.

'You look like what's-her-face, off that reality show, y'know, before the skanky years.' Sienna's so giddy she's lost her ability to do detail.

The kitchen has been turned into a bar, complete with waist-coated staff. A man and two women. The man shakes cocktails like his life depends on it. The women look tougher than he does. Sienna shoves a cocktail into Beth's hand and, once out of sight, glugs some vodka into it.

'Trish has applied the three drink rule…' Sienna explains, hauling Beth towards a door leading to the cellar. Or, at least what was once a cellar.

The door opens out onto an open spiral steel stairway.

Downstairs is one huge den with throws, beanbags, psychedelic lighting and a gleaming sound system. The ceiling is black and the walls are lined with a blood-red, padded velvet fabric. The carpet is plush and a nightmare of dark swirls, the pattern seeming to step up at you.

They are alone in its womb-like quiet.

'Tonight, you're just Beth okay? No grief, no tears. You're just my best friend.'

They click glasses as the door opens above them and strikingly beautiful Japanese girl descends, carrying boxes.

'DJ,' Sienna offers. 'She'll do requests.'

Half an hour and two cocktails later, Beth is buzzing and the DJ, who turns out to be called Mio, is playing Childish Gambino, to greet the guests

Sienna has invited loads of their friends and has obviously told them to shut up about her mum as they say their hellos and hug Beth. Not a word. Not a sniffle. Just cocktails, fruity shots and the bounce of the bass from Mio. Beth looks around as more people drop down the stairway into the party. A familiar looking boy squeezes himself past the people lingering on the stairs.

'Isn't that Olly?' Beth asks.

Sienna looks over. 'Oh, yeah.'

'I thought, err… you and him…'

'That was then.'

Olly suddenly reminds Beth of Will. That same rugby player's stance, saying, come on, get past me. The neck and the shoulders, the confidence. She had forgotten about Will. And Susie for that matter. And Trev.

Rhys however, is still in her mind. The kiss, the bliss and

then the horror. She reaches for the St Christopher and twists it between her fingertips. Olly comes straight over and kisses Sienna. He dips his huge frame to kiss Beth too, on both cheeks.

'Wow!' he says. 'Can you walk in those?'

'Not really.'

'It's good to see you back.'

'Thanks Olly.'

He smiles disarmingly and she feels a surge of warmth towards him. Sienna's obviously told him as well, they're not doing grief tonight. Beth scans the room, thronging with dancing bodies, most of them from school. Her old school. Even though she never counted any of them as real friends, they're here now.

She takes a big sip of her shot and feels the oily texture of the vodka. The buzz she felt is sliding into something deeper; everything looks warmer. Everyone's smiling and laughing. Mio cranks the music higher, something that sounds like a train crashing down the stairs. The room goes bananas. Olly points at her drink and tips his empty hand to his mouth; does she want another? She shakes her head and covers the top of the glass. He laughs and mouths something over the mechanical beat. She can't catch it over the shouts of the dancers as the big shouty vocals kick in.

Sienna catches her arm and spins her into the middle of the dancers. At the last second Olly snatches the glass from her hand and laughs as she disappears. They're caught up with the crowd, crashing together, arms in the air. Oblivion; this is what she needs, pure oblivion.

~·~

Beth feels slightly dizzy holding the rail as she attempts to get up the stairs without attracting attention. Sienna has an arm around Mio behind the decks, glass aloft, chanting, as the room shakes. Beth pushes the door open as Sam swings his massive shoulders down the hallway, an empty plate in one paw. He's left the front door open to a cool night and she gulps in fresh air.

She looks up for the stars and then remembers; she's in a city. The sky glows orange with sodium. She can hear a distant siren, car tyres hissing on glassy roads, a jet landing nearby. The air smells of kebabs, engines and wet tarmac. She rubs her naked arms and turns back inside.

Sam fills the hallway again. 'Everything okay, miss?'

'Yes thanks.' And it is. Sort of, right now, it is.

She walks through to the kitchen where the bartender is leaning on a marble counter, chatting to one of the tough women. They jump to attention as she enters.

'S'okay, just water please,' she tells them.

'Allow me.' He runs a tap, scoops in some ice, unasked for fruit, and offers her the glass.

'Thanks.'

'And for you, sir?'

Olly arrives at her side. 'Beer please. Sapporo.'

Olly opens his beer with a hiss.

'Jesus,' he says, 'you *do* look amazing. Come on.' He gestures towards the kitchen's exit into a conservatory the size of a small country. Trish calls it her orangery. In here, it's almost dark and she can feel the lacquered oak floor pulse to the rhythms below them. Outside a huge garden disappears into the gloom beyond the rear doors.

'Could do with a break,' Olly says. 'Sienna said not to, but it seems bit shit to me – sorry about your Mum.'

'That's okay, thanks. She's just looking out for me, I s'pose.'

'Yeah.'

They sit in a huge sofa, the shape of a pair of bright red lips. Very Trish. Her dress rides up and her boots creak as she sits. She twists sideways to try and make the dress show slightly less skin. The boots creak again.

'Will you stay here now?' Olly asks.

'Dunno. It's up to Dad really.'

'What's it like in Wales?'

Where to start? Certainly not with the truth. 'It's alright.'

'Doesn't the school suck?'

'It's a school isn't it?'

He laughs and takes a deep swig from his beer.

'I've only ever been to Abersoch.'

'That *is* in Wales…'

'Doesn't feel like Wales though; all my mates are there – may as well be back home.'

'You were there this summer?'

'Yeah, when Sienna dumped me.'

'Sorry.'

'Don't be.'

'Are you back together now?'

'Not really. She thinks I've got the hots for Trish.'

'Haven't you?'

'God no! Well yeah, in a way… the kind of way you have the hots for Susanna Reid, y'know, they're *there*, and like, I so

202

would but, like, never in a million years…'

Wow, she's having a normal conversation with another teenager.

'Didn't see you as a Susanna Reid kind of guy?'

'I'm breathing aren't I? Here, check my pulse!'

He offers her a chunky wrist and she pinches the veins there.

'Yep, you're alive.'

He grins. She lets go.

'Your dress is smiling at me.'

'It's not mine.'

'It fits…'

She tugs at the hem.

'Sienna make over?'

She nods.

'Yeah, well, you deserve it.'

'What, for having a dead mum?'

Olly looks stung, like a huge puppy who's just had his bone taken away.

'Sorry,' she says.

'Hey, forget *that*!' he says. 'I've always liked you best, out of Sienna's mates. You're *real*. Like what you just said. No bullshit, no posing.'

'Yet, here I am, sitting in Versace.'

'Thought Trish said this was an orangery?'

'No, you fool…'

But his lopsided grin tells her he's joking.

'Do me a favour, I'm not that stupid.'

'No.'

'Another drink? Apart from water?'

'Yeah, okay…'

'I'll surprise you…'

And he rises really easily for someone his size. He's wearing ripped jeans, she hadn't noticed that before. They look like he's actually ripped them just by putting them on. Sienna said he was a proper gym junkie. But then, she said a lot of things about him.

She decides to twist her body away from his seat. Squeak, squeak, go the boots. Now I'm all leg, she thinks, wondering further if she's ever going to cut it in haute couture. Olly's back with two cocktails. The red-lipped sofa seems to close its mouth as he sits.

'Something I picked up in Cambodia.'

'What is?'

'Femme Fatale. Fizz, brandy and strawberry.'

'You've only done this so you can say…'

He holds a finger against her scarlet lips.

'So I can say I once picked up a femme fatale in Cambodia… you're right. But it is delicious…'

'Sooooo cheesy…' She smirks, raising the rim of the glass to her lips.

She sips it. It is. The brandy kicks in under the sharp strawberry and fizzy wine. It warms her throat and seconds later she feels it hit her stomach.

'What were you doing in Cambodia?'

'Dad took me on a "coming of age", bonding sesh.'

'But you're not… "Of age" yet?'

'Excuse for a trip. For him, not me. At least I get to go again when I'm eighteen.'

She takes another sip.

He drains his glass. 'You staying over?'

'Yes.'

'In your own room?'

'Dunno. I mean, Sienna didn't say.'

'Not like they're short of rooms.'

'No.'

'Want to go find one?'

Her brain doesn't seem to be working properly. 'What?'

He takes the glass from between her fingers and places it carefully on the floor. He takes her chin in his hand. He tilts her head up. He leans across the gap between them. His hand slides under her hair, steely fingers grip the nape of her neck. He kisses her full on her mouth. For a beat she is transfixed, letting him kiss her. Then she feels his tongue push past her teeth.

Beth feels a slight resistance as she tries to break away and for a second she's afraid he's going to fight back. Then she's free and looking into his hurt-puppy eyes again.

'No, Olly.'

'I thought…'

She's aware that she's breathing normally. She looks down at her hands. Nothing but pink skin, red nails. No spinning; just the taste of brandy in her mouth.

'I'm not – I don't like you that way…'

'Okay, no worries. Just thought it might – take you out of yourself y'know?'

'What? You having sex with me?' She feels a sense of growing anger.

'Yeah. Nothing complicated. One night.'

'Oh, sort of doing me a favour?'

'That's a bit harsh.'

'Is it?'

'Look it wasn't my idea, okay?'

Her anger goes up a notch. 'I'm sorry?'

'Right, don't say anything though? It's not like I don't fancy you. I do have that pulse remember?'

Breathe deeply, breathe deeply.

'Whose idea was it?' Like she needs him to tell her.

'Right, Sienna said…'

In an instant she has swept the cocktail glass up from the floor and tosses the contents into his face. It doesn't feel very original but it helps.

'Oh, fuck's sake…' Olly jumps up, brushing the strawberry from his too tight shirt.

She doesn't hang around for more humiliation. She's had enough for several lifetimes. If she can only keep on her feet in these boots. Screw the boots! She thinks. She sits on the lacquered oak and peels them off, not giving a toss if Olly can see up the dress. She leaves them where they lie and stomps barefoot down the cellar stairway.

Mio is playing what sounds like Tiesto. Sienna is snogging some other rugby-sized waste of denim. Beth grabs Sienna off him and doesn't know what to do next. Sienna's shouting something, wild-eyed, but Beth can't hear it above the music. Beth shouts back.

'How could you!?'

Sienna mimes not hearing. What am I going to do, thinks Beth? Slap her? No, that's stupid and immature. Sienna smiles at her drunkenly. Beth slaps her.

Beth pushes her way through all her 'friends.' Did they all

know? They grin at her as she goes past, so she pushes harder. She's out, slamming the cellar door behind her, tugging at the zipper on the dress. Sam looms over from the door.

'Everything okay, miss?'

'Not anymore! Can you get me a taxi please?' Then she's annoyed at herself for being polite whilst incandescent.

'Sure, when?'

'Now!' That's better.

Sienna has the good sense not to come up as Beth packs, discarding the Versace on the floor. There's no sign of Olly either as she almost trips downstairs, out into the cold air and into the warm taxi. She spits out her address at the driver and they slide off into a drizzly Manchester night.

It's only when she's home, in bed, that she re-lives Olly's kiss. Olly's unwanted kiss. She didn't change. She didn't feel like she did when kissing Rhys. It's whilst she's trying to work out if this is a bad thing or not that she falls fast asleep.

CHAPTER 26

Seriously, does Sienna think she can fix things with a few emojis? Beth texts back.

'Real friends don't pimp each other out.'

She wanders the empty rooms, chats with Grannie Annie in the kitchen and asks where Dad is.

'He's popped into work, hun,' Annie says. 'You want to go shopping or anything?'

'No thanks.'

'Not seeing Sienna today?'

'No.'

'I'm doing shepherd's pie for tea.'

'Great, thanks.'

They look at each other for a while. Grannie's always been the pragmatic one; a peck at Christmas, bit of a back rub on birthdays, odd ruffle of the hair. Then she surprises Beth.

'Bit of a cliché I know,' she starts, 'but it takes time. We all have parents, some go too soon. I know for a fact that I don't want anyone moping around when I'm gone. I also know that there's not a bloody thing I can do about it. Everyone will cry at first; well they better had do! But if I was around to tell you all to stop it and get on with things, then I would.'

Beth's not used to this amount of emotional honesty from Grannie Annie. They don't normally get beyond cooking (Beth doesn't), boys (there never were any), and shopping (not really her).

'That's probably crap advice! Oops and bad language, but I

don't care, it's how I feel. If I could take your place and take your pain I would.' Annie looks at her, eyes as big as moons under an unruly mop of greying ash blond.

'Thanks Grannie, it's not crap advice.'

'Okey dokey, well I'm guessing you've had enough hugging and crying to last a lifetime so I'll crack on. I've got shepherds to mince.'

She turns to the cooker, rolling up her sleeves.

Beth goes into the lounge and finds Max there, Mario-karting on his own. She sits next to him and he speaks without looking from the screen.

'I miss Sadie.'

'Really? Why don't you…' Then she remembers that Max has no real friends here, he's alienated them all by being weird. By being himself. Like me, she thinks; oh God, where *do* we belong?

Joe comes back later in the afternoon. His car is stuffed with boxes and files and he's talking to his parents about a further sabbatical and wanting to be nearer Mum. Grandad nods solemnly and Grannie dishes out steaming hot shepherd's pie. They promise to come and visit, see Christmas too.

'When are we leaving?' Beth asks.

'You enjoy yourself this week,' her dad replies, 'there's no rush.'

She looks sideways at Max. 'I'm not fussed Dad, we can go when you're ready.'

Joe flicks a look at his parents and at Max. Everyone eats.

'Okay, how about tomorrow?'

'Tomorrow's good.'

Max nods, chewing.

Tomorrow it is.

~·~

Shifting under her duvet, surrounded by all the stuff in the bedroom she's called hers for years now, it all feels a bit weird. She feels so far from her mum that she begins to understand what her dad meant. Mum isn't here anymore, she thinks; here, as a presence in this house. Beth thought her mum would be and, yeah, there are loads of pictures and clothes – mostly hidden by Grannie Annie – but Beth doesn't *feel* that she's here.

It's confusing. She's not sure that being in Wales where she *does* feel her Mum's presence so strongly is a good thing. She catches herself feeling guilty at having such bad thoughts. Her only consolation is that it's not up to her, she's still a teenager. Okay, not a normal teenager. In fact sometimes she doesn't feel like one at all, not with what she's seen and done. Sleep beckons, she can sense it settling on her.

She dreams of kissing Olly, on Trish's red-lipped sofa. When she breaks her face from his, he becomes Rhys and when Rhys kisses her, she surrenders. The red lips part with a sigh and they are sucked into its opening mouth where everything is black and where all she can feel are Rhys' arms around her, carrying her to somewhere dark and unknown.

CHAPTER 27

Porthmadog hasn't changed in the days they've been away and Grandad Christmas can't hide his pleasure at seeing them pull up in the yard. He leans heavily on his stick, Rags at his feet, ears up. Grandad sidles up to Beth as Dad and Max carry things inside.

'Had a gentleman caller for you, young lady.'

She tries to conceal her feeling of dread. 'Really? Who?'

'Lad called Will, big feller, Karen's son.'

'What? *He* did?'

'Oh, not who you were expecting?' There's a mischievous glint in his eye.

'I wasn't expecting anyone, Grandad.'

'Having a driving lesson. With his mam, thought they'd call by, say hello and that…'

'Did they ask after Dad?'

'Might've done, can't recall.' That glint again.

'So not for me at all then?'

'Oh yes. I might have to use this stick but it's not for my brain, or my eyes for that matter. I know what I see…'

'What did you tell them?'

'That you'd be gone all week.'

'That's okay then, isn't it?'

'If you say so.'

She reaches in the car for another box of Dad's work and smiles sweetly at Grandad as she passes him. Then she hears him calling.

'Alright there, Trev? Elwyn?'

She puts the box down and turns to see Trev and four other men strolling slowly down the lane. The others are grown men, in their forties and older. They wear a kind of uniform; battered, greasy, age-old waxed jackets, muddy-coloured trousers and mud-caked boots. All have ruddy-red, wind-blown faces and all have shotguns cradled in their arms, broken and pointing at the ground. Even Trev.

'Christmas,' Elwyn nods the greeting at Grandad. He seems to be the leader. 'We're after that dog, police can't do a bloody thing and some of us are up to a sheep a day.'

Trev doesn't take his eyes off her.

'I'd heard,' Grandad replies, 'they said so when they were here. For Eve, you know?'

Trev looks at his boots and Beth scans the others, weighing them up.

Elwyn speaks for them all. 'Shock to us all that. Bloody joyriders. I'd use this on them. If it was up to me.'

He idly raises the gun, all black-blue metal with two dead eyes at its end.

Elwyn carries on. 'So you've not seen anything?'

'Not here, no. I'd've shot the bugger myself.' Grandad looks levelly at them.

Elwyn replies for the men. 'Police said to stay away but where does that get you? If we all stayed away from the things that threaten us, we'd never leave the bloody house.'

There is a murmur of agreement from them, even Grandad is nodding. Elwyn has said enough and he turns to go. 'Let us know yeah? If anything occurs?'

'Will do,' chirps Grandad, coming back towards the

kitchen door. Beth keeps her eyes on Trev as the group stride back up the lane. As Grandad passes, her he speaks plainly.

'Bloody idiots, more likely to shoot each other.' He winks and starts to limp towards the farmhouse.

The thought of that dog, lurching into the yard, makes her skin crawl. 'Would you, Grandad? Shoot the dog?'

His calm gaze settles on her. 'In a heartbeat, lovely, don't you worry.'

'I mean, the size of it...' She tails off as Grandad's eyes harden at her slip. 'I've heard, at school, y'know...'

He cocks his head, working something out.

'When's the last time you shot anything?' She attempts a light tone, slightly mocking.

'Probably that spy plane, during the war...'

'Had they invented planes by then Grandad?'

He snorts and turns away and she wets her lips with relief, taking one last glance at the group of men slouching up the lane.

She watches and it's not until the last moment, when the men turn at the end of the lane, that Trev quickly shifts his thick neck and chances one last look at her. She matches his look until he too, turns with the others, and is gone. Then she goes inside.

CHAPTER 28

For the first few days back at school she has practically sprinted to the bus with Max. She has even got Max to climb over the wire fence at the back of the school field. It didn't take much effort, Max loved it.

On one occasion she thinks she saw Rhys down a side street, in the shadows. Perhaps he's avoiding her as much as she feels the need to avoid him? He must be really upset if all the things he's said about her are true. He didn't feel like she did though, didn't have her translucent hand…

Today though, she feels like she may never see him again and she's really confused. She knows where he lives but, then again, he knows where she is too.

It starts to drizzle with rain. Max arrives – late as usual with Sadie tagging along – when a car pulls up alongside them and Will jumps out. He's grinning and holding something in his hands, which he rips up with a flourish. It's his L plate.

'Passed today!'

'Congratulations.'

'How was Manchester?'

'Good.' Liar.

'And how's Max?'

'You're massive,' Max tells him. Will's grin broadens.

'Want a lift?'

'No thanks.'

'Please?'

She looks around, for a way out.

Will sounds so reasonable. 'It's dark, wet and I don't smell. Much.'

'Cheers,' says Max, reaching for the door nearest him.

'Max!' But he's inside, staring at her through the window and she knows there'll be a scene if she tries to get him out.

'Baby brother's got sense, even if you haven't.'

She tries glowering at Will but is not sure she's carried it off. With a deep sigh, she slips into the passenger seat. The car sits on its springs as Will drops in behind the wheel.

'Great, you're my first passengers. First drive solo, if I'm honest.'

'Oh, what?' But she doesn't feel properly angry. Or worried.

'Just got to pop home, get my training kit alright?'

'Oh, wait a minute...' Now she is worried.

'S'okay, Susie's not in. If she was, I'd put her in her place. I'm bigger, older and better looking, in case you hadn't noticed?'

There's a confidence Beth just can't argue with.

'Won't take a sec, honest?'

'It's your car...'

He clicks his seatbelt into place and they glide away from the kerb. She looks out of her window at the street lamp-lit pavements and every person she sees, huddled against the cold and the rain becomes Rhys, watching her drive off at Will's side.

Will lives at the top of a hill, somewhere behind the high street, with views over to Tremadoc and down the estuary towards the farm. He pulls up into a short drive. There are no other cars there.

'Come in, need to dig my stuff out of the washing.'

'We'll wait…'

'My mam would kill me if she knew you'd come here and not come in!'

'Is she in?'

'No, all out. Just me.'

'Then she'll never know…'

'Jokin' aren't you. Half the neighbourhood's just watched you drive up.'

'Did you plan this?'

'What? Living next to a bunch of nosy old bags? This lot think "Neighbourhood Watch" means they have to sit all day, *actually* watching the neighbours.'

He looks past her, through the window and puts his thumb up, nodding his head and grinning. She spins quickly enough to see a pair of curtains actually swing back together. Will nods in the direction of the curtain- twitcher.

'Mrs Davies; might as well take out an ad in the Gazette.' He looks at her. 'Come on, show them you don't give a toss.'

Inside, the house is spotless. Will leads them through to the kitchen and flips on the kettle. There's not a pot out of place. The living room is several shades of grey, with an impressively large television. Will bends to pick an Xbox controller from the floor, which he hands to Max whilst he flicks the screen on with a remote.

'Is he allowed Halo?'

'No.'

'Yes,' Max pipes up.

'Big sis says no mate, sorry.'

'And anyway, we're not stopping.' Amazingly Max doesn't

argue. Will swiftly slips the disc out of the Xbox and loads another.

He winks at an entranced Max. 'Assassin's Creed. No monsters, just random acts of extreme violence, bit of Geography thrown in'

'Look, Will…' She is definitely feeling trapped now.

'Neighbourhood Watch will be timing this visit. Just a quick kettle on, tea brewed. Splash of milk. C'mon? There are reports to be filled in. Anything less would be a scandal?'

'You're not funny.'

'Actually, there's something I wanted to show you. God, now I'm not sure?'

He seems genuinely conflicted. 'Okay, I'll tell you first, then you can make your own mind up.'

'Go on.'

'My mam and yours were really close, years ago…'

'I'd heard.'

'You've been here before, when you were tiny.'

She doesn't mention Susie's little chat.

'We've got pictures see? Thought you might want to have a look…'

'Oh…'

'Course, you don't have to! I mean, I don't want to cause any upset?'

She hears Assassin's Creed loading and watches Max settle in front of the screen.

'Where are they?'

Will nods to a door. 'Dining room.'

'Okay.'

They leave the adjoining door ajar and Will asks her to sit, whilst he goes to a sideboard to fetch several packs of photographs. He lays them out on the dining table in front of her and sits by her side.

'They were all on our computer, I'm guessing.'

She looks at him quizzically.

'I'd never seen most of them before, Mam's just had them printed.'

He takes a fistful out of a sleeve and begins to slide them over one another. The first few are of what looks like a younger Karen, posing in a bikini, on a large rock. The rock looks familiar. It's by a river. The next photo is blurry, revealing a pool with several heads bobbing on its surface. Oh God, is it?

Then the undeniable truth is shown to her. Eve and Karen, sharing a towel, hair dripping wet, heads together. They look about sixteen and her mum radiates happiness. Beth can feel her eyes stinging.

'Aw, God, I'm sorry.' Will places a hand on her arm. 'This is so typically *stupid* of me.'

'No, I'm alright. Honest.'

'You sure?'

She nods and his hand slips off her arm. She takes the pictures from him and starts to shuffle through them. Slowly Karen gets older in them and often, her mum's there, always seeming to be glued to Karen's side. Always laughing. More and more, a dark haired boy appears. He never smiles, it's as if he resents the camera being there at all. In most of them he has a proprietorial arm around Karen.

'Dad,' says Will simply.

They finish one pack and there are at least another six to go at. Will scoops them out and gives them to her.

'What about your training?'

'What training?' he replies, smiling.

In this pack Karen looks like she's in her thirties, Beth thinks. She's so pretty, it's hard to tell. She looks like she's in a school, often sitting with teenagers. Four or five pictures go by, all are of the same scenario; they're in a hall, like it's a rehearsal for a school play.

'Ah, sorry, must have the wrong pack. Mam taught at the school, years ago. Total MILF, or so Dad's mates say. Thank God I was too small to get it.'

He's reaching out to take the pictures back off her when Beth sees it.

Karen is sitting on the edge of the school stage, in a short dress that hugs her figure. She has an open manuscript in her lap and is surrounded by a group of attentive teenagers; most of them are boys.

She is smiling at the taker of the photo and the flash has whitened her teeth and given her red-eye. Beside her, closest, is a boy wearing a bright red Porthmadog baseball cap. The peak is down, hiding his face, but the flash has caught something else.

The boy is wearing a medallion on the outside of his T-shirt. It's the size of a fifty pence piece and looks like it's round. The T-shirt under it is dark but with several circular objects on it. They look like moons.

She's aware that she's blinking rapidly. 'When, err, when was this taken?'

Will takes the picture off her and peers at it. 'Well, she doesn't look pregnant, and she's still teaching, so it must be at least sixteen, seventeen years ago?'

'Does she still teach, I've not seen her in school?'

'God, no, Dad made her give that up years ago, when she fell pregnant with Susie. I know that sounds a bit Neanderthal, but that's more or less what he did.'

She's beginning to feel light-headed. 'Did I see you put a kettle on?'

Will smacks himself on the forehead. 'The neighbours, what am I thinking of? Coffee or tea?'

'I don't care.'

'What?'

'Err, sorry, coffee please.'

'Okay, back in a bit...'

She hears him move across the living room. 'Alright there Max?' Of course, he gets no reply.

She stares at the picture and suddenly stuffs it in her blazer pocket. She quickly shuffles through the rest. Face follows face but she thinks she knows what she's looking for. The boy in that red cap, that T-shirt, *that* medallion. The one around her neck. Oh God, she panics, I think I'm losing my mind, what *am* I doing? She reaches inside her blazer, about to put the picture back when Will bounces back in and she jumps so much that the other photos spill from her trembling hand.

'Jesus, you alright?'

'Yeah...'

'Kettle's on...'

'Listen, Will. I'm sorry but, I need to go. Now.'

'I *have* upset you, haven't I?'

She sees an escape and shamelessly takes it. 'Yeah, a bit, but it's not your fault.'

'I meant it, about the lift home.'

'That'd be nice, thanks.'

They leave the scattered pictures where they lie and walk over to Max.

'Time to go little feller.' Will says it with such authority that Max simply obeys. She marvels at Max's utter lack of resistance.

She can't meet Will's look all the way home, even though he talks through much of the journey. Rugby. Music. Manchester. How, first chance he gets, when he's eighteen, he's out of here. They reach the lane and he swings down it before she can say stop. It's raining harder now and she pauses for a moment as Max runs inside.

'Thanks, Will.'

'Anytime. Seriously. And sorry.'

She finds herself smiling at him before slamming the door and jogging inside; with that photograph, burning a hole in her pocket.

CHAPTER 29

O kay, St Christophers aren't that common. But she's not sure that the thing in the picture *is* one in the first place. The T-shirt? Could have been a Topman best seller sixteen years ago. She wouldn't know, she wasn't around.

All these things run through her mind as the bus rattles along the lanes on the way to school. Max is ill, says he's got a temperature and Dad's not going to argue.

As the bus pulls up outside the railway station she sees a familiar figure waiting. Rhys looks pale and, somehow, shrunken. At least he's wearing a jacket against the cold. She doesn't want to face him but there's no way she can avoid it either. The bus doors hiss open sucking in the cold air.

'I need to talk to you.'

She tries walking past him, avoiding those eyes.

'Look Beth, was it that kiss?'

'Yes.' It's not a lie, not the whole truth either.

'I'm not sorry.'

To be fair, there's no reason why he should be, she wanted that kiss as much as he did. They're crossing the road, another few yards and she'll be in the school grounds. Suddenly she feels his hand on her shoulder. She can feel his strength as he spins her around to face him.

'I'm scared. Okay? I *need* your help.'

'Why?'

'I've lied to you…'

'Right, that's a great start…'

'But, I need you to understand. I need *me* to understand.'

'Rhys, I can't help you.'

'And *I* can't believe you won't.'

He still has hold of Beth, but the grip is gentler.

'I'll be waiting for you. After school. No matter which way you slip out...'

They spend another second looking at each other and then he lets go of her shoulder. She walks into school without looking back. She thinks of the medallion, the picture, still in her blazer. Then she wonders what on earth she's going to do.

She spends the whole school day in a daze. People simply come into her orbit and then spin away again, making little impact. She might as well be on Mars. It's only when she's leaving and decides to walk out of the front of the school that she knows what she's going to do.

~·~

She walks with Rhys up the path to his house, which looks even more sinister in the early evening gloom. They haven't spoken a word since she met him outside school. He soon has a fire going in the grate, but she keeps her blazer on.

'Are you going to sit down?' he asks. She stays on her feet.

'This might sound a bit off its head?' He looks at her for a sign that he can continue, and then continues anyway.

'I have no idea who I am. All that stuff about my parents – I made it up, out of, like, *tiny* fragments of memory. The blackouts – that was me trying to make sense of what has happened. And, then, when I *did* blackout, I was like, *glad*!'

'Why?'

"Cos it made what I'd lied about into the truth..."

'Is your name Rhys?' She's actually thinking of sitting down now.

He guides her by her elbow to the kitchen door that leads into the rear garden. Or what was once a garden. He opens the door and points to a line of scratched markings on the doorframe. Each mark is an indicator of height, someone has etched a child's growth into the wood. Rhys kneels and points to the lowest mark. She kneels too. It's about a metre off the floor and has the name 'Rhys, 18 months' written next to it. Standing, she can make out the final mark. 'Rhys, 14.'

Rhys watches her for a reaction.

'How do you know it's you?'

'My head's like one of those snow globes that's been shaken up. There are all these tiny bits spinning around. My earliest *proper* memory is seeing you. The day your mum died.'

Now, she does make her way to the sofa and sits. Rhys stands over her, agitated.

'In that *moment*, I knew you. It was so weird. I found my way here by instinct. Every step seemed to make sense. And when I got here, I knew it had been my home. I found these marks on the second day here. The name fitted. Catching animals *fitted*. I found I was good at things I can't remember ever doing. I didn't want to freak you out so I made all the rest up. At least, I think I did.'

'Sit down, Rhys.'

He does. But sitting doesn't make him any less manic.

'I must have amnesia. Maybe I've been in an accident, maybe my parents are in a ditch somewhere? Maybe I *should* go to the police?'

She takes the photo from her pocket and lays it between them. Rhys stops gabbling and looks down at it. He picks it up, holds it up to what light is coming from the fire.

'Looks like you, don't you think?'

'When was this taken?'

'Sixteen years ago.'

'I've got a T-shirt like that... well, I found it here, in this house.'

'And what about this?' She uncoils the St Christopher from her neck.

He squints at the picture. 'I can't tell. Anyway, that's yours.'

'I found it.'

'Where?' he asks.

'On a run.' Before she can work out whether to tell him exactly where she found the medallion he spits out another question.

'And the photo?'

'Boy called Will had it. At his house. He gave us a lift...'

Rhys flicks a look at her. 'Oh right. Big lad, dark hair. Must've been nice for you?'

His face has hardened into a jealous mask.

'He's Susie's brother. The woman in the picture is Karen, remember? You saw her driving from school?'

'Yeah, so?'

'He was being *nice*. His sister's a bitch and he was making up for her.'

She knows this isn't the whole truth but reckons it's about as much as Rhys can take right now.

Puzzlement now flickers across his features and she feels hugely sorry for him.

'Our kiss made me feel alive,' he says without warning. 'Then you went and I had no idea where you'd gone. I mean I looked, but you'd disappeared…'

'We went to Manchester, I told you.'

'Did you? God…' He sweeps his hair off his forehead, leaving his hand there, cradling his head.

'Will you help me find out who I am?'

'Yes.' She means it.

'How?'

She realises she'd already worked this out. 'I'll go back to Karen's. She used to teach at the school. You reckon you went there, she might have some kind of information?'

'What if I didn't, what if I made that up too?'

'One way to find out…'

'Does this mean seeing that Will again?'

'Yes.'

They lock eyes again and she recalls that dream, the red sofa, those lips…

Rhys leans in close, breath brushing her mouth. Their lips touch, but it's like a spark of static hits them and she jumps back. Nothing like Olly, nothing at all.

'I can handle Will,' she says. More to get out of the moment than anything else. 'But I'll need that back.'

Rhys reluctantly gives up the photo and she slips it back into her pocket.

'It's dark,' he says, 'I'll walk you home.'

Beth wants to reach out and hold him, tell him it's all going to be fine. He beats her to it by taking her hand and helping her up. They hold hands all the way back to the farm. She reassures him that getting invited back to Karen's will be okay, she's been asking to help ever since Mum died. All she has to do is avoid Susie. That easy.

CHAPTER 30

She seeks Will out at break. He's not difficult to miss.

'Sorry I shot off like that.' She tries a smile.

He's oiled and in his Rugby kit, smelling of liniment. She's worn it herself on cold runs. It always reminds her of winter and ground, as hard as iron.

'I said, no worries.'

'I'd like to have another look at your mum's photos? If that's okay?'

'Better than okay, she's mad at me for scaring you off.'

'You didn't.'

'That's good to know.' He smiles, kind of knowingly.

Uh oh, she's finding this dishonesty a bit tough. It's a minefield. Everything gets bent out of shape, people get the wrong ideas.

'Tonight okay?' he asks.

'Yeah, great. Max is off...'

'Ahhh, just the two of us then?'

Shit, not again...

'Erm, no, I thought...'

'Teasing,' he grins, 'Mum's dying to have a chat.'

And he jogs off, leaving her feeling more stupid than ever.

~·~

The car ride is short. He parks on the drive behind what she recognises as Karen's car. Is that a street full of curtains twitching she can sense behind her?

'Your dad in too? she asks.

'Nah, he's away a lot. Works in nuclear plants, Middle East and stuff.'

'Wow, does he glow when he gets back?'

Will snorts out with laughter. 'I have *genuinely* never heard that one before.'

She's trying to sound relaxed. Inside her stomach's like a hamster on a wheel. They go in and the first person she sees emerges into the hall in a rush. Susie's steaming and looks murderously at Beth. Then Susie shoves past her and shoulders Will out of the way too. The front door slams in her wake.

Will shrugs as Karen comes in from the living room. She looks like she wants to hug Beth, but settles for an awkward handshake instead.

'Ignore Susie,' Karen says. 'She's a Daddy's girl, misses him loads and gets a bit lairy every now and then.'

'That's a shame,' Beth says.

'I am *sooo* glad you're here! Will told me you'd been...'

'And half the street,' Will joins in.

'I've got the kettle on, come on through.'

Karen leads her into the living room where she has spread out a table full of photo albums and stuff to eat.

'Best biscuits, eh Mam? Tell we got a guest.'

Karen flushes a bit, caught. It makes her look prettier, Beth thinks.

'Sit here, next to me.'

She smells nice too, something fresh and flowery. She's wearing a loose seventies-style psychedelic top and black leggings. Long blonde hair is tied back into a ponytail. She still looks young enough to keep her hair long. As Beth sits, she can feel the photo she stole, against her chest. Somehow she has to put this back.

Karen waves a hand at Will, shooing him off. 'Go and make tea, Will. Or coffee, what d'you want love?'

'Tea's good, thanks.'

Will bows and backs out of the room.

'Idiot,' Karen adds, affectionately. 'Is he pestering you?'

'God no!' She is quick to answer.

'I loved your mum, I really did.'

Beth doesn't know what to say.

'You're so like her, around the eyes. Definitely got her shape. You run, don't you?'

'Yes.'

'Your dad told me. Lost touch with Eve after a while. Life gets in the way. Kids, marriage, day-to-day stuff and then you take a breath and see that years have flown by. Best intentions and all that, gone.'

Beth looks down into her lap.

'Bit rubbish eh, having to stick around here? After Manchester?'

'I'm getting used to it.'

Karen flashes Beth a smile and reaches for the nearest pack of pictures. It's the one she stole her photo from, the one with the school hall and the stage.

'I was going to try and sort this lot out and then I realised how many I've got. Can't be doing with them on the laptop, you never bother looking at them do you? And, so, what's the point? Pictures are meant to be looked at. Remembered.'

Karen looks at Beth and seems to sense her nerves. 'Where's bloody Will when you *actually* want him? Stay put, I'll get us that tea.'

Karen rises and goes as far as the open doorway into the kitchen, which she hangs onto, swinging her head through and calling.

'Will? Get a move on!'

Beth reaches for the photo but snags it on the inside of her pocket. Don't pull it, it'll crease. Try again, let it go. Try again. Karen stands on one foot, leaning further in.

'Will?'

Now it's coming out. Quickly, slip it into the pack and...

Karen swings back round to face her. Beth's hand hovers with the picture in it.

'Useless, never have boys... oh, have you found one?'

'Yeah, just, one of you, I think...'

Karen crosses back over and sits as Will steps through the door with a tray.

'Sorry. Was trying to find the best china.'

Karen shakes her head at him and turns to her, taking the photo out of her hand.

'We don't have any china. Oh God, that's me alright. What a sight!'

Karen quickly drops the photo down on the sofa beside her. 'Don't want too many of those! Here...'

Karen hands her about five photographs as Will sits the other side of Beth, nudging her with his thigh.

'Shove up.'

She is squashed between mother and son, looking down at a picture of Karen; in school again, but this time with a heavily pregnant woman, dark hair, blue eyes and a swollen tummy. It's her mum.

'She was carrying you at the time. I was dead proud, the running you know, the medals… I got her in to do some motivational speaking.'

Mum's glowing in these pictures; Beth has never seen her look as happy. She looks at her mum's bump. At her future self. She shuffles the pictures, bringing up the next. Eve's up on the stage, arms held out – this is how you do it. The next picture is taken from the side, showing some of the audience. In the second row, someone is wearing a red baseball cap.

'Some of my kids needed more than motivating! Eve was brilliant; local girl, born here, done good. More than most of us can say…'

'Not me.' Beth had forgotten Will was there. 'Eighteen, I'm gone…'

Next picture. A queue forming in front of Eve as she signs books. The boy with the red cap's there, three from the front. It's definitely a boy. In the next picture, Eve poses with a few girls, all holding books and smiling.

'Yeah right, Will, believe that when I see your bus ticket.'

'Not a bus ticket, Mam, *plane* ticket. Thailand. One way.' Will seems to be losing interest, in the pictures anyway. 'Back in a sec…' He slides out of the sofa and from the room.

Karen smiles after him. 'Never still…'

They go back to the pictures.

Next photo. Eve poses with Karen. Professional smiles. Next picture, her mum poses with a bunch of boys. One has a red baseball cap. His T-shirt has moons all over it. He has a medallion. He has the deepest green eyes.

'Who's that?' Beth manages to say.

'Baseball cap?' Karen asks.

'Yes.'

'Rhys Jones.'

This can't be right, this is sixteen years ago.

'He was one of the ones I got your mum in for. One of the worst.' There's a catch at the back of Karen's throat, but Beth doesn't register it. Instead, she begins to feel hot, as if her clothes are getting too tight.

'The worst?' Beth asks.

'Tried all sorts with him. In the end he was caught trying to set the school on fire. Expelled…'

'Why him?' Karen asks Beth. And now, Beth hears that tension in Karen's voice.

Beth literally tugs at the neck of her blouse, loosening her tie.

'Err, it's the medallion. I've got one…' She quickly undoes the tie altogether and almost snatches her top button off. She pulls the medallion out, trying to regulate her breathing.

'Oh love, it's gorgeous. It's the same, don't see that many today. Didn't he get downgraded or something?'

'Who?' asks Beth.

'St Christopher, patron saint of travellers…'

Beth squeezes the medallion in her palm, feeling its heat as Karen continues.

'Not that it did poor Rhys any good…'

'Why?' Beth hears herself ask.

She catches Karen glancing at the wad of pictures before she carries on.

'A bit sad love, that's all…'

Then, as the room shrinks around her, as the walls close in, as her pulse slows to a boom, boom, boom and echoes around her head – Karen tells Beth a story.

CHAPTER 31

She thanks Karen and lies to Will, telling him that her Dad is picking her up.

The edges of her vision have closed into black halos. She steps carefully, feeling the tilt of the road down from their house. She feels herself totter, feels her knees buckling. She throws up into someone's garden. She staggers to her feet, afraid a neighbour might have seen her and might try to help.

No one can help. Touching hedges, fences and lampposts, she feels her way down the hill. There are footsteps behind her, getting closer, starting to run. There's an arm under hers, holding her up. A face looms in but she tries to shake them off violently. They're talking but there's this humming in her head. Then the black halos converge. Then there's nothing.

~·~

She's bumping along and streetlights come in and out of her clearing vision. The sky between the lights is of the darkest blue. She's being carried, feels strong arms under her shoulders and legs. They start to descend steps. Slowly Rhys' features are lit by the sodium glow off the lights. She can taste bitter tea and bile in her mouth as she unsticks her tongue to speak.

'Rhys.'

He stops.

'Put me down.'

He gently lowers her to the ground. They are in the small square overlooking the harbour. The tide is full and shimmers with the lights coming from the surrounding houses. Cables snap and click against the swaying masts of the many yachts there.

'Are you okay now?' he asks, leading her to a bench by the railings.

'No,' she tells, him, arranging the insane thoughts in her head.

'What happened?' He looks wild with worry.

She unhooks the medallion from around her neck and places it in his hand.

'This is yours.'

'What are you on about?'

She feels for a photograph, the one Karen gave her before she left, having pressed it into her hand. There's just enough light to see clearly who is in the picture. She gives it to Rhys and he looks down, confused.

'That's you,' she tells him.

'Yeah…' he says uncertainly, 'that's that teacher, Susie's mum. And who…?' he tails off, shaking his head.

'That's my mum with her and that's me inside her.'

'I don't get it…'

'This was taken sixteen years ago. Before I was born, just.'

'Okay, it *looks* like me…'

'It *is* you. You're Rhys Jones, Karen taught you.'

'But, surely I'm sixteen *now*, so what? So, what you saying? You think I'm *thirty* two years old?'

'No Rhys… Not that…'

'What then!?' He's shaking his head.

'I'm saying that I think you're dead.'

He switches his gaze from the photo in a heartbeat and locks his eyes onto hers.

'Right, that's bollocks and, what, this is some kind of a joke? Something you and *Will* cooked up?'

'No. It's what I've worked out. It has to be.'

'But, I'm talking to you. I've held you, carried you, I've *kissed* you..!'

There's an edge of hysteria in his voice and she begins to feel afraid.

'Rhys, remember I told you, I can make bad things happen, weird things?'

'No, no, no. I'm not having that emo shit. You're cut up about your mum dying and things have got a bit dark for you…'

He stands up and Beth looks around. At first she sees no one, then a couple walking a dog appear from behind the yacht club wall. They are hunched against the chill wind. She stands.

'Take this back!' He holds out the medallion, still clutching the photo. She shakes her head. The couple have heard his raised voice and have stopped, their dog straining on the leash, starting to yap.

She's trying to stay calm. 'I'm going now, okay. I'm catching my bus. Don't follow me.'

'You can't say all that and run.'

'I'm scared, Rhys.'

'No. You can't be scared of me! I love you Beth…'

But she doesn't wait. Once again she's running. Running from her own nature. Running from what she has created.

CHAPTER 32

The bus coughs a cloud of warm diesel fumes at her as she gets on. The driver asks her if she's okay. Please don't say I look as if I've seen a ghost, she thinks. He doesn't. She sits at the back, thoughts whistling around her head. Maybe I shouldn't have blurted that out to Rhys? What if I'm wrong? What if I'm losing my mind? He could be right, the grief has sent her off on some mad tangent.

Assembling her thoughts, she sifts through the meeting with Karen, everything she said; but Karen's words refuse to take shape. There's a splitting pain growing behind her eyes and the muggy air inside the bus feels toxic. She almost throws up again and has to lean her forehead against the cool metal of the rail in front of her.

She's transported out of the streetlights of the town and into tunnels of darkness. To home and to sanity, or at least to the only kind of sanity she has left to her.

~·~

The bus drops her at the top of the farm's lane. The dark wraps itself around her as she walks towards the farmhouse and only accentuates her suffocating feeling of dread. She reasons that there must be someone who can help her unravel the secrets of what she has learned.

Of course there is; Grandad. She's both hopeful and wary in equal measure.

Her dad has cooked again but she can only pick at her meal. She knows they're looking at her.

'Karen said you'd dropped in,' Dad prompts. She looks at him sharply.

'She texted…' he offers defensively.

'She showed me pictures of Mum.'

'Ah…'

'When she was pregnant with me.'

Grandad joins in. 'That was the spring she had you… when she went into school. Your grandma was so proud…'

'She did a talk,' Dad adds, 'I was at home. In Manchester.'

Beth puts her fork down. 'There was a boy in some of the pictures… Rhys Jones.'

Grandad stops eating too and looks intently at her.

'I think it was his medallion I found.'

Grandad carefully lays his knife and fork by the side of his plate. 'The Saint Christopher?'

'Yes.'

'Could be. You still got it?' Grandad asks.

'No. I lost it. Running, it fell off.'

'Shame.' Grandad picks up his fork and starts to push his meal around his plate, separating stuff. Head down.

'That's a pity,' Dad says, 'you could have given it back.'

'No Dad, he's dead.'

'God, when?' Poor Dad looks really upset.

'Sixteen years ago. Wasn't it Grandad?'

Grandad looks up from his plate. 'Lots of Rhys Joneses around here.'

'This one disappeared.'

'Did Karen tell you that?' Now Dad's alarmed.

'Yes.'

'She shouldn't go upsetting you…'

'She didn't,' Beth lies. 'This boy's blood was found in a car. He was supposed to have crashed it.'

'*Sixteen* years ago? I don't get it.' Now Dad has stopped eating and only Max chews away, not missing a trick.

'Ah,' Grandad says, 'that Rhys Jones.' He prods a piece of chicken and waves it absentmindedly as he speaks.

'Owen Jones' son. Owen was a poacher. On top of a load of other things. Police never found the boy.' Now he pops the chicken into his mouth and chews along with Max.

Annoyingly, Grandad doesn't look like he's got any more to say.

'Poacher?' she prompts.

'Just a bad lot, Beth. Wife left him, son died joyriding. Weren't too many that upset when he buggered off.'

'Joyriding?' Trying to keep the edge out of her voice.

'Some reckoned he was just like Owen. Didn't look like he lived long enough to prove it one way or the other.'

Now Grandad rises from the table to scrape the remains of his meal into the bin. 'Look at me,' he says, back bent to his work, 'eating like a bloody bird.'

Max titters and gets his phone out.

'Not at the table,' Dad's warning is useless.

'I'll have to tweet you, Grandad.'

'You can try…' Grandad says and winks at Max before he limps over to the kitchen door.

'Where did he crash the car?' she asks.

Grandad stops and turns in the open doorway. 'Didn't Karen tell you?'

'No.'

He looks into her, grey-blue eyes shining brightly. 'Not sure I remember. Not sure I ever knew…'

And he leaves, stairs creaking under his feet.

Karen didn't tell me, Beth thinks. But when *she* said she didn't know, I believed her.

~·~

She helps clean and clear away the dinner things, working silently alongside her dad. He's lost weight, she can see where his clothes droop. She can also see flecks of grey in his hair, just above his ears. She wonders what it will be like, watching him grow older. He catches her staring at him and cracks an unfelt smile, probably for her benefit.

He waits for a few seconds before he speaks. 'I can finish these Beth, thanks,' and he roughs up her hair, like he used to when she was small.

There's a floorboard just outside Grandad's room that creaks louder than the rest. Because his room is at the end of the landing they always know when he's up and about. Beth steps on it now and instantly winces at the sound.

'Come in Beth,' his voice comes through the closed door.

The old door fights against stubborn hinges, slowly revealing Grandad, fully clothed and sitting at the window overlooking the yard. She hovers in the doorway, unsure what to say next. Grandad beats her to it.

'It was that same bend. Where your mum died.'

'Where I found the medallion…'

'Yes, that makes sense,' Grandad ponders. 'Lying there all

these years… those who reckon they know, said the boy was thrown out of the car, didn't have his seat belt on.'

'Did you ever meet him?'

'No. I only didn't say… about that road… 'cos I didn't want you upset, see?'

'Yes.'

'Why so interested?'

'The medallion. I, um, felt it had a story to it…'

'And it did eh? What a story. No need to tell Max and your dad though?'

'No.'

'You're a great little girl. Strong like your mum, and your Nan… spirited…'

''Night Grandad.'

''Night sweetheart.'

The closing door slowly slides him from view.

Lying in bed, she can feel the dreams crowding in on her, rolling over each other, fighting to be the first into her sleep. Let them come, she thinks, they can't be any more gruesome than my reality.

CHAPTER 33

One day melts into the next. She seems to bump in to Will a lot and Susie has taken to staring super-hatefully at her, especially if her brother's there. He's asked Beth back for a meal, but she said no, thanks. Karen thinks she's upset Beth and she's right. It's not Karen's fault but Beth still wishes she'd stop texting her dad.

The more Beth thinks about her last meeting with Rhys, the more all she can remember is him telling her he loved her. She finds herself standing where he said it, trying to make some sense of what, and how, she feels. He's right, she *did* kiss him. She has felt his strength and his warmth... his *alive*ness. All she did in return was to run and leave him.

When Saturday comes it will have been over a week and he hasn't turned up once. She knows she has no choice, she can't avoid what she's done and there are things she needs to tell him.

Beth tells Grandad that she's taking Rags for a walk. Dad's taking Max to Sadie's 'for tea' and spending some time in town. Beth's pretty sure which part of town too...

Rags is almost giddy to be out in the fields and Beth feels guilty that she doesn't walk him more often. It's only when they reach the entrance to the woods that he stops dead. She calls him sharply and his instinct is to obey, but he's not happy. He's not the only one. She's afraid, but ploughs on, Rags now staying close.

They're soon in the clearing at the front of Rhys' cottage.

She sees the front door is cracked open and stops. There's a low growl from Rags, ears flat against his skull. She walks up and pushes the door fully wide. The air is stale and cold, no sign of any fire in the hearth. She calls out his name. Nothing comes back. She hisses at Rags to follow her, but he's not moving a muscle.

Her footsteps seem to make too much noise, no matter how carefully she treads. The sofa looks like it's been torn apart, tipped on its back and cushions scattered all over the room, stuffing spilling from their covers.

There are congealing plates in the kitchen sink, bits of fur and dried blood on the worktop. Some plates lie, smashed on the tiled floor. Their flakes crack under her shoes. She walks slowly back through the lounge until she's standing at the bottom of the stairs. She calls out his name again, into the darkness at the top of the staircase.

The stairs creak at every step and her heart pounds in her ears. At the top of the stairs to her left, is the bathroom, door wide open. Empty. To her right is the landing leading to the three bedrooms. In the middle of the landing is something she's never seen before. There's a stepladder wedged up against the ceiling and disappearing into what must be a loft.

'Rhys, are you there?'

The silence presses in on her. She looks back down the stairs, where light floods in through the front door. Where Rags is waiting. She could be home in half an hour, if she runs. But she's not running. Not this time.

She tests the ladder and takes a first tentative step. Then another. And another, until her head is level with the yawning mouth of the roof space. She squints into the blackness. After a second or two she can see the odd crack of light, between uneven tiles, but they don't have the strength to filter down. She steps up, her shoulders filling the space, and peers around. There's a slight noise to her right, a shifting of something. She whispers, her foot already feeling for the nearest rung down the ladder.

'*Rhys..?*'

Suddenly a light blinks on and, for a second, she almost slips as her foot misses the rung and she grips hard on to the sides of the hatch.

Rhys is sitting, curled into a ball, in a far corner of the attic. In the stark light of a single bulb, he looks white. She clambers in and instinctively crouches as she covers the distance between them. When she gets closer she sees he *is* actually white. He sits by an open cardboard box, playing with a red cap, twisting it with his fingers. As it turns she sees it says Porthmadog FC. There's a greasy sheen to his skin, despite the cold up here, and his once vibrantly green eyes stare dully up at her.

'I'm sorry,' is all she can say. For everything.

Rhys reaches back inside the box and hands her a picture. The damp has yellowed the edges and curled the photo, but the image remains. It is of a couple beaming at the camera. The man is dark, swarthy, with broad shoulders and a scruffy, half trimmed beard. He has a purely vulpine look about him, as if he'd devour you as soon as look at you. The woman has long, corkscrew hair with ash blonde streaks in it. She has the greenest eyes and is holding a tiny baby. The picture has caught the child with its mouth open, wailing, eyes tightly shut.

Rhys gently takes the photo from her and turns it over. On the back is someone's small, neat writing – 'Rhys Owen Jones, DOB March 1988. Love Mum and Dad X.'

She's shocked to hear the dry rasp that is Rhys' voice.

'You were right. I'm not thirty two, so I must be dead.'

He looks deeply into her eyes, pleading, help me, help me...

She sits next to him and takes his head onto her shoulder, combing the hair off his forehead with her fingers. It's as if she can feel her energy flowing into him. She watches as his waxen hands turn pink. She can *sense* life flooding back through his veins. This time his voice is more than a croak.

'I looked and looked until I found this. It's full of stuff. Then I just sat here. I was dying, I could feel myself dying. Until now, until you came back. It would have been better if you'd stayed away...'

She tips his face up to hers, smells his now-sweet breath. She brushes her lips against his and knows this is right. This is meant to be. This is what she wants.

'I couldn't have stayed away. I love you.' The words sound strange and she hadn't even realised that she was going to say them, let alone mean them. She feels weak and exposed, like she's let some vital part of herself loose. She feels that only Rhys can gather her up and make her whole again.

He sits up into her arms and leans his forehead against hers. Their noses bump.

'Tell me again. Then tell me everything,' he asks gently.

'Tell you what?'

'That you love me.'

'I love you.'

He smiles at her and runs his hands through her hair. 'I've loved you since the moment I saw you.'

They share a nervous laugh. She's almost feeling overwhelmed, like something huge is about to wash over her.

'Do you believe that you did *this*?' he asks, of himself.

'I'm pretty sure I did. I mean I've done it with small things. That seal in Criccieth…'

'That was *you*?'

'Yeah.'

'How?'

'I don't know.'

They sit back, at arms' length and she watches his very-much-alive face shift as he thinks.

'Do you *know* what happened to me?'

She nods. His hands slip from her shoulders and he takes her hands into a firm grip. His gaze is even, ready.

'You died in a car crash, or at least that's what the police said. That was your medallion I found, by the roadside.'

'So, where are my parents?'

'Your dad left after the crash. Just disappeared.'

'Mum?'

'Don't know. Karen told me she'd disappeared days earlier. Seems your dad drank a lot, some said your mum had run off…'

'Jesus…'

'You were…' She stops. Would it really help to tell him he was expelled? Is he the same person now? He interrupts her.

'Right, this is stupid okay, but, I don't *feel* dead. I can't actually believe I'm saying these words but…'

'I know. I was the same all through summer. In fact, ever

since my gran told me… about what I can do. But I've been forced to believe it.'

Suddenly he's up on his feet, pulling her with him effortlessly.

'Come on, show me…' He pulls her by the hand and drops through the attic door, waiting for her to join him.

'Show you what?' she asks as she descends the ladder.

'You're asking me to believe in something so mad… I want proof.'

'Rhys, I can't…' But they're rushing down the stairs, across the mess of the lounge into the kitchen. Out through the back door.

A kind of garden has been reclaimed by the forest at the back of the cottage. Someone has cleared a space where logs lie, half chopped, axe standing proud in the ground. Hanging from a hook in the wall are two pheasants, feathers shimmering in the breeze. Dead, of course.

'Go on then,' he prompts, nodding at the birds.

She feels angry with him. 'It's not a party trick.'

'I have to see.'

'You don't believe me?'

'It's more that I don't *want* to believe you.'

She looks from him to the birds. He still has her hand in his. I guess I'd do the same if I were him, Beth thinks.

She lets go of Rhys and walks up to the birds. She tries to remember what she did with the butterfly. She reaches out and touches the soft feathery side of one of the birds, closing her eyes. She's waiting for that feeling, those sounds. What if nothing happens?

Now she's beginning to feel foolish. She can smell the

birds, they must have been hanging here for days. Oh God, he'll never believe her… perhaps he shouldn't, maybe there's something else she's missing? The seal, imagining it whole?

'Oh my God…' Rhys' voice comes from behind her and she opens her eyes.

The pheasant is twitching into life, twine around its neck, beating its wings furiously. Rhys is over in a second, lifting the bird up, taking its weight. He slips a knife from his back pocket and skilfully slices through the twine. Then he tosses the bird up into the air and they watch as it flaps off, bumping awkwardly back to the floor before careering up and over the brambles at the edge of the garden.

'Oh. My. God.' He sits down, knife still open in his hand. She sniffs, aware of the blood now. Just a trickle.

'Does that always happen?' he asks of her sniffling.

'Yes. Sometimes a tear. Sometimes I taste it.'

They sit in silence. Rags appears cautiously around the corner, grumbling. She calls him over and he trots to her side, never taking his eyes off Rhys.

'You said your gran told you?'

'When I was younger. She said that with the blood, comes the gift.'

'Blood? What blood?'

Beth gives him a look.

'Oh, *that* blood… sorry.'

'Don't be.'

'Could she do it?'

'Yes, I saw her. With a mouse, up on the blood rock.'

'The *what?!*'

'It's up by the farm. I was kind of… initiated there.'

249

'By your grandma?'

'This is fucked up.'

'You're telling *me*…?'

There is a moment of silence between them and Beth feels a surge of pure understanding flow from her. At last she can share all the awful things.

'Wow… We should go in, it's freezing.' Rhys stares vacantly after the pheasant. She rises and offers him her hand. He takes it and springs athletically to his feet, making Rags jump.

'S'okay boy…' Rhys squats to face the growling dog. Then he reaches behind Rags' ears and gives him a little tickle. The growling stops. Rhys shuts the knife away, pockets it and leads all three of them back inside his home.

He sets the sofa back on its feet and shrugs at the state of the room.

'Guess I lost it for a bit…'

They sit and stare at the empty hearth.

'S'pose I should light a fire. Now that I'm alive again?'

It's ridiculous, but she smiles.

'How do you do it?' he asks.

'I don't know. And I have no real control.'

'The pheasant was real.'

'Okay, yes. But most of the time it just happens whether I plan it or not. Like, *you* weren't planned. And there have been loads. Random.'

'People?'

'No. Just you.'

'Lucky me.' Deadpan.

'Do you feel lucky?'

'Yes. Honestly, I do.'

Seconds tick by. She breaks the silence. 'So?'

'So, what do we do now?'

'Dunno.'

'This is weird for me.'

She nods.

'I mean, there are so many things I need to know.'

'I can help.'

'Thanks.' He reaches out for her hand, interlinking their fingers. 'Now that we said we love each other, does this mean we're *seeing* each other?'

She can feel herself blushing. 'I think we're past that…'

He blows out through pursed lips. 'Whoo, in a relationship then.'

'Yes. It's weird for me too, knowing what I knew, to feel that way about you, despite… y'know…?'

'You mean it was easier for me to tell you I loved you because I didn't know I was dead?'

'Oh, God, I don't know!' She can hear the tension in her voice.

'It's complicated…'

'I can't live without you. I mean, *literally*…'

'I know that now.'

'It's a massive ask?'

'I'm here. I'm not going anywhere.'

He reaches out and brushes her hand away from her mouth.

'You shouldn't do that.' He raises a finger and traces the contours of her lips. They tingle where his touch has been.

Then Rhys leans over slowly to kiss her. At first the kiss is tentative, but it soon grows and she can feel the pit of her stomach falling away. She thinks of her dream, the red-lipped sofa swallowing them, a fall into darkness. She kisses him back, intensely. Her eyes are closed but she can feel the room spinning. She's falling away from him and tries to lean back, but there's nothing there, just the falling. Nothing.

CHAPTER 34

'Beth? Beth?'

And with a whoosh of light she's back. Rhys is leaning over her, frowning. He's black and white. She can hear Rags whimpering.

'You had some kind of a fit. Jesus, you scared me. Shush boy.'

Rags stops. Rhys presses something cold to her lips and tips water against them. She drinks greedily.

'Beth? Are you okay?'

Rhys' face slides into pink, like a child was colouring him in.

'Yeah, did I faint?'

'After a bit, you had, like, spasms.'

She sits up shakily, the sofa still feels like it's on wheels.

'It felt like the last time...' she tells him, 'the last time we kissed.'

She checks her hands. They are like x-rays. This time she simply holds them up for him to see.

He takes a hand, turning it over, looking through it.

'Oh,' is all he says.

'That's what happened the first time we kissed.'

'No wonder you legged it. I thought it was my breath.' He's smiling but she doesn't feel like joining in.

'I can't kiss you.'

'What?'

'Not like that...'

'Oh. Right. You sure?'

'I think so. It's not the same with other people...' Oh, really? That was clever.

'Other people? Like who?'

'In Manchester. A boy kissed me, it was my friend's idea...'

'Okay. And you kissed him back?'

'No. I didn't feel anything at all. Not like with you...'

'When you become translucent and pass out?'

'Yes.'

'Great.'

'No one said this was going to be easy.'

'I don't care. Well, obviously, I *do*, but I mean... I still love you.'

As she hugs him closely there's a question forming in her mind, a question that takes a few moments to take shape – yes, but for how long?

He interrupts her thoughts.

'Can we visit my grave?'

'Err...'

'What? Was I cremated?'

'No! They, um, they never found your body.'

'What?'

'The car you were driving, went over the wall and into the river. They said you'd been thrown clear. Your medallion was there.'

'What was I doing driving at sixteen?'

'I don't know. Sorry.'

'Sounds like I had a pretty messed up life.'

He looks so sad she can't tell him what Karen said, oh, and by the way you were expelled for trying to burn the school down.

254

'So, my mum and dad are out there. Somewhere.'

'Karen told me there'd been a group of your mates, from school, laid flowers and that. By the road.'

'God, really?'

'Someone found a note, from your mum, in amongst them.'

'Why did she leave? Was it 'cos of me?'

'All I know is what Karen and Grandad told me...'

'Did your grandad know me? Can I talk to him?'

'Rhys, you're not thinking clearly...'

'Oh, I'm *sorry*...' There's anger in his voice.

'Please don't get mad.'

He's up from the sofa, arms spread wide, searching for words.

'Okay, genuinely sorry now...'

'Grandad knew your dad. A bit.'

'And?'

'No one liked him.'

'Great.'

'I get the idea he might have been mean to your mum.'

'Oh.'

He paces over to the front door and hangs from its frame, looking out into the trees.

'All this time, I've been walking round town. Anyone could've seen me.'

'I'm surprised Karen didn't. She was there, outside school that day.' Now Beth knows why Rhys had thought he'd known her. He did.

'She'd have had a shock.' He tries a small smile. 'So, I'm stuck here aren't I?'

'It'd be pretty weird if you just walked into town and said, I'm back...'

'Not a day older...'

He's still looking out, framed by the wood beyond.

'What about your parents?' New questions fill her head.

'If I was them, I'd want to know. Wouldn't you?' There's hope in his voice.

'Yes.'

He turns and looks at her. 'We'd be famous.'

'We'd be freaks.'

He nods. 'Yeah, s'pose...'

He wanders around the room, picking things up, putting them right, fixing the mess.

'Okay, if we found my mum and dad, we could like, swear them to secrecy? And, right, they must live miles away, could even be another country...'

'Yeah...'

'So no one would know about me, I could start again?'

'Yeah...'

'Would you come with me?'

'Rhys, I'm not sixteen yet. My mum's just died...'

'I'm sorry. Just got all these thoughts...'

'I know. Me too.'

He gathers up sticks and paper from the hearth and begins to set a fire. 'Can we at least look for them?'

'It's your life...'

'No, not really. Not without you, remember?'

'It's a mess isn't it?'

The damp wood hisses as Rhys puts a match to the paper. The room begins to fill with a sweet, sooty smell. He doesn't answer, bending to his task, breathing on the flames. Rags lifts a drowsy head from his paws and sniffs the air. Rhys speaks, kneeling as the fire crackles into life.

'So, all the things you've brought back, they were, like, just dead?'

'What do you mean?'

'Like, they were *there,* in front of you?'

'Err, yes, I think. Mostly.'

'Like the pheasant?'

She nods. Then remembers. 'There was this dog. The night Sienna nearly drowned.'

'What?'

'My friend…'

'The one who sends lads to kiss you.' This isn't a question.

She rolls her eyes at the thought. 'I saved her and there was this huge dog-thing. It came out of the ground, like from bones. There was this horrible noise…'

'So, it came up from where it had died?'

'I suppose…'

He stops to think.

'Where was I then? When you first saw me?'

'We were by the river…'

'Where I'd crashed?'

'Yes. Where my mum was killed.'

He crosses from the fire on all fours and lays his chin in her lap, looking up at her. 'Okay?'

She nods, when will it ever be 'okay'?

'Was I like, dripping wet?'

'No. You were muddy.'

'Oh right, yeah, course I was. I came here, got tidied up.'

She instinctively runs her fingers through his messy hair. 'You need a trim.'

'Don't they say your hair and nails keep growing after you die?'

'Yes, but you're alive now.'

'Yes, I am, aren't I?'

'I'll cut it for you.'

'You cut hair?'

'How hard can it be? I'll bring scissors next time.'

Rhys hauls himself up onto the sofa and they cuddle, heads lolling together.

'I need more…' he says and she wonders what he means. 'More about me, my life before…'

'We could try the library, go back through local papers?'

'The library?'

'Well I don't see any internet around here…'

'Need electricity for internet.'

'You can't come round to ours, there'd be too many questions.'

'Crap boyfriend aren't I?'

'You don't choose who you fall in love with.'

He snorts with laughter. 'Understatement of the year.'

'Understatement of any year.'

The warmth from the fire fills the room as they fit together like a pair of gloves. Right now, she feels like nothing else matters and she doesn't want that to go. But she knows it will, she knows it must. Outside life is going on and there are secrets to be kept and secrets to be discovered. Nothing will ever be the same again.

CHAPTER 35

Walking home, Rhys throws sticks for an enthusiastic Rags. Until the old dog looks how far he'll have to run and clearly thinks, enough is enough, barking at the stick instead. Rhys laughs at him, swinging Beth's hand in his.

They stay as close to the fields where they can, scattering sheep, which Rags looks longingly at, probably remembering a time when he bossed them around. It's bitingly cold but Rhys doesn't seem to feel it, his hand is warm around hers. She looks up at him, all sorts of emotions flooding through her. That's when she sees them.

From here, they look like stick men, fanning across a field. At least eight of them, carrying guns. Rhys has noticed her alarm and looks over too.

'Hunting,' he says, simply.

'I know – they've been to the farm. Let's go another way.'

'I'm not scared.'

'I am.' Trev will be there and the thought of Trev meeting Rhys with a gun makes her feel sick to her stomach.

'What are they looking for, do you know?'

'A dog. A big one.'

Rhys looks at her. 'A stray? I'd have seen it…'

'I think it's the one I told you about, the one I brought back.'

'Oh. Okay,' he squints at the men, closer now. 'They'll leave us alone then…'

'Trev's there.'

'So?'

Why does he have to be so stubborn? 'One of the older men might know you…'

A hardness settles on him. Is this the Rhys who tried to set the school alight? There's a tension in his grasp. But, just as quickly, it's gone and he smiles at her.

'Come on, I know another way.'

He leads them downhill, away from the group. They cross a small stream, ducking under spidery trees and treading carefully around the edge of an old quarry.

'So, I'm not the only dead thing walking through these woods?'

'There are loads.'

'Wow.' He looks genuinely excited.

'Promise me you'll never go near that dog.'

'Hey, perhaps we're like, related; kindred spirits, you know?'

'It's a dog, Rhys.'

'All the same?'

'Promise me?'

He laughs. 'I promise.'

~·~

They leave each other at the top of the farm lane, Rags turning circles in excitement until she tells him to go and he's off, helter-skelter.

'Will I see you tomorrow?' Rhys asks.

'Of course.'

'Bring something warm to wear, and boots.'

'Why?'

'We're going for a walk. A long one.'

He stoops to kiss her, gently. It's only for a few seconds, but the buzz is there, like static. He strokes her hair, pushing it off her face and she wants the kiss again. Instead, he lopes away, bending to pick up a large, branch-sized stick. Without looking back, he calls out.

'For your big dog, if I see him…'

'Not funny!' she calls back, but she can hear him laughing until he's out of sight.

CHAPTER 36

It's cold enough to snow as their bus twists its way slowly up a road that snakes away from them, occasionally giving views of an impossibly high Snowdon. This is to be Rhys' idea of a long walk. Snowdon in December.

He's like a kid. 'You been up before?'

'Yeah, years ago. Mum dragged us up.'

'Which way?'

'Err, the Miners' track, I think?'

'That's for tourists.'

'Didn't feel like that.'

'You were a kid though.'

She peers at the mountain, between passing pines. 'Think it might snow?'

'You're not getting out of it. Hey, thought you were a runner?'

'I am. Was…' She hasn't run in weeks.

'You'll be up it like a goat.'

They step out of the bus into a car park which seems to sit in a saddle, as the road dips away steeply in both directions.

'We're going up Crib Goch.'

'If you say so.'

'I do.'

He hitches an old rucksack onto his back. It looks weightless in his hands.

'If you'd said Snowdon, I'd have brought something else with me.' She peers up at the mountain.

'What, like Sherpas?' He jogs on the spot.

'Ha, ha.'

'If I'd said Snowdon, you'd have stayed in bed.'

Rhys has worn his red cap on the bus, with a pair of old shades he found in the attic. Now, he asks her to stuff them in the bag, shaking his hair loose. They set off along a rock-fringed path. Everything is so clear up here she feels like she can see forever.

The path turns out to be a trick, as if to say; it's fine, I'm a path, what can possibly go wrong? It soon disappears and they walk on rough grass with bits of rock and sandy soil poking through. Beneath them, in a huge bowl, is a glassy lake, bottle green. It looks a million miles away. She realises that, even with just a few weeks of non-running, her chest feels tight.

'We're going along the knife edge,' Rhys cheerfully announces.

'That doesn't sound good. Where is it?'

He stops and points up, way ahead. Towering above them is what looks like a sheer face of rock. Boulder on boulder, stacked up to the sky, forming a narrowing ridge. It doesn't look possible. It definitely doesn't look safe.

'Great...' she says, without enthusiasm.

'Look,' he points, 'it's full of people.'

She can just spot occasional pinpricks of colour on the mountain, not seeming to move.

'I've seen people run this.'

'When?'

'Must've been a kid, I don't know.' He stops, hands on hips. 'I'm pretty sure I came here with my dad. Pyg's for tourists, he used to say…'

'What pig?'

Rhys points to the other side of the immense bowl. 'Pyg track, there, above the Miners'… wow, I *can* remember…'

'You said, the Miners' for tourists…'

'I did, didn't I? Got that from my dad too then; wonder what else I got?'

Beth wonders too, but doesn't say anything.

Rhys leads. The knife edge is a jagged curve, barely wide enough to stand on. It tops what looks like the back of some mountain-sized prehistoric reptile as it fans and bends towards the summit. At times she has to straddle it to get a foothold, often bending to keep her balance. The rocks are precariously and haphazardly piled on top of each other and the drop is sheer. Horribly sheer.

'God, if you fell off here…'

'You'd die,' Rhys finishes her sentence. 'Ironic isn't it?'

They stop and she cautiously turns through three hundred and sixty degrees. She can actually see cloud forming under them; flimsy, wispy strands of it.

'We're on the roof of the world,' he says proudly.

'That's Everest?'

'Okay smartarse, the roof of the world in Wales.'

She sucks in air and looks off into the hazy distance.

'I wonder what would happen if I fell?' Rhys is looking down to the lake. She looks down too and feels vertigo rush up through her legs to her head.

'You'd die.'

'I'm already dead.'

'What, you think you're immortal?'

'I dunno, I'm new to this resurrection business.'

She reaches out and pinches his bare arm.

'Ow!'

'So, that hurt?'

'Yes!'

'Then you'd die. Painfully.'

'Then you'd have to bring me back again.'

'What if I couldn't? What if it only works once?'

They look intently at each other, thousands of feet tumbling away beneath them.

'Better watch my step then?'

'Yes, you'd better.'

He smiles, eyes twinkling, hair lifted by the breeze. Impossibly gorgeous, impossibly alive.

They occasionally have to step aside, literally on the lip of the drop, to let people past. Rhys grips her hand tightly and always nudges her back first. Yes, she thinks, I'd bring you back; or at least try.

The summit feels safe and, after the wildness of Crib Goch, the restaurant seems incongruous; lattes in the clouds. She pays for steaming coffees, which they take outside and then find a rock big enough to sit on. Rhys drops his rucksack to the ground and fishes out two apples, water and some fruitcake.

'We'll go back down the Miners'.'

'What, with all the tourists?' She's smiling.

He laughs. 'I owe all of this to you.'

'What?'

'Up here, the knife edge. Feeling alive; just that actually, feeling alive.'

She holds the coffee up to her face, feeling the steam collect on her nose.

'No one else up here feels like this.'

'They might?'

'No. Not like I do. They can't.' He gazes over the lid of his own drink. 'Can they?'

'No.'

'Thank you.' His eyes are moist and greener than ever. He reaches over and flicks at her nose. 'You're dripping in your coffee.'

'Lovely.'

He laughs.

They sit and drink in silence until the faint chatter of those around them shrinks into nothing and she feels they're alone. Side by side, invisibly bound together by something no one could ever possibly understand.

The Miners' track is almost deserted as they traipse down its hundreds of steps. The day has that kind of sharpness that only winter days can bring and at some points it feels like the whole of Wales is laid out in front of them, like some richly patterned carpet. Her calves feel the burn of dropping from one rock to another; she really needs to start running again.

~·~

It's still quite early in the afternoon when they get back to Rhys' home. She watches his back as he lights the fire, the way his too-long hair curls against the nape of his neck, the way he flicks it absent-mindedly away from his face. She wants to hold him again, wants to kiss him again. He turns from what he is doing and, when she sees his eyes, she knows he's feeling the same way.

He stays on his haunches and they look at each other for what feels like minutes, the unspoken desire almost physical between them like some magnetic pulse. Then he turns back to the small flames, blowing them into life. She curls into a ball on the sofa, hugging her knees to her chest, keeping everything in, everything dangerous.

Rhys stands, rubbing his hands together. He speaks lightly.

'I'll fetch something to eat. You stay put before you start bringing my dinner back to life.'

He cooks the other pheasant over the fire, with some kind of beans and carrots and they sit together, eating side by side on the sofa. He pauses to wipe something from the side of her mouth, then traces her lips with his finger.

'You're literally making me burn up.'

'Am I?' she says, feeling it too.

'In my stomach, in my chest…'

'That'll be your food.'

'Ah, you're kidding, surely once we've eaten the bloody thing…'

She laughs. 'No, I didn't mean like that…'

He puts his plate down on the floor. 'Are we going to be like this forever?'

'Like what?'

'Apart.'

'We're not.'

'You know what I mean.'

She looks away. 'I don't know.'

'Really?'

'Yes, really. There are loads of things I don't know, I'm still only fifteen.'

He takes her hand. 'S'pose, we just muddle along then?'

'See what happens?'

'Yeah. That.'

Suddenly the words 'only fifteen' flash in her head like a neon sign. All the things that have happened to her since she came to Wales. There have been times, she sees now, when she has had the weight of a lifetime hung around her neck. And, now, here she is with her boyfriend and she feels fifteen. Gloriously fifteen.

CHAPTER 37

They're breaking up for Christmas and Beth can't wait. More time with Rhys; long walks, the pleasure of just sitting and eating with him. She's lost some of her sharp shapes. Her hips don't jut out any more, her ribs have softened.

She still has the tone in the legs, which she reckons is a good thing. She's tried the odd run, mainly as an excuse to get out and spend time at his house. The proximity can be as bad as it is good. Being so close, physically, is like… difficult. They get by.

And then, there's the not-so-small matter of her sixteenth birthday, weeks away in February. Her dad has mooted the possibility of a party, back in Manchester but Beth has said, no. Okay, Joe had said, but there would be one surprise for her; Octavia is going to visit and Beth should listen carefully to what she has to say, he adds mysteriously. Suitably intrigued, Beth has googled Octavia Joseph.

Haitian by birth. Adopted at an early age. Educated in France and England. Boarded at Benenden. Read PPE at Cambridge. Olympic Gold Medallist in the High Jump. Recently appointed CEO of the late Eve Gray's gym empire. Just turned thirty. The online pictures are rare and luminous.

Beth has no idea what the exotic Octavia could possibly have to say to her, but remembers that promise, made at the funeral; she would visit. And now she's on her way. Beth has been told Octavia's treating her to lunch and so her dad has taken Beth to a cool, tiny back street shop in Pwhelli and bought her a beautiful print knee-length dress. Beth has ordered herself a pair of glossy black Docs and opening the box gives her a pang of regret over Sienna – silent now for what seems months.

She appraises herself in the bedroom mirror; I should stop being so stubborn, she thinks and makes a promise to herself to get back in touch with Sienna. Then she hears a car's tyres rippling down the farm lane.

She peeks out of her window and takes in the most beautiful car she has ever seen float into the yard. It's lipstick-red, vintage and gleams with chrome grills. Unexpectedly, the driver's door lifts away from the car vertically and Octavia unfolds her long frame smoothly from a plush interior.

She wears a slate-grey, short-skirted suit, immaculately tailored. It doesn't seem possible that anyone can exit a car like this, elegantly and with such modesty. But Octavia does. Joe appears, offering a hand, which Octavia takes, radiating a smile as bright and wide as the car's grills.

Beth trots downstairs past Grandad and Max, who are both glued to the window, gawping. The second Beth emerges into the yard, Octavia switches her attention from Joe to her like a laser.

'Darling Bethan, how are you?' The potentially trite greeting makes Beth seem like she's the only person in the world at that moment, or the only person in Octavia's world.

'I'm, good, thanks,' Beth answers.

'I'll leave you girls to it.' Her dad smiles shyly and pads back to the farm.

Octavia's eyes are magnetic, daring you to look away. As if

anything could be more beautiful to behold than she is.

'Shall we get the car out of the way?' Octavia offers.

'What is it?' Beth asks.

'1957 Mercedes Gullwing.'

'It's stunning.'

'Thank you. Your mother always said of me that I couldn't "do" understated if my life depended on it. I do try, honestly I do, but I'm afraid that cars are a weakness.'

Beth seriously cannot conceive of this woman having any weaknesses.

'Shall we?' Octavia nods to the Mercedes and Beth mutely nods. 'I adore your boots,' Octavia adds.

'Thanks.'

'The dress… did your father choose it?'

'Erm, he was there…'

'He has good taste.'

It seems impossible that Octavia can fold herself back into the car so swiftly, but she's in before Beth is and whips the car around and back up the lane. Out on the road, Octavia steers with one hand whilst sliding her sleek black phone into a slot under the dash. Music throbs from unseen speakers.

'I had a few modifications made,' Octavia purrs. 'Do you like the music?'

There is a breathy female voice under insistent, pulsing electronics.

'Err, actually, I don't think I've ever heard this before.'

'I'd like them to score our next campaign. We're going to branch out into spas.'

Beth nods. 'We?' she asks.

'Your mother's company. Gray's Anatomy. I'm CEO now.

Not replacing her, no one could; but we couldn't afford to remain rudderless in today's climate. You understand?'

'Yeah, sure... Beth is beginning to feel about twelve years old.

'You have a boyfriend.' Octavia pitches her remark half way between a statement and a question.

'No, um, yes.'

'And you're sixteen in a few weeks.'

'We're not... err...' Oh my God, this is torture, she feels.

'I don't mean to pry and I'm getting ahead of myself. I apologise.'

'No need.'

Jesus, Beth thinks, she's driving *really* fast.

'I'll shut up and let you listen. You must let me know what you think when we get there.'

'Get where.'

'Where we're going,' Octavia answers, as if this is obvious.

The dry stone walls blur past, feet away from Beth's window.

'Could you slow down, please?' Beth asks.

Octavia actually curves her long neck to regard Beth, eyes decidedly off the road.

'Of course. How crass of me, your mother must have died near here. And I find myself having to apologise. Again. I must be nervous.'

Beth settles back into her seat, aware she'd been on the edge of it for the duration of the ride. The recently polished leather squeaks beneath her and the blissful music pulses on.

Ten minutes later they suddenly swing from the road onto a single-track, purple-slate drive. High laurel hedges practically shut out the sky until they give way to a Gothic Mansion fronted by a huge fountain. They have climbed away from the main road and, from her window, Beth can see across a river estuary, dotted with inlets and small islands.

Octavia brings the Mercedes to a discreet stop outside two huge wooden doors at the entrance of the house. Before the wheels can stop turning, one of the doors opens and a bear of a man descends the wide stone steps leading to the drive. He wears a battered bikers' jacket over kitchen whites and has an impressive salt and pepper beard. If he was carrying a cleaver, thought Beth, the image would be complete.

The rising gullwing door almost takes him by surprise, but he recovers in time to take Octavia's hand in his and raises it to his be-whiskered lips.

'Miss Joseph…' A deep, rich Welsh voice.

'Please Jonno; Octavia?'

'Octavia.'

He offers Beth a paw, which she takes and become enveloped in.

'And your lovely guest.'

'This is Bethan Gray,' Octavia speaks, before Beth can.

'Miss Gray. Welcome to my hotel.'

'Thank you.' Beth is beginning to think she's has just stepped into a Bond movie.

Jonno leads them into a vast reception, high as a church and flanked by grandiose, curving stairways. The interior is eclectically decorated with vibrant pieces of art hidden in gloomy spaces and picked out by subtle spotlights. There is a lot of steel on show, vying for attention with meaty oak beams.

He pushes a ceiling-high door open with a flourish to reveal a circular dining room the size of Grandad's farm. Four ceiling high leaded windows leak light in through heavily-swagged drapes. In the middle of the room is an intimately sized round table, dressed for two. It is the only piece of furniture in the room.

Jonno seats them at the table and lumbers from the room, leaving them in a hushed silence, as if in a library.

'Well?' asks Octavia.

Beth doesn't know where to begin. She opens her mouth like a fish.

'The music?' Octavia prompts.

'I loved it.'

'Good. I will offer then.'

'What? On my say-so?' Beth's mouth remains open.

Octavia shakes out her heavy linen napkin. 'Bethan, are you aware of what you can do, once you're sixteen?'

Beth looks down into her lap.

'Apart from that,' Octavia teases.

'I can leave home,' Beth announces, remembering how she'd almost threatened it to her Mum.

'You can marry. Join a trade union. Drive a moped…'

'All at once?' Beth asks mischievously.

'I don't doubt that *you* could,' Octavia's eyes seem to glow, a deepest ochre. 'And that is why we're *here*.'

A slender, coat-tailed waiter walks in briskly. He is carrying two pieces of what looks like ancient parchment, rolled and held together with black ribbons. He hands them one scroll each and takes a step away, hands clasped behind his back.

He speaks with the barest hint of a Midlands accent. 'Good

afternoon ladies, my name is Rikki. For your drinks?'

They both order water and, with a nod of assent, he turns on dainty heels and wordlessly leaves.

'I asked for discretion but I feel Jonno may have gilded the lily. This must all seem a, little *ridiculous* to you?'

'Bond movies spring to mind.' Beth smiles and Octavia laughs out loud. It's a gutsy, deep-throated laugh that Beth doesn't deem possible coming from such a willowy, elegant person.

'Oh, I'm sorry. I have such a dirty laugh.' Your mum used to say it was my secret weapon.' And she does it again and this time, Beth laughs with her.

'Eve wanted you to eventually run the company. Be my boss.'

Octavia's voice is honeyed. She never blinks.

Again, Beth can feel her mouth open into a wordless circle.

'I want you to be the new face of the business. Starting on your sixteenth birthday. Please, just let me talk for a few minutes?'

Beth nods.

'From the look of you, the running has stopped. This is a shame, but not irredeemable. People loved your mother. Clients did. But here we can apply the law of diminishing returns. This will not last and we need to rejuvenate the process, the whole brand. You were to be the successor, so, why not start now?'

'I don't want to.'

Octavia doesn't actually pause. 'That was rhetorical. Of course this would be your choice and I don't want an answer today. Talk to your father, talk to your friends, to your boyfriend. All that I ask is that you do just that. Talk. No decisions. The details can wait'

Beth let's her words sink in. 'Okay…'

'Marvellous, Bethan. Thank you.'

Octavia slides the parchment from its ribbon and begins to unravel it. Rikki slips in with iced water and slips out again without actually disturbing the air. The whole day is beginning to have an unnervingly unreal feel to it.

'I recommend the skate,' Octavia announces.

Octavia is holding the menu out in front of her in a decidedly regal manner. She catches Beth's eye.

'Sorry, I must look I'm about to pass some awful judgement! Bethan Mary Gray, I bestow on you, fathomless wealth and happiness!'

She roars that filthy, infectious laugh and Beth laughs too.

The meal is ludicrously good; the skate wings melt in her mouth. Octavia talks Beth through her life with the preface, 'I expect you've googled me? I would you.'

Octavia's life sounds like a fairy-tale and Beth finds herself thawing as she begins to bask in Octavia's glow. She is *impossible* not to like, Beth thinks.

When the meal is over, Jonno himself guides them through to the front doors, a tattooed arm draped surprisingly delicately around Octavia's shoulders.

'And, of course,' she whispers to him, loud enough for Beth to hear. 'We were never here, Jonno?'

Jonno puts a finger to his lips and Octavia allows herself to be kissed on both cheeks. Jonno barely has to stoop.

It's only when about a mile from home, the same music subtly playing in the background, that Beth remembers she's planned a walk with Rhys. She checks her phone for the time. He's been waiting fifteen minutes.

And, sure enough, Rhys is propped up against the gates at the top of the farm lane. The wind is blowing his moppy hair into a halo around his face and he has his arms folded against the cold. Beth can see him register the car first, beginning to unfold his arms and to stand up straight, paying attention.

'Actually, Octavia, could you drop me here please?'

'Ahhh, the boyfriend,' she purrs.

'Yes.'

'Does he model?'

'No!'

'Oh. Well, he should. I'll leave that with you.'

Octavia stops the car and Beth opens her gullwing. If only she had a picture of Rhys' face at this moment.

Octavia leans over and embraces Beth. Both cheeks are kissed and, as they break, Beth feels that static charge again.

'Leather seats,' Octavia says apologetically.

'It's okay,' Beth says.

'Thank you for listening, Bethan.'

'Thank you for lunch… and the offer.'

Then Octavia looks deeply into Beth's eyes. 'Stay safe,' she says simply.

Beth offers a wan smile in return and swings herself, legs first, out of the Mercedes, noticing for the first time just how cold it is. But then, Rhys is there, in the doorway, smiling.

'Hi, I'm Rhys,' he beams at Octavia.

'Of course you are darling. Look after her, she's precious.'

Then Beth closes the door and the Mercedes muscles its way down the road, away from them.

'Wow,' Rhys says. 'Just wow.'

'Octavia or the car?' Beth asks

'Both, if I'm honest.'

She can see that he's teasing and reaches up to kiss him.

'Well?' he asks.

'It's a long story,' Beth says. 'I'll tell you on the walk.'

'Dressed like that?'

'Good point. Wait here, be right back.'

'Keep the boots on!' he jokes at her retreating back.

She feels light footed and light headed as she practically skips down the lane. Crazy, crazy day.

So far.

CHAPTER 38

Rags loves their walks, Grandad says the old dog is rolling back the years. For Beth, it's another excuse to be alone with Rhys. She does feel guilty, but it's not like she's lying to her dad. Just not telling him everything.

Today is the coldest of the year by far. It started with a frost and hasn't got any warmer. Even when low, grey clouds roll in off the sea, all they bring is snow. Beth catches herself thinking of Octavia in her sleek, ancient Mercedes, sliding round those forest lanes.

They tread through the snow now, where it has fallen lightly on the hard sand of Black Rock. Snow and the sea don't seem right together somehow. Rags runs off ahead leaving sandy, snow-rimmed paw prints, chasing the gulls. Beth has told Rhys everything about Octavia.

'What about us?' he asks.

'I'll wear suits and you'll wear practically nothing.'

'Ha. Ha.' Sarcastically.

'I'm too young. I'd have to leave here and I'm not going to do that.'

'I wouldn't want to hold you back.'

'You won't.' Beth hopes she is sufficiently reassuring.

He smiles.

'I feel sorry for you, in the cold at home...' The recent warmth of the hotel is still with her.

'I don't feel it so much.'

Beth had insisted that he put on as many layers as he could

fit into and he looks oddly beefed up. He catches her watching him and stops to flex his biceps, body-builder style.

'Hench or what?' he asks.

'It's all padding…'

They set off again as Rags starts digging at the sand, scattering lumps of it everywhere.

'Leave it boy,' she tells him. Like he's ever done anything Beth's ever ordered him to do.

They're the only people out in this weather and when they reach the curve of a small bay the wind picks up. Little flurries of snow prick at their cheeks.

'What's this beach called?' she asks.

'Samson's Cove.'

'That's not very Welsh…'

He draws her to him, arm around her shoulder and points off towards the cliffs at the end of the bay.

'See that rock?'

'It's a cliff, there are loads of rocks.'

'Okay smartarse, that one, massively huge rock. The one that is obviously a *rock*?'

'Oh, that rock, why didn't you say?'

He ignores her. 'See how it looks like it shouldn't be there?'

He's right; there is a large rock, like a giant sugar cube, sitting precariously above the beach. As if someone has carelessly dropped it there.

'Yeah…'

'Samson dropped it there.'

'As in Delilah?'

'The same.'

'Why?'

'I dunno.'

'Eh?'

'Never asked why.'

'Your story sucks,' she teases. 'Wasn't Samson from, like, the middle east or something?'

'Probably came here for his holidays.'

'Oh, right, 'cos of the weather?' She arches an eyebrow.

'Yeah, *obviously*. Brought that rock with him…'

'He'd never have got it through customs.'

'Right. Now you're just being daft.'

She looks around to call Rags again and in doing so, catches a glimpse of something moving in the gorse behind them. Up above a small white house. Something or someone. She stares through the shifting flakes, trying to focus. Nothing moves.

'That's the powder house,' Rhys helps. 'Been empty for years.'

She shifts her eyes to the house, small and white with rust patches around the windows. The glass in them looks darkly out to sea.

'Thought I saw someone…'

'Not in there. Unless it's got squatters?'

He sets off towards the house.

'Leave it.' She tries to say this without betraying the fear in her voice.

'It's okay…' Rhys says. 'Oh, there he is…'

Rags comes haring around the corner, trailing seaweed in his mouth. He skids to a halt in front of Rhys who starts to play tug-of-war with him, wrenching at the seaweed.

'Don't let him eat it!' she calls, 'he'll make himself sick.'

'Give!' Rhys calls and Rags does. Annoying animal, Beth thinks, whose dog does he think he is?

'Come on.' She feels that she wants to go.

Rags has other plans though and races off towards the house. He sets more gulls off and barks up at them, as they wheel around above him.

'Ridiculous dog will chase birds all day.' She starts to walk off.

'You love him really,' Rhys states as he joins her.

She casts a last look at the gorse behind the roof of the small house; then it disappears as they round the dunes. Rags is still craning his head, eyes flicking forlornly from one gull to another. As she watches, he sits back down, tail wagging against the sand, eyes now fixed elsewhere, away from the gulls. She walks on.

'You call him,' she tells Rhys, 'he'll come then.'

'He's having fun. Let him catch up.'

Rhys puts an around her waist. 'You can crawl under Samson's rock.'

'*Why?*'

'It's a laugh.'

'Okay, you've possibly been living in Wales too long.'

'Come on, we'll do it.'

'No chance. Seriously.'

He laughs and steers her along the curve of the small bay. The tide is flooding in, rippling against the flow of the river. She works out that this river must be the Glaslyn. The river that flows under the bridge in Porthmadog harbour. The river that crashes down the gorge in Beddgelert. The river that carried both her mum and Rhys away. That river.

She stops walking. 'Okay, where is he?'

They both look back along the beach. Just the snow and the sand. She looks down and sees where their footprints have traced their walk from the powder house. Her small size fours against his size tens. His strides against hers.

Then she notices another set she hadn't seen before. Bigger than Rhys' and leading away from them, towards the powder house; not yet filled in with snow. Recent. The image of something flashes back into her mind. In the gorse; that movement.

'Rags!' she calls. Then again, louder. But she's shouting into the wind, swallowing snow. 'Will *you?*' she asks.

'Rags! Come on boy!' Rhys puts his fingers into his mouth and pierces the air with a whistle. It seems to bounce back off the dunes. He does it again. They scan the edge of the bay for Rags, and she expects he'll come rocketing back, with something he shouldn't have clamped in his teeth, expecting to get away with it. But nothing.

'We'll have to go back,' Rhys says.

Every bone in her body resists this, but she steps along with Rhys as they retrace their steps.

The black eyes of the powder house still look out over the endless sea. The snow's getting thicker now as the clouds grow darker and fatter. They find Rags' prints leading up, past the house and into the dunes.

'He'll have seen a rabbit…' Rhys squints against the snowy sky and then whistles again. He takes her hand and sets off towards the house.

'What's up there?' she asks.

'It backs onto the golf course. Be deserted now.'

She clutches his hand as they skirt the house and plunge into a tunnel of tall gorse. This opens out onto a high dune, the house now beneath them. She can see all the way along Black Rock. In the distance, smudged by the snow, she can see the castle at Criccieth. She remembers their walk and wishes she was back there.

'He's not here,' Rhys states. 'The course is full of rabbits, he could be anywhere…'

She swallows her fear. 'We should look, he's too far from home.'

They drop down onto the course, away from the wind, and follow a path between the bunkers and greens, all tinged white now. They are the only ones here; it seems that all other life has done the right thing and got out of the snow. And, she thinks, we're still half an hour away from the bus.

'He's an old dog,' Rhys says, 'he won't stay out in this, even if he can't get home. Someone will take him in, or he'll find somewhere safe.'

But she doesn't want to leave, not without Rags. They search until she's too cold and Rhys' face is pink with the chill. They work their way back to Samson's bay where even the gulls have packed it in.

'Seriously Beth. Someone will be feeding him biscuits by now and we're out here, freezing to death.'

She nods and they set off along the coast, climbing up into the dunes and watching as the tide races into the estuary, forcing the river back on itself, creating wild currents that are fringed with dark foam. The snow is now coming in off the sea in horizontal waves, making Rhys laugh.

'This is *mad*!'

She knows she should believe him, Rags is safe somewhere, but there's this sense inside her, growing. She tries smiling at him, joining in. He's right, the snow seems comical; how can the skies hold so much? His hair is thick with it.

'You're all frosted,' he says. 'Beautiful…'

They reach a steep dip in the dunes and run down it, out of the wind. Beneath them there is a tiny inlet, littered with boulders, which have fallen out of part of the cliff that shelters the inlet from the sea, creating a cavernous peephole in it.

Rhys looks down at the small cove, deep in thought. 'I'm pretty sure I used to swim here. It's weird, reminds me of suntan cream…'

She looks at the sea, foaming at the base of the cliff. The tide is pushing froth and seaweed into the cove, where it swirls, caught in a whirlpool. She watches as a plastic bottle bobs on the choppy surface, inching its way to the small, pebbled shore.

'I can almost smell it…'

'What?' she asks.

'Suntan lotion.'

The bottle gets a little kick from the current and tips onto its side, rolling over, nearly ashore now, bumping against something else. A dark shape. Looks like a rock fringed in weed. There's something about the weed though; it's too thick. She peers more closely. It can't be, she thinks, watching it move as the waves lap at it. She squints again, through the snow, almost at whiteout.

'Coconutty kind of smell…'

'Rhys?'

'Had a palm tree on the bottle. I think.'

A larger wave rolls in, washing the dark shape sideways. It opens out. It reveals itself.

'Oh God, no…'

'Beth?'

She doesn't wait for Rhys, she's running down the dune, slipping over snow-soaked boulders. She feels the skin rip from her shins. Feels the pain through her knee, up into her hip. She doesn't stop.

A final jump lands her on the rocky beach and a few metres from the sea. She can't take her eyes off the shape, silently pleading to be wrong, to have seen the wrong thing. Suddenly Rhys is beside her, passing her, skidding to a halt as he plunges into the freezing waves, knee deep. In a second she's there too, looking down at Rags as Rhys turns him over, fighting to get at whatever is tied onto his collar, anchoring him to the shore.

'Bastards…' Rhys hisses.

He is frantically fumbling with what looks like a carrier bag of rocks. Someone has clumsily lashed them through Rags' collar and they scatter across the beach as Rhys finally rips through the plastic. Rhys rises from the sea, with Rags cradled in his arms.

Something hits her in the chest. It feels physical but she knows it isn't. A huge sob erupts from her, something almost animal. She begins to chant…

'No, no, no…'

Rhys lies the old dog down at her feet. Rags is lifeless, his tongue lolling uselessly out of his mouth. Snowflakes turn to mush as they fall silently and thickly on him.

'Sick bastards...' Rhys looks at her as she kneels beside Rags. She starts to run her hands through his matted and sodden fur.

'Do it, Beth.'

She looks up at Rhys. He nods at her.

She tries to get her breathing under control, forcing it through her nose. She concentrates on Rags, planting both hands on his cold, wet flanks. She thinks of him, bounding across the beach, just a short while earlier. Barking at the gulls. In the yard, circling Grandad. She thinks of him, *alive*.

She blinks tears out of her eyes and stares at him, *willing* something to happen, waiting for that feeling again. The rushing, the scent of blood. They stay like this, all three of them, for what seems like hours. Rags doesn't move, doesn't breathe. Rags just lies there. Dead.

Why now? She thinks. Why this time? She lets go of his fur and sits back on the rocks with a bump.

'What's wrong?' Rhys asks.

'I don't know. I can't do it.'

'Try again.'

'I can't.' She sounds so pathetic.

'Let's get him off the beach.' Rhys lifts Rags easily up and over his shoulder so he can climb back up off the shore. She follows them, slipping on the snowy rocks again, starting to feel the pain from her first fall. They reach the dunes and she puts a hand on Rhys' shoulder.

'Let me carry him now.'

'He's heavy. It's the water...'

'Please.'

Rhys slides Rags off his shoulders and offers him to her.

She takes the old dog and hugs him to her chest. She lowers her face into his neck, seeking out his scent. All she gets is wet fur. Wet, salty fur. They set off, Rhys slightly behind her, up and out of the dunes.

'Tell me when he gets too heavy…'

But she doesn't answer because she's started to cry again. This is my fault, she thinks. She could almost wail. Bringing him, leaving him at the powder house. *Seeing* something and being too scared. *I* didn't tie those rocks to him but I made him die.

The sand drops away from them as they start across another small bay. There are houses on the tops of the dunes. Lights are on inside. People are at home. Safely going about their lives. No crises, no deaths. Watching the soaps, getting their dinners ready…

Her crying intensifies, but now she's angry. Her shoulders begin to ache with his dead weight and her chest heaves and with every step, she chants silently. My fault, my fault; all my fault.

'Wait… Beth?'

There's something wrong with Rhys' voice and she turns awkwardly, Rags' weight almost tipping her over. Just in time to see Rhys drop to his knees, arms dangling uselessly at his side. He looks puzzled. His mouth opens but no sounds come out. His eyes roll into his head.

Now she tastes the blood. Now she hears the rush. Rags twitches in her arms and she looks down to see her tears of blood dripping onto him. Rhys pitches forward into the sand, not able to put a hand out to stop himself.

Rags coughs up gouts of saltwater, head rearing back, legs

frantically churning against her, forcing her to drop him. He hits the ground as she runs over to Rhys. She quickly pulls Rhys' face out of the sand, brushing it from his mouth and nose. She strains to tip him onto his side, he feels *so* heavy. Rags is barking now, pushing up against her, nuzzling her.

'Rhys!' She gets him over, face up to the snowy sky. 'Rhys!' She cups his face in her palms, thumbing the sand from his eyes. His lips are bloodless. She presses his mouth to her own lips and has to cradle his head against hers. She concentrates on letting her life bleed into his; allowing it to flow from her.

He blinks, then coughs. Eyes now wide open, scared. He sits up, almost pushing past her, but she keeps hold of him.

'Jesus, I just went…' he starts. 'I felt everything *leave* me…'

Rags licks his face, forcing him to wince and turn away.

'He's alive? You did it?'

'I'd stopped trying…'

Rhys reaches up and wipes blood from her nose and cheeks. 'What just happened?'

'I don't know.' She can feel herself getting upset again, feel tears coming back. Rhys hugs her, pushing Rags aside. He barks in protest.

'Shall we go home?' he asks.

And she can only nod.

CHAPTER 39

By the time they reach town the snow is settling in and the streetlights have stuttered into life. And they're wet, all three of them. The bus is taking forever to come.

'Maybe the roads are closed?' Rhys asks.

She sees him shiver.

'Thought you didn't feel the cold?'

'There's cold and there's *cold*...'

He's put his cap back on but the shades would look ridiculous so he pulls the peak over his eyes. Rags sits obediently at their feet and only occasionally lifts his head to sniff the air. Passing cars have turned the snow to mush and their tyres hiss with it as they drive by. A few pedestrians huddle against the snow, shuffling along.

'Could you phone your Dad?' Rhys asks again.

'What about you?'

'I'm fine, I can wait.'

'I'm not leaving you.'

'Look...' he begins, but suddenly Rags is up and barking wildly at a car that has just turned onto the high street. It's a black hatchback with garishly orange wheels. The car is low to the ground with darkened windows and throbs with bass heavy music.

'Shush boy...' Rhys stoops to calm him, but two things happen at once.

The car drifts alongside them and, although the windows are opaque at first, it passes the lighted window of the shop opposite and Beth gets a glimpse of who is inside. Faces hanging in the window, like Halloween lanterns, expressions of horror and shock written all over them, are Trev and Susie. They stare back at Beth.

Rags shakes Rhys' hand off and launches himself at the car, jumping up to snap at the windows.

The engine roars and the wheels spin uselessly for a moment in the slush, then the car fishtails and squeals off, Rags charging after it, in the middle of the road.

Rhys sprints along the pavement, far too fast for her to keep up. People are turning to see what's going on, nudging each other. Rhys' cap flies from his head and lands in the street and she quickly leaves the safety of the pavement to stoop and pick it up.

She hears car horns and shouts but ignores everything, concentrating on keeping up as best as she can. The car slides across the incoming traffic, back end going round, and for a moment she thinks it will slam through the windows of the Big Rock cafe on the corner. At the last moment it grips the road and disappears. Rags attempts the same corner and his legs go from under him. He slides uncontrollably into the path of the next car coming towards them, which brakes hard, immediately skidding.

Rhys hasn't stopped sprinting, somehow surefooted when everything else is going sideways. The car loses it completely, spinning, facing the wrong way, not stopping. Rags is scrambling, trying to get some grip. There's another scream growing in her throat... not again...

Rhys dips almost to his knees, slipping a bit now, and scoops Rags up before taking them both into a tumble that sees them spill over onto the pavement and up to the door of the Big Rock. The car slides to a halt, facing backwards and in the middle of the street. She arrives just in time to look down the side road and see Trev's car squeal around another corner and out of sight.

Rhys slowly gets to his feet, still with Rags in his arms. She races over, clutching his cap as people rush up to them; there are angry shouts, other cars are stopping. She looks wildly around as other people arrive. In any moment there will be a crowd, questions will be asked... the police...

Then a car she knows comes across the halted traffic and stops right alongside them. The door opens and her dad steps out. Max presses his face up against the passenger window. She looks from them to Rhys and back again. And she opens her mouth to speak.

Rhys beats her to it.

'Here, do you want your dog back?'

Is he pretending not to know her? She realises that she has his cap in her hands.

'You dropped this.' She offers it to him.

Rhys puts Rags down and takes the cap, quickly fitting it close to his eyes.

'Are you okay?' Joe asks, walking round the front of the car.

'Yes, it was Rags, he chased a car.'

'What?' Joe kneels to check Rags. 'He's soaked...'

Rhys speaks again, starting to move away. 'Right, I'll be going...'

'Thanks,' she mutters. Then she hears a window slide open in dad's car.

'You're that Rhys, one that battered Trev.' Max has spoken

292

and everything now changes. Her dad stands to look Rhys in the eye.

'In fact, you're all soaked. Get in.' Joe is being cool and she can't tell if he's angry or not.

'No, you're alright thanks…' Rhys starts to edge away again.

'Please,' Joe says, 'I insist.'

'I should be getting home…' Rhys protests.

'You saved our dog, least I can do is give you a lift.'

She turns her back on Joe and tries widening her eyes to express the panic she's feeling.

'It was nothing, honest…'

'Are you two going out?' Joe suddenly asks.

'No,' they say, too quickly.

Her dad smiles to himself. Max helps things along. 'They so are.'

Then their minds are made up for them as the driver of the backward facing car comes over. He's furious.

'What d'you think you were doing?' Others follow him.

Rhys shrugs calmly. 'I was saving the dog.'

'I could have killed you!' The man's face is turning puce.

'But you didn't.'

A woman from the back of the small crowd calls out. 'Should keep the bloody dog on a lead!'

Another voice pipes up. 'You want I should call the police?'

Her dad speaks. 'Is anyone here hurt?' Nothing. He speaks directly at the driver. 'Are you hurt?'

'No, but…'

'Is your car damaged?'

'No. Not that I can see…'

'Okay then.'

Joe opens the rear door of the car and looks at her and Rhys. 'Coming?'

~·~

Max grins at them from the front seat as they drive out of Porthmadog. They have Rags squashed between them, his head in Rhys' lap. Dad talks as he drives.

'Will you come back for something to eat, to ours I mean?'

'No, thanks…' Rhys doesn't look at her.

'I'd like to say thank you.'

'The lift is fine, honest.'

'I'll take you home then.'

'Err, no. There's no need. You can drop me. Anywhere through Tremadoc.'

'Is that where you live?'

'No. Not exactly…'

'Where exactly then?'

She butts in. 'Dad…'

'Dad what?' he teases her.

'It's a bit out of the way. Where I live…' Rhys tries to take the heat out of things.

'Wouldn't be any bother,' her dad insists. 'Look, in fact, and I'm not being rude or anything, but… it's either back to ours or to your doorstep. You're drenched, it's snowing, you saved Rags and you're going out with my daughter.'

'No, I'm not…'

'No he's not…' God, they're sounding like twins.

'Just good mates?' Joe offers as Max sniggers.

'Yes,' she speaks first to stop Rhys.

'So what's wrong with a mate coming round for a bit of tea?'

'Nothing…'

'And it's not like you've got anything to hide is it?' Joe seals it.

'No.'

Max is starting to pull weird faces and she wonders if she can cross her legs, kick him and pass it off as an accident. He's too far away.

'Do you need to call your folks?' Dad asks.

'No, it's okay thanks.' Rhys sounds calm.

Now Rhys and she look at each other, but Beth's aware that her dad can see them in the mirror, so smiles as sweetly as she can, pretending that everything is just grand. That everything *will* be okay. That they have nothing to hide. That Grandad won't have any idea who Rhys is. It was sixteen years ago, Beth thinks. He won't remember. Will he?

CHAPTER 40

'Chasing cars eh?' Grandad ruffles the fur on the back of Rags' neck. 'Silly old bugger.'

Rhys stands in the kitchen doorway, cap pulled down as far as he can without it appearing rude.

'Come in lad, you're letting the winter in.'

Rhys slides the door shut. It clicks with a kind of finality.

'I'll get the kettle on,' her dad says, busying himself by the sink. Max sits at the head of the table, loving every second of this.

'Been in the sea boy?' Grandad asks Rags. He feels under the dog's collar and unfastens the buckle, slipping it off. He looks up at the two of them, dripping on the stone floor. 'You shouldn't encourage him...' But something changes in his voice as he runs the collar through his hands.

'It was an accident,' Beth says. 'We threw his stick too far.'

'What's this?' Grandad has found a small piece of string, still tied to the collar.

'I don't know,' Beth lies.

He tugs at the string, testing its strength. 'Someone's tied this on...'

Dad talks over the boiling kettle. 'You need to get changed, both of you.'

'Err, this is all I have...' Rhys objects.

Dad eyes him up and down. 'I've got some old stuff you can have. I'll go and set it out for you.'

'Welcome to the nineties.' Beth tries to sound glib.

'Oi…' Dad calls as he crosses to the stairs. 'Cargo pants are back in again.'

'Only in *your* head.' She looks at Grandad, who has managed to get the string free. He squints at it.

'Can we have a shower?' Beth calls to her Dad, stopping him in the doorway.

'Together?' Max is soooo annoying when he's like this.

'No, Max.' She can see her dad isn't amused.

'Yeah, help yourselves.'

Rhys shuffles towards her as she makes for the stairs.

'Need to take your cap off…' Grandad speaks softly, 'for a shower…'

'Yeah, course…' Rhys almost mumbles and then reaches up and slowly slips the cap from his head. As he does this he turns away from Grandad and almost starts shoving her out of the kitchen.

'Here, lad…'

Rhys stops in his tracks.

'Pass me your cap. And your jumper, I'll dry them by the hearth.'

Rhys turns and faces Grandad, who has stood up from fussing over Rags. Beth watches as Rhys and Grandad look straight at each other. Grandad's face gives nothing away. Rhys hands him the cap and tugs at his sweatshirt, pulling it over his head.

She starts to look away, not wanting anyone to catch her staring at Rhys shirtless, but then she sees what is about to happen and realises she can't do anything to stop it. As the sweatshirt clears Rhys' head and he shakes his hair loose from it, something else drops into view. His medallion.

Rhys smiles sheepishly at Grandad as he hands over his wet clothing. But Grandad isn't smiling back. He simply takes the sweatshirt and hangs it over a chair, which he then drags up to the hearth. He then hooks the cap over the chair's shoulder.

'What d'you think of them, since relegation?'

'Sorry? Who?' Rhys is oblivious.

'Port...?'

'Relegation?'

Grandad looks so calm as he questions Rhys.

'Do you not go so much?'

'Ah, no. Not since I was small really, with my dad...'

'Cap still fits you though?'

Rhys nods. 'Yeah, it's like... adjustable...'

'Grandad? Rhys is standing here with no top?' Beth pulls at Rhys' arm.

Grandad shifts his face into a smile. 'Course, you get up there. We can talk about football when you're dry.'

Rhys gives a nervous laugh and follows her onto the stairs. They hiss at each other in whispers.

'He *knows*.'

'Rhys, he can't.'

'The cap, football; oh, and what the hell, when were we *relegated*!?'

'You're asking *me*!?'

'He couldn't take his eyes off my medallion. Weird.'

'Err, not really. He fixed it for me and we talked about it being yours, and the crash and that...'

'Oh my God, you're kidding..?'

'These do?' Joe makes them jump, appearing from his

298

room with several shades of beige hung over his arm.

'Thanks, Mr Gray.'

Joe smiles at him. 'I'll have your tea ready when you come down.'

They all stand awkwardly at the top of the stairs until Beth realises that she's supposed to go down with her dad.

'Okay,' she says, too cheerily, and heads off back to the kitchen.

'Bathroom's through there...' She hears her dad tell Rhys as she descends the stairs.

Grandad's sitting in his chair, still clutching Rags' collar. 'Wish I still smoked,' he mumbles.

'No you don't Grandad.' Max is deadly serious.

'Bloody well do.' Still mumbling.

'Rhys definitely battered Trev.' Max smiles gleefully, switching in an instant.

'Did he now?' Grandad stops fiddling with the collar.

'That's a lie.' Beth stares hard at Max.

'It's all round school,' Max explains.

'Ah, right. Must be true then...' Grandad smiles to himself. And Beth knows they've dodged that one.

'That medallion..?'

'It's mine,' she says. 'I gave it Rhys.'

'Thought you'd lost it?'

'Found it again.' Lame. Really lame.

Grandad nods slowly to himself as her dad breezes in.

'Giving her the third degree?' he asks of Grandad.

'Of course.'

'Good, you can fill me in later.'

Beth sits at the table and thinks, there's no way Mum

299

would have let me off so lightly. She'd have had addresses, dates of birth, next of kin. Rhys would have been begging for mercy by now. She plucks at her soaking top.

'I'll get changed.'

Joe throws her a look.

'I'll be straight back down…' she adds and rises to leave.

She throws on fresh joggers and a zip top, tying her still-damp hair back. She can still hear the shower running as she passes the bathroom.

'He's in there longer than you,' her dad teases. They all sit in silence, all those questions hanging in the air, unasked.

Rhys trots downstairs, hair slicked back, eyes shining green. Wearing chinos that he has to hold pinched in at the waist, to keep them up. And a collarless shirt.

'Great shower,' he enthuses. Grandad adds Rhys' remaining wet clothes to the chair and they sit as Dad serves them a pot of tea with a plate full of biscuits. Max eats them like he's never seen biscuits before.

'You'll be sick…' Dad tries to calm him.

'Don't care.'

Dad ignores him. 'So, where did you two meet?'

Here we go, Beth thinks. 'On a run,' she's in quickly, telling the truth. 'Over by Beddgelert.'

'You're not in the same school year?'

'He's not in our school,' Max speaks through a mouthful of biscuit.

I'm err…'

'Rhys is home-schooled.' She tries to save him.

'Are your folks teachers?' Grandad joins in.

'Err, no…'

'Would I know them?'

'Shouldn't think so,' Rhys is quick to reply. 'We've not been here long. From Wrexham…'

'Oh aye?'

'Near Wrexham. Tiny place.'

Beth spots a mistake and takes a breath to speak.

'Had to travel to see Port,' Rhys is quicker. 'My Dad's Dad and all that. Only get to support one team…'

'Could've been worse,' Grandad answers, 'could've been Wrexham.'

Rhys laughs. Too loudly.

This is torture. She wants to escape, be alone with Rhys again.

'Have you lived here long?' Rhys is trying to be subtle and change the subject.

'Generations. Dad's Dad and that…' Grandad replies.

'Oh, course yeah, farming…'

'What does your dad do then? If he's not a teacher?' Grandad isn't letting go.

'He's err… he's not at home any more. Just me and Mum.'

'Oh, I'm sorry,' her dad says, polite as ever.

'We don't really… talk about it…'

Everyone nods, except for Max, who uses the awkward pause to grab another biscuit. Then, through the crumbs…

'Is he dead too?'

'What?' asks Rhys.

Max continues. 'Your dad, is he dead like our mum?'

'No,' Rhys regards Max. 'I'm sorry. Sorry your mum died. She sounds like she was a brilliant person.'

It's like a huge weight has descended on the room. They all

look down, or away. Max's eyes are like saucers as he looks at Rhys. Rhys looks helplessly at her, searching for the right thing to say. She tries to help him out but all she can think about is her mum, cold in the ground.

It's a real shock when Rags suddenly yelps and begins growling. The old dog leaps at the closed kitchen door, clawing at the wood. Grandad gets up as quickly as he can.

'Now then Rags, settle!' He fumbles with the latch as Rags becomes more frantic. 'Must be a fox…'

Grandad gets the door open and Rags is through it in an instant. Outside it has stopped snowing but the sky is scowling; grey and fat with fresh snow. Rags has disappeared and they lean out to see what he was after. Grandad kneels in the snow. By the set of Rags' paw prints, there are some other marks and Grandad tuts to himself, scratching behind his ear, confused.

'Is it a fox?' Beth asks.

'No. But…'

'Wolf?' Max calls out, hopefully.

'Trotters, like a pigs. Can't be a pig though.' Grandad squints into the gloom around the yard, then stands and whistles loudly. They all stand huddled in the doorway, but the snow has thrown a blanket over the countryside and the silence is deafening.

'I'll go and look.' Rhys turns back inside looking for his shoes.

'No,' says Dad, 'you've done enough for today…'

'Really, I don't mind.'

'Rags is great with Rhys, does as he's told…' Beth chips in, sounding pathetic.

She can see it's his chance to escape. He slips his shoes on and takes his damp sweater off the chair. She desperately wants him to stay, but all she can do is watch as he pulls the sweater over his head. He reaches out and brushes her arm with his hand. They smile at each other and then her dad tosses something at Rhys, which he catches.

'Take my old coat, might as well go completely nineties.'

'Thanks, I'll get them back to you.'

'Course you will,' Dad says, 'you'll be back in a while won't you?'

'Yeah. I will…'

Rhys closes the door behind him and she feels a sharp pang, high in her chest. Fear.

'I'll get the dinner on,' Dad tells them.

It's only when he's slicing the onions that they all jump at the scratching at the door. Grandad is first over and opens the door to let a panting and snow-drenched Rags back in. Rags is straight over to Beth, jumping up, greeting her. Grandad leans out, calling. 'Rhys?'

But she knows he's not there. She just hopes he's home and safe.

CHAPTER 41

The night and the first few waking hours have been torture for her.

'I found him barking at some trees,' Rhys explains when they meet at the top of the farm lane. They walk, hand in hand, the crusty morning snow crunching under their boots.

'I was worried about you,' she says.

'Why?'

'Did you see a massive pig?'

'Think I'd've noticed…'

'Huge dog?'

'Oh, not *that* again.' He shakes his head.

'I'm serious.'

'Nothing, honest. The pig yours?'

'Not sure, I think so…'

'Could start your own zombie zoo…'

'That had occurred to me.'

'Does this mean *I'm* a zombie?'

'No Rhys, it does not.'

'Well, what am I then?'

'Zombies are all rotten, vile and crusty with bits hanging off.' Like I'm the expert, she thinks.

'Kind of dead behind the eyes, bumbling around..?'

'Yes.'

'Like Trev?' Rhys holds his arms out in front of him and starts mumbling, rolling his eyes. 'Must find other brain cell…'

'You're not funny.'

They climb high above the valley and look down its steep sides to where the sea glistens in the distance. She can see small swirls of smoke coming from the farm's chimney. They hang, almost still in the freezing air.

'I went to the library,' Rhys says simply.

'What? When?' She is genuinely alarmed.

'The other day.' He looks down at her and squeezes her hand.

'Did anyone see you?'

'Loads of people. None who recognised me though.'

'How d'you know?'

'Think they might've said. Look, there's that dead lad. The one who tried to burn down the school…'

'Ah…' She's caught.

'You knew?'

'Okay, you didn't actually burn it down.'

'Only 'cos they caught me. And expelled me.'

She looks away, cheeks burning.

'Anything else you want to tell me?'

'No.' Her voice sounds small.

'Who told *you*?'

'Karen.'

He nods, as if he already knew. 'Why didn't you say anything?'

'I don't know. Well, I thought you'd got enough to deal with.'

'So have you.'

'Yeah, but…'

'I don't need protecting.' She slides his hand from hers. 'I

305

need help. Remember?'

'Yes.'

They both stare down the valley for a second.

'So, my dad beat my mum up and I'm a wannabe arsonist…'

'You don't know he hit her.'

'I do now. Went through the criminal section in past papers. He got arrested, but Mum bailed him. Withdrew charges.'

'God, Rhys, I'm sorry.'

'So what if I'm just like him?'

'You aren't.'

'You don't know that.'

She takes his hand. 'Yes, I do.'

'That's probably why she disappeared.'

'I wouldn't blame her.'

'Left me though.'

'You weren't a child…' She searching for crumbs of comfort.

'No… no, I obviously wasn't.'

'I said I'd go with you, to the library.'

'I know; couldn't wait… you know me, hot-headed.'

He tugs at her hand, leading her off.

'There've been times when *I've* wanted to burn the school down…' Beth is telling the truth.

'With Susie in it?' He's smiling.

She laughs.

'Least I tried it at night, when it was empty.'

'Good of you.'

The smile fades from his face. 'Why though? Why would I

306

want to do that?'

'I don't know.'

'Doesn't it make you worry about me?'

'How?'

'What kind of person I am?'

'I can see what kind of person you are.'

'You know what I mean.'

'Okay. It did. But you're *you* now, alright?'

'I honestly don't know who I am. When I read those things, it messed me up… it was like reading about someone else.'

'That's because it *was* someone else.'

His half-smile tells her he's not convinced.

They walk on, breathing hard as they climb a steep hill, sometimes stooping to gain a handhold in the frozen grass. They reach the crest of the hill and she can see a valley sloping away from them, scooped out by a glacier. The windows of a distant Porthmadog wink at them in the winter sun.

'Did anyone at yours say anything about me – after I'd gone?' he asks.

'No. Just how nice you were.'

'Really?'

'Yes, really.'

'What, like, "he's dead nice..?"'

'You're in a funny mood this morning.'

He looks at her, eyes big and green enough to stop her heart. 'I'm all alone.'

'You've got me.'

'Yeah, sure, but my family… it's okay for you, you've got…'

But he trails off.

She picks up, '…most of mine.'

He smiles weakly. 'We make a great pair, don't we?'

'I think so.'

He shields his eyes from the sun, squinting down the glacial valley. 'I keep getting flashes of memory. Like, this place, it feels like I've been here before.'

'Hunting with your dad?'

'Maybe. Come on…'

They set off down a slope, heading towards a veil of skeletal trees, lining the valley's side.

'What will you do for Christmas?' Rhys asks.

'I don't know. Hadn't thought about it and no one's said.'

'Hmmm, thought I'd throw a zombie party, y'know, get all the dead things round, few drinks, bit of karaoke…'

'Sounds great, I'll bring a cake.'

'But you're not dead.'

'But I *have* provided all the guests. As long as the pig doesn't come. Or the dog…'

'You think the pig's dead?'

'I've kind of worked out that it has to be. There was this pig attacked me when I was small. I have dreams about it. In fact, I have dreams about lots of things.'

'About me?'

'No. Not properly.'

'What about then, what kinds of things?'

They dip through the bony shadows cast by the bare trees.

'Well, there's this baby…'

'Dead?'

'No. It's crying, it's all at night…'

But Rhys has stopped walking and is staring at something. Something hidden from her by the twisted trunks and spidery branches.

'Rhys?'

'I know this place.'

'Yeah, you said…'

'Oh Jesus…' He's raising his hand to his mouth, covering it.

She leans in to him, getting onto his eye line, getting a sense of his fear. All she can see is a huge, square rock, jammed in between two trees. It's about two metres tall and at least half that across. It sits crookedly between the trees, like it's had too much to drink and has slumped there, unable to move on. Maybe Samson dropped it there. It has a beard of dark green moss.

'Rhys, what is it?'

He lets go of her hand and runs over, hurdling fallen branches. She goes after him, dreading every step. They stop, side by side, feet from the rock. Rhys suddenly drops to his knees and vomits. She instinctively stoops to place a hand on his back and that's when she sees it.

At the edge of where the rock sits on the grass, there is a hollowed out opening, leading under the rock itself. Roots have been snapped and hang like a curtain. It looks like it's been dug out, by some animal. Some large animal. She thinks back to the night with Sienna. And the dog. She remembers how it tore itself from the ground, that awful noise and the snapping of roots and bones as it rose up in front of her.

Rhys is spitting and catching his breath. 'Oh God,' he says, 'I think I was here…'

An image of him snaps into her brain. The first time she saw him, covered in mud and dirt; and then, of course, she knows.

She slowly walks to the rock and peers down at the hole. There are dead leaves in it now, but of course there would be, especially if the hole had been made in the summer. On that day her mum died. On that day Rhys crawled out of here, barely alive… newly alive…

'Oh shit…' she hears him say, 'was I buried here?'

She looks back at him, still on his knees. 'I think so. Yes.'

'Why? I don't get it…'

She puts her hand on the rock, testing its weight. It's solid, immovable.

'Maybe this fell on you?'

Rhys looks wildly around. 'From where?'

'I don't know. It could have rolled.'

'What, whilst I was lying around? Under a couple of trees?'

She can sense the distress in his voice.

'Okay, I don't know. I'm trying to help.'

'Right, and then, my parents, they just give up and move on?'

'Rhys, we don't even know if this *is* where you were.'

'*You* know.'

He catches her looking away. 'I'm not sure…'

'Yes you are.'

He stands and walks up to the mossy face of the rock, placing both hands firmly against it. And then he starts to push, arms slowly folding into his chest with the effort. Unbelievably, the rock begins to shift.

'Rhys, don't…'

He just grunts, sinews straining under the skin of his arms and neck.

She can feel things under her hands, under the soil. Worms wriggle in between her fingers and bugs scurry across her wrists. The hole under the rock begins to yawn open, black and horrible, full of dead things that she can only feel and can't yet see.

'Rhys, please…'

With an awful animal howl he releases the rock which slams the hole shut again with a final rush of dank, foul air. Rhys is stalking around the rock, looking for weaknesses and gaps.

'Someone put me there. Must have done.'

'*Under* the rock?'

'Yes.'

'No. They can't… it's too heavy.'

'Left me to die. If they didn't kill me first.'

'But no one would do that.'

'Okay, how else?'

'Maybe it was like that other place, Samson's rock. You climbed under, got stuck?'

'At sixteen? Climbing under rocks?'

She shakes the bugs from her hands and gets to her feet.

'Wait a minute. What about the car crash? The river?' Rhys is frantic. 'My medallion!?'

The thoughts whizz about in her head, trying to settle into some pattern. 'Maybe it isn't yours after all. The crash though, that's documented. The crash is what everyone thought…'

'Well they thought wrong then didn't they?' He's flushed

with anger.

'We need to think calmly…'

'You think calmly, I'm trying to get my head around being murdered.'

'I could speak to the policeman, the one who came round after mum died.'

'What for?'

'He's been here for years, he'd know.'

'And why would he tell you?'

'I don't know. Why not?'

Rhys towers over her, breathing deeply, clenching and unclenching his fists. There are tears at the corners of his eyes and all she wants to do is take away his pain. She stands on tiptoe and kisses one of the tears away. She runs her fingers through his hair, brushing it off his face. She takes his head onto her shoulder, feeling its weight. She feels that current, low and heavy, inside her.

'Seriously, why not?

CHAPTER 42

'I'm doing this project...'

It's early morning and PC Hughes peers at her across his desk. Beth thinks he's only putting up with her because she mentioned her mum's death. He nods at the cup of tea he's just placed in front of her and she stops to take a sip.

'Lovely, thanks.'

He nods approval.

'It's for school. Well, really, it's more for me...' She can't believe she's actually using her mum's death like this; she feels cheap. 'I'm looking at road accidents, y'know, people dying, and, like, the reasons...'

He picks up his own steaming mug. 'Is this, erm, part of the process?'

'Sorry?'

'Grief. Working through it?'

'I don't know yet. It might be.'

He nods again. 'Okay.'

'I've been to the library, gone through stuff. Going back a few years.'

'We don't get that many road deaths. Not here. You'd have to go over Wrexham, Llangollen way. They're all in some god-awful rush see, to get to the sea. That's where it all happens. Mostly bikes.'

'It's not so much the "where", it's more the "what happens after"...' She takes another sip to hide her discomfort.

'Ah, course. Well, we clean up...' She sees a spark of alarm in his eyes. He thinks he might offend her. 'Erm, check the vehicles… with your mam…'

'You said, joyriders.'

'That's still open, but the chance of finding anyone…' he tails off. 'They come over from Manchester, Liverpool, lots of them. For the day, see, bit of fun.'

'What about in the past? Wasn't there a car in the Glaslyn once; a boy?'

'Yes. There was. Local tearaway. His dad's car I think. But then, if you've checked, you'll already know that?'

'There wasn't a lot of information. Just said, trouble in the family, being expelled; no body ever found?'

'That's right.' PC Hughes folds his broad arms across his chest, matter closed.

'I mean, how did the parents cope? With his death?' Shamelessly she looks down into her tea, but finds that she doesn't have to pretend, she actually is becoming upset.

PC Hughes notices. And compensates.

'Oh right. After. Well, the dad was in here, told us his lad had been drinking, stolen the car. It all came out, after. The boy's mam had been driven out by him; that's what the dad said. The school, getting expelled… you know about that?'

She nods.

'The dad said she'd been ashamed, took off, and left them to it – but the boy, Rhys something or other, was out of control. The dad was given to violence himself, bit of a bully. We asked him about that, he said he'd needed to be strong, keep his kid in line.'

PC Hughes stops to take a deep sip of tea. She can see he wants to say more, but can't.

'End of the story... the dad was the only one around to ask. Boy dead, mam disappeared.'

'I thought someone laid a wreath?'

Hughes snorts derisively. 'So she comes back but doesn't attend the service? Doesn't call here, asking questions? She was no stranger to this place.'

'The father had hit her, hadn't he?'

Hughes just gazes ahead, mug in hand.

'Did he hit the boy too, did he hit Rhys?'

Hughes' mug is placed firmly on the desk.

'Are you getting proper counselling?'

She shakes her head. 'Didn't want it.'

'I'm not just saying this as a policeman. Get some. As soon as you can. Other peoples' stories might not help.'

'It's just the coincidence, same bend in the road. It felt like I'd known the boy. Do you see what I mean?'

Hughes breathes deeply.

'I interviewed him, about the school and that. Seemed angry, but then again, he was a sixteen year old lad, they're all angry. I was worried what was going to happen to him, after he was expelled. Looks like I was right. See it all the time around here – nothing to do, loads of time to do it in.'

'But, he was okay?'

'How d'you mean?'

'He was an okay boy? Not nasty?'

'No. Not nasty. Troubled, wouldn't talk about things.'

'What kind of things?'

'Any kind of things... why aren't you writing any of this down?'

'Got a good memory. I'll make notes when we've finished.'

315

'Like now then.'

This isn't a question. Hughes rises behind his desk, so she stands too.

'Thanks, PC Hughes.'

'You're welcome, I hope it helped.'

He crosses to get the door for her and she takes the chance to finish her tea. Buying time…

'What happened to the dad?' she asks as she puts her phone away.

'Whole thing broke him. Like I said, the boy's actions drove the wife away. Left the two of them alone in that cottage.'

'Must have been a sad time?'

'Yes. At first, it looked like he was making a fresh start. He'd even started clearing the grounds, borrowed a tractor off his neighbour. Then the boy died and he upped and went. Been empty ever since. Waste eh? Waste of lives too?'

'The poor man.'

'Turned up here regular like, drunk more often than not, accusing her of having an affair. Think his mind was going. Tragic.'

'Yes. It sounds awful.' Something is beginning to ring in her head, small and insistent. 'A tractor?'

'Yes. And chains. Pulling trees down, he said. Storm damage.'

'Aren't you supposed to cut trees down?'

Hughes now has the door open and is checking his watch. 'Who's going to argue with a man whose wife has run off? About trees? He wasn't the most popular around here, but we help where we can; it's a small community.'

'No, of course. Sorry. Thanks again. You've been a real help.'

He smiles, barely parting his lips. 'You take care now.'

'I will.'

The door closes quietly behind her and leaves a thousand unanswered questions.

~·~

The cold outside hits her as soon as she steps out of the station and starts to walk alongside the building, down a narrow path back to the main road. She hears an engine and then sees a tow truck turn off the road onto the path.

On the back of the truck is a burnt out car, paint peeling off what was once a black hatchback. The tyres have burst, leaving sticky messes of shredded rubber around the wheels. It's a tight squeeze for the truck to get past her, so she flattens herself against the wall.

The driver raises a hand to thank her as he inches past. The car's wheels come into view, almost at her eye level. They too are blackened with heat, paint peeling. Flakes of it still fluttering in the wind. Orange flakes.

She shuffles quickly along the wall and slams her palm onto the passenger's window bringing to truck to a sudden halt. The driver's alarmed face turns to see her. An electric window slides down.

'What the hell you doing?' Deeply Welsh.

'Sorry, I...'

'Thought I'd hit you!'

'No, no. I'm okay.'

'What then?' Not happy.

'Where d'you get this car from?'

'Aldi, where d'you fucking think?'

'I think I know the driver.'

'It was stolen. Few days ago.'

'I think I saw someone driving it.'

'Get inside and tell Hughes then.' He looks questioningly at the window she's leaning on. 'Alright if I go now is it?'

'Sorry.' She leans back and the window slides shut.

The truck lurches forward and she looks up in time to see a police car pulling away on the main road. She clearly sees PC Hughes behind the wheel.

What would she say to him? I think I saw Trev driving a stolen car? Trev says he didn't. I say I've got another witness, only he's been dead sixteen years?

She walks out onto the main road and watches as the police car pulls away towards Tremadoc, over the rail crossing. She knows that she doesn't have enough information for Rhys. Just more unanswered questions. Part of her thinks they should stop here, that something dreadful is waiting.

You don't bury someone under a rock like that unless you've murdered them; unless you don't ever want them to be found. Especially if you then go through the pretence of seeing them 'buried' in a ceremony miles away. That's if the murderer turned up, if they knew Rhys. Didn't she read somewhere that many murders are committed by people known to the victim?

Then it hits her and she can't understand why she hasn't thought of it before. Rhys' dad told the police that Rhys stole his car, drunk. He can't have, not if he was under that rock.

Okay, that leaves two alternatives. Either she's wrong about the rock or Rhys' dad put him there. She feels sick and literally stops in the street to steady herself against a wall. That's when Beth smells her before she sees her.

It's a mix of cherries and chocolate. Something so sweet coming off someone so foul. Susie slaps her lightly across the back of her head as she comes into Beth's view. Skin-tight, stone-washed jeans, high-top converse and a black denim jacket over a lacy, low-cut slip. In winter. Hair spilling over her shoulders.

'What's up skank, time of the month?'

Beth stands upright, head swimming. Susie looks different today. There's a manic look about her; like she knows something...

'Boyfriend not looking after you?' she sneers. 'Not enough for him eh? Wouldn't surprise me, you reek of virgin.' She sniffs the air around Beth, pretending to recoil.

'Me? I wouldn't let him out of my sight. Might call on him one day, when you're at school, show him what he's missing.'

Beth wants to say something, something smart – but the words won't come.

'Could ask him some questions while I'm there, after I've shagged him, y'know?'

Susie reaches inside her jacket and shoves something right up into Beth's face. Beth steps back and bangs her head on the wall. The pain is sharp and she reaches quickly under her hair, fingers coming away smeared with blood.

'Who d'you think that is?'

Beth squints at a photograph, hand pressed back to her head, breathing through her mouth. It's of a boy, red baseball cap, at a school.

'Found it in my mam's book. Will told me you'd been nosing around it. I'm like, gobsmacked 'cos it looks so real. I mean, it's him isn't it? Except it can't be.'

Beth can feel the ground slipping away from under her feet. Sliding, sliding…

'Oh my days, get up, virgin…'

Beth's on the ground, on her knees. 'My head…'

'There's nothing wrong with you, except you're a freak. Freaky boyfriend, freaky dog…'

'What did you say?' Beth looks up.

'You heard.'

Black windows, orange wheels; that look of surprise when they saw them with Rags. The string round his collar, the hatred, the sheer hatred… peeling paint, blistering as it burns, a kaleidoscope of images; cherries and chocolate.

There's a roar that Beth doesn't recognise as her own and there's something in her fist; it's hair. She's twisting it; raging and spitting. Beth slams Susie against the wall, hearing the breath leave her. She has Susie's head in her grip, yanking it, making to smash it into the bricks. Susie's neck is arched, her mouth is open, pretty, pearly teeth gleaming. Beth thinks, I *am*. I'm going to kill you. Then, just as quickly, Beth's back on the floor again, but this time it's her who can't breathe.

Trev stands over her, sausage fingers clenched into fists. Her chest lurches as the air whistles in and out. She looks up in time to see Susie swing a leg at her, foot flashing. A sharp, dizzying pain in her ribs. She brings up this morning's cereal, her nose is full of it. Susie's screaming something unintelligible and Trev is holding her back. There's a car horn being blown. She sees Susie kicking out as Trev literally carries her off, around a corner. The car pulls up and Beth hears a voice.

'You're a bloody disgrace, fighting in the streets like dogs! Bloody kids!'

A squeal of tyres, the milky sky coming into view as she lies on her back, breath returning in spasms. Susie's words come to her now, 'I'll fucking kill her!' That's funny, Beth thinks, that's what I was about to do.

CHAPTER 43

They've arranged to meet at the rock again and that's where she finds Rhys. He's sitting on top of his own tomb. Her head's thumping and her throat feels raw. There's a raggedness to her breathing, ribs stabbing at her as she walks.

'You alright?' he calls.

Where does she start? 'Yes,' she calls back, 'stitch, not as fit as I used to be.'

'What did he say?' Rhys lets her lie slide, or hasn't heard it.

She starts to tell him, laying it all out, trying to remember every word, knowing Rhys will pounce on any ambiguity. She watches his face, looking for signs that her words are hitting home.

It's when she gets to the part where his dad borrowed the tractor that he stops her and holds out a hand. He wants her to join him so she tentatively reaches out, wincing as she does. He frowns.

'Stitch,' she lies, again.

Rhys easily lifts her onto the rock and shifts aside so that she can sit by him.

'I found these.' He gestures to places where something has scraped and gouged at the rock, leaving scars.

'What are they?' she asks, thinking that she already knows the answer.

'Something's been put around the rock, to move it.'

'Chains?'

'Yeah, could be.'

'Your dad asked for chains too, with the tractor.'

Rhys nods.

'Said he was pulling down trees.'

They sit in silence and she places a hand on his arm.

'That's not a stitch, is it?'

'No.'

'What then?'

'Susie kicked me. I tried to kill her.'

'No you didn't.'

'Yeah, think I did. And I think she and Trev drowned Rags. They burn out cars.'

He nods and then turns his gaze to the sky, growing dark with rain above them. 'Your mum?' he asks softly.

'I think so.' And only now does she admit what has been seeping through her mind ever since the fight, her loss of control. 'That bitch and that monster killed my mum. '

'And you think my dad did this to me?'

'I don't know Rhys…'

'Well I do. He did.'

The first drops of rain fall through the trees, pit-patting softly on the rock.

'First I'm going to kill them, then I'm going to find my dad and kill him too.'

'That's stupid.'

'Is it? You don't think I can do it?'

'I know you can. I don't want to lose you.'

'Your own dad doesn't kill you for no reason – I've must have been beyond bad. Then I turn up the moment your mum dies and I'm dead.' It's like he's listing reasons for something. 'You can't touch me. Ever. What's to lose?'

She strokes his cheek. 'You are.'

'What if I came back to you? After I'd killed them?'

'You wouldn't be the same person.'

The rain falls in great fat blobs now. Rhys looks at her again and she shivers. She's not sure whether it's the cold or the look in his eyes. Icy, full of harm.

He drops lightly to the ground and reaches out to help her down. She winces as she holds out a hand.

'Jump,' he says.

She does and he catches her effortlessly. She feels the heat through his sodden shirt and he holds her close, eyes inches apart. Instead of lowering her to the floor, Rhys takes a tighter grip, one arm under her knees, the other under her shoulders. She snakes her arms around his neck and he starts to walk.

She lowers her head into the crook of his neck, smelling wood smoke and wet cotton. She closes her eyes as he carries her, weightlessly, through the woods.

Rhys kicks the door to the cottage open and lowers her onto the sofa.

Without taking his eyes off her for a second, he peels off his dripping shirt and stands before her, his chest rising and falling. She feels her throat tighten as she stands too. She peels her own sweatshirt off, snagging her hair before it spills loose around her shoulders. Her T-shirt is sticking to her. She feels an intense ache, a tugging and her whole body is alive with it. Rhys stands impassively, eyes on hers still. She makes to pull off her T-shirt, feels its clammy hold on her stomach.

'I think you should go,' Rhys says.

'I don't want to.'

'Then I think you should stop.'

She slowly lowers her T-shirt. She feels stupid.

'Susie said she could have you any time she wants.'

'She's wrong.'

'Maybe not Susie then. One day… someone…'

Rhys breaks their look and walks close to her, so close she can feel his breath as he leans past her. She touches his bare shoulder, tracing the muscles. Then, quickly, he wraps a blanket around her and stands back.

'I've got dry stuff. Wait here.'

Beth gazes blindly at the wall once he's gone. Her body is still vibrating with desire. But even this feeling is curdling inside her; churning into something toxic. She drops the blanket and snatches up her soaking sweatshirt. She makes for the door and starts to jog through the pelting rain, feeling splinters of pain in her ribs as her pace increases.

Her face streams with a mix of rain and tears. It's all too much. Everything feels so… *heavy*. And endless. She's not sure where she's running to now, there's just the splash of her feet hitting the ground, and the green and the grey of the land passing. Then, as the grass gives way to a road, she knows. It's where I should have gone before, she thinks. As soon as I could, if I hadn't been so selfish and scared.

Only now, maybe it's too late.

CHAPTER 44

The rain has eased as she walks through the church gates. Somewhere, thousands of feet above, the wind is shredding the clouds, and a strong winter sun is blazing through, painting everything in brilliant colours.

The graves loll against each other. Nearly all are mossy and grey, even Mary's. Except for one.

Her mum's stone is a modest one. A slab of granite with the words simply chiselled in white. The sun is so strong that a slight steam rises from the wet stone. She walks right up to it, running her fingers over its gritty edges. Someone has filled the small square in front of it with jagged green stones.

'I'm sorry, Mum.' The words are too late, and they feel useless. She leans her arms over the top of the stone and lays her cheek against it. This, she thinks, is where I've always known I will end up.

'What do I do, Mum?' Beth needs to hear her words.

'You should do it.' Rhys' voice makes her jump. 'Either I'm getting faster or you're getting slower.'

'Both, I reckon,' she replies.

He strolls up to her.

'You can't keep running away.'

'I'm sorry.'

'Nothing to be sorry for. What's stopping you?' he adds, looking to Eve's grave.

'I was scared.'

'Of?'

'Well, first of all, I didn't think I could do it. Not until I realised you were mine... and that felt like an accident.'

He jumps up to sit on a crooked tomb by the side of her mum's grave. Like he hasn't got a care in the world. Like he's decided something and has relaxed.

'Ahhh, okay, that makes sense. Me, I'd have tried to get her back, like, as soon as I knew that I could do it.'

'It's not that simple. I've thought loads about it.'

'Go on...'

'For a start, what would my dad say, and Max... Grandad? There's no explanation.'

'Would they care, as long as she was back?'

'I don't know.'

'You're over-thinking, just act.'

'Okay then. You, right – you were under that rock, just managed to struggle out. I saw that dog, and it had to peel itself out of the ground...'

'Yeah?'

'Mum's in a box. Sealed.'

'Oh.'

She feels her eyes start to fill. 'I've thought, all this time, that I might have already done it... you know...'

'Oh. You mean she might have come alive and been down there all this time?'

'Yes.' She can barely whisper.

Rhys jumps down and puts strong warm arms around her. 'I'm sorry, I wasn't thinking...'

She's starting to snivel and bury herself into him, trying to find safety from her thoughts.

She mumbles against his chest. 'And there's something else...'

'What?'

'I think this is the worst part.' She pauses for breath. 'It's you. When I brought Rags back, when I was really trying, with someone I loved... you passed out.'

She can't see his face, but his grip on her never falters. She keeps going.

'And when we didn't see each other for all that time, you looked so ill...'

She can feel him resting his head on hers.

'I think... that if I tried to bring Mum back, it would kill you...'

The sun is warm on her neck. Rhys selects a strand of her hair and winds it around his finger, slowly.

'You mean, it's like some kind of... transfer?'

'I don't know. Possibly. Maybe?'

'Well, okay. Let's think about this. If you think you might have brought her back already... well, I'm still here.'

'Yeah?'

'So, chances are, you can't have done. Or else, according to you, I'd be dead. Again.'

'It's too much. I can't take it. No one should have that choice.'

He eases her off him so he can look her in the eyes.

'This won't go away. You're going to have to face it.'

'No I'm not.'

'I don't see how...'

She interrupts him. 'Right, you just said, if it was *your* mum, you'd just do it?'

'Yeah.'

'If it meant killing me?'

'No, I didn't say that…'

She's getting angry. 'But if that was your only choice?'

'Whoa, it's *way* different. For a start, I can't do the things you can…'

'But if you *could*? You just said so yourself.'

He shuffles back, putting a small distance between them. 'It's impossible to say.'

'That's because it's an impossible choice. My impossible choice.'

He stares at her mum's stone. 'Maybe things were fated to be this way?'

'I've stopped believing in fate. You kind of do, when you can change the way things are meant to be.'

They hear a gate creak and both look over to see a man and a boy making their way into the cemetery. It's her dad and Max.

Without thinking she grabs Rhys' arm and hurriedly leads him off. They duck down behind a huge family crypt, mossy and unreadable. They sit in the thawing grass and Beth can feel the cold seeping through her trousers.

Rhys hisses in her ear. 'Why are we hiding?'

'Shhh!'

She can hear their footsteps as they approach Mum's grave. Then Max's voice.

'Why didn't Grandad come?'

'I don't know Max,' Dad replies. 'I think he comes on his own.'

'He doesn't bring flowers then.'

'What?'

'There aren't any flowers.'

329

'Well, we've brought some, haven't we?'

'Yes.'

There is a lull. Then Max again.

'What will she be like? Now?'

Dad clears his throat. 'Asleep.'

'But she's dead...'

'Like she's asleep then.'

'Only rotten?'

'No Max. Not like that. Lay the flowers.'

A brief silence.

'I can still see her. In my head.'

'That's a good thing, Maxie.'

'Can you?'

'All the time.'

'That's a good thing for you then, isn't it?' Max's logic is irrefutable.

'Yes.'

'Will I ever get another mum?'

'No...'

But she can hear Dad choke on his words. Whatever he was going to say dissolves into small wheezes. Beth stares straight ahead through cloudy eyes.

'I don't like it when you cry,' Max states, a matter of fact.

Beth sees something small and green spinning away, over the cemetery wall. Then another. He is throwing the grave's green stones as far as he can. This is Max's way of dealing with emotions he can't handle. She can hear the little grunts he gives with every effort.

'Don't Max.' Dad has regained some control.

'Why?'

'Let's go. Come on.'

She can hear the scrabbling together of the stones and imagines Max stuffing them into his pocket. Footsteps are fading.

'Someone's got white ones over there. Look.'

'Oh yeah,' her dad says.

'Like pearls.'

Their voices disappear just before she hears the gate creak again.

Rhys speaks first. 'We'd have to dig her out. The box, I mean.'

She turns to Rhys, wiping the tears from the corners of her eyes. And shakes her head.

'I'll do it on my own,' he offers.

She kisses him fiercely on the lips, accepting the small swoon that always comes with it. Then drags herself up, wiping the wet grass from her legs.

'I need to get home.'

'Yeah, course. Do you want me to walk you?'

'No. It's okay. I'll come round yours tomorrow?'

He nods sadly and this makes her want to stay. Makes her want to go back to his instead; want to do lots of things she can't. She walks off without looking back. Suddenly Beth feels like she has to be with Dad, Max and Grandad. She knows they need her there more than ever.

CHAPTER 45

The kitchen windows are steamed and the room smells of lamb stew. Grandad is just sitting in his chair. He seems out of breath.

'Ah, the wanderer returns.'

'Hi Grandad. Dad back?'

'They've been to the cemetery.'

'I know.' Too quickly.

'Do you?' Grandad's answer feels like an accusation.

'Yeah, they said, didn't they?'

He shifts the cap on his head without taking it off.

'Don't know about that. Is your phone flat?'

'Oh, yeah. Probably.'

Grandad knocks his stick against the side of the hearth.

'Stick the kettle on, there's a girl?'

She picks the kettle up, running the tap.

'Your dad said something about popping to the shops, y'know, 'cos they were in town.'

'Uh huh.' The water drums at the kettle's sides. She casts a glance back at Grandad to see him wipe his brow, momentarily lifting his cap to do it.

'You been out, Grandad?'

'Bit. Getting the blood going. Dog doesn't walk himself.'

'Told you, I'll do that.'

'With Rhys?'

Was there an edge in that? She looks at him again. His eyes bore into her.

'Sometimes, yeah.'

'That dog's different...'

She looks away as she places the filled kettle on the hot plate. Hairs prickle on her neck.

'How d'you mean? Older?'

'No. If anything, seems to have gotten a second wind. Can't put my finger on it... tell you one thing though, if I knew what it was, I'd be having some myself.'

He's smiling now. 'No fun, getting old.'

'How's your leg?'

He shakes his head with disgust. 'Ahhh, I never wanted to be one of those old buggers who can tell the bloody weather by the feeling in their joints. And yet, here I am. May as well stick me on top of the town hall so everyone can share it – there goes old man Williams again, looks like snow.'

She sets two mugs down on the draining board and lifts the head off the porcelain chicken that holds the tea bags.

Grandad talks behind her. 'No. No, if anything, I'd say Rags was a new dog.'

She almost drops the pot chicken on the floor.

'Mary never lost an animal. I told you that, didn't I?'

'Yes.'

'And, back in the day, if there was any problem with the ambulance, before there was a station here, she'd be asked to attend babies' births. Like yours.'

Beth turns slowly to face the old man.

'I mean, self–taught. No YouTube then. No training.'

'She had a gift,' Beth says slowly.

'She did that. The day you were born...'

'You told me.' Beth realises she's trying to stop him from

talking.

'Listen. I didn't tell you it all. Now I think I need to.'

Beth grips the edge of the kitchen top; leans on it.

'I was outside the bedroom door, like I said. I heard your mam going through the labour – no pain killers, nothing. Then I heard her cry out, I remember it clear as day, clear as I do now.'

Beth moistens her lips from a rapidly drying mouth.

''She was practically screaming, 'the cord's round her neck, the cord…''

He stops to gather his thoughts. Beth's dream insinuates itself into her brain. The kettle begins to whistle shrilly.

'Mary told her to shush. Like a child. I couldn't help it, I cracked open the door, I might have been able to help. Mary had you, dripping wet and your colour. It wasn't right. I've seen dead things Bethan, I've seen them. Mary pulled at the coil with her teeth. That's what stopped me from going in. She spat it aside. Took you up to her mouth and breathed the life back into you.'

'Yeah, so. That's what she did then. It's like… normal.'

'There was nothing normal about it.'

'What are you saying, Grandad?'

He just looks at her. She struggles not to look away.

'What happened to Rags? Why did he have that rope around him?'

All good lies contain a grain of truth, she thinks.

'We think Trev tried to drown him. Rhys saved him.'

'Not you?'

'No.'

They stare at each other and Beth is preparing herself for

334

this to go any of many different ways. None of them good.

'I never asked your Grandma about that day. I was afraid of the answer. I still am.'

The kettle begins to scream. It rattles wildly on the hot plate. Neither of them move.

Then the latch on the kitchen door clicks and her dad pushes it open with his hip, arms laden with bags.

'Every time I forget the damn bags,' Dad says as Max follows, pretending that his bags are heavier than they actually are.

'Swear to God I should have shares in them. Hello stranger.'

'Hi, Dad.'

'Jesus, what's with the kettle? All okay?' Joe asks.

Beth strides over to flip the whistle off the boiling kettle.

'We've been to see Mum,' Max says and starts rummaging through his carrier, pulling out a box of Frubes.

Dad has folded back the fridge door and is carefully slotting his shopping inside.

'Make a pot,' Grandad suggests to Beth. He slides the cap from his head and smooths his hair down. Now that the moment has been broken, Beth finds him difficult to look at, avoiding his gaze.

'*You* should go,' Max tears at a Frube with his teeth and the yoghurt inevitably squirts out over his sweatshirt with Finn the Human on it.

Beth opens a cupboard to reach for the teapot. 'I've been.'

'Not with us,' Max rubs the yoghurt into his top, giving Finn a pink quiff.

'No...'

Max sucks at the opened yoghurt.

Her dad speaks over his shoulder. 'We can all go, next time.'

Beth hears a small clattering sound. Max has emptied his pocketful of green stones onto the kitchen table. He spreads them apart and then begins to sort them into some pattern only he can see. She knows she's not supposed to know where they're from.

'They're nice,' she manages to say.

'They're Mum's,' Max replies. 'She has green ones, other people have white.'

'I've seen blue ones,' Grandad gazes indulgently at Max.

'Dark or light?' Max asks.

'Dark. Like sapphires.'

'These are emeralds.'

'They are that.'

She looks at her dad, but he's hunched over the fridge, one hand gripping onto its edges. He stoops to fish another package from the bag at his feet.

Beth's voice cracks. 'I miss her too.'

'We know sweetheart,' Dad answers.

'No one's saying anything…' Grandad is rising creakily from his chair and Dad turns a tear-stained face from the fridge.

'We'd do anything to get her back, goes without saying,' Grandad's words stab at Beth before he envelops her in arms full of warm wool.

Then she feels other arms around her. Dad has encircled them both and squeezes them tightly. Beth's crying again. She feels a nudging at her waist and peers down to see Max trying to wriggle into the middle of them. She reaches down and drags him in, burying his face under her arm.

They huddle there, rocking slightly, for minute after minute. Silently. The quiet is broken by a high whining sound from Rags. Grandad is the first to speak.

'Damn dog wants a cuddle now.'

Max breaks away and throws his arms around an anxious Rags, who licks him enthusiastically in the face.

'He's only after your yoghurt,' Grandad teases.

But Grandad's eyes are fixed on Beth. You know, he's saying. You know what to do.

She wipes a sleeve across her nose. 'Think I'll have a bath.'

'Okay,' Dad says. He looks broken.

As she passes out of the kitchen she reaches out and sweeps one of the green stones off the table. She clutches it tightly as she climbs the stairs and keeps it in her palm all through the running of a steaming bath.

She slips out of her clothes and looks at herself in the tall mirror. I was dead, she thinks. Mary brought me back to life. I'm just like Rhys and all the other dead things. Only, I'm not really, 'cos I can do it too. So, what does *that* make me?

The water stings as she lowers herself into it. It feels cleansing. She takes the stone in her hand again and lowers it into the water. It's dark now, a real emerald. Dark, like me, she thinks. My family don't know me anymore. Not really, not who I have become. Only the dark things know me. The things I have resurrected. Six feet under the green stones, my mother lies, grey flesh falling from her bones, skin pulsing with tiny insects. Not yet a dark thing.

She squeezes the stone until it digs into the palm of her

hand. The pain feels good, not like the other pain she feels, the pain that never goes away. Would bringing Mum back ease that pain or make it a thousand times worse? The thoughts crowd her muddied mind. Then everyone would know my true nature.

Queen of the dark things.

She lies back in the bath, her head slowly slipping under the water, the knot in her hair sliding undone, eyes wide open. Her hair floats over her face, shutting out any light. She could be anywhere. Strands of it drift across the surface of the water, waving; like weeds, she thinks. Like weeds in a river, tugged by the current. She closes her eyes and allows images to bloom in her head.

That day in the river, with her mum. The pool. Her dive. The weeds on the bottom, rooted by the rocks, undulating. The cold. The breath burning in her lungs. Breaking the surface. Mum making the 'loser' sign at her. Feeling how light Eve was as she pulled her from the pool. Her words...

'Help an old lady up, will you?'

A kind of light dances over Beth's closed eyelids. She needs to breathe. Then her mum's face crashes into view, through the surface of the bath water and it's *her* hair waving on the water. Her eyes bulge wildly at Beth. Her mouth opens – help an old lady up, will you?

Beth's up, spluttering and spitting water, sloshing it over the edge of the bath. She hears it hit the floor, rubbing it from her eyes. She's gasping, looking around crazily. She's alone. Was I asleep, she thinks, for an instant? Did I dream? Oh my God, did I fall asleep in the bath? Her pulse pounds at her temples.

She gets quickly out of the water and wraps herself in a towel. The plug belches air as she yanks it out. She pads across the landing, leaving wet footprints there and shuts her bedroom door quickly. She sits on the bed, pulse slowing a little.

It's only a few minutes later, when her breathing has levelled out, that she opens her fist of a right hand and looks down. She sees that the little green stone is still there, its shape almost cut into her palm. She quickly places it on the bedside table. It's still there, slowly drying to a duller hue when she slams the door shut; dressed and with somewhere to go.

CHAPTER 46

The door to Rhys' cottage is wide open and shifts squeakily on its hinges in the wind. She steps in warily. The fireplace looks neglected, charred logs sitting in its grate. She calls out his name and it just echoes back at her.

He's not in the kitchen but a skinned rabbit glares at Beth from the sink, lidless eyes dull. She turns quickly away and goes to the stairs, taking them two at a time.

The ladder to the loft is down and she calls uselessly up into the dark attic. She's seen the rabbit, he'll be out, checking his traps. This doesn't feel right though. The ladder shifts queasily under her weight and the gloom of the attic dulls her sight for a second until her eyes adjust.

There's no-one here. The old case is open and its contents have been gone through. She squats over it, shifting the old memories over one another. Faded, yellowing envelopes have split, past lives spilling out. She stands, almost hitting her head on one of the roof beams, something brushing her forehead. It's a letter, pinned to the beam. It starts, 'Beth.'

Scratchy writing; *'No one should have to make that choice. Thank you for making me feel so alive. Rhys.'*

Her mouth dries in an instant, tongue clacking against her teeth. Where is he? She screams his name at the top of her voice.

She screws the note up and pushes it into her jeans. She's down the ladder too quickly and slips at the bottom, almost turning an ankle. She uses the banister to lurch down the stairs, head reeling. Where can he be? She plucks the note out of her pocket, feverishly unwrapping it.

'*Thank you for making me feel so alive.*' Please don't let this be his end, not to see him again, Beth anguishes. She *did* make him feel alive again. He said so, he'd never felt so alive and neither had she. Did I ever tell him this, she wonders? No. I should have… I will when I find him. If I find him.

She's standing at the front door, scanning the woods, horrible thoughts scrambling her mind. She needs to think calmly, if she's to find him. He has nowhere to go. She's all he's got. Yet, he has gone.

Where would *she* go, if it was her? Without me, he'll die; she convinces herself. So, he's gone off to die somewhere and he doesn't want her to find him, to try again. He's making the choice for her. The sea? No, he might wash up. Like Rags did. Okay, okay. If it *was* me, she reasons. I'd want to feel *that* alive again, even if it was only for a short while. For one last time. Go somewhere they'd shared together? Criccieth? That was fun, they had a great day, but did he say that, about feeling alive, to her there? God, this isn't helping.

He'd thanked her – for giving him life. Of course he did. Now she remembers. The wind, the fear and the sheer scale of it. That feeling of being so alive yet so near to death. Snowdon. Crib Goch.

Now she runs with real purpose. His life depends on it.

CHAPTER 47

I t's about four miles to Porthmadog, two of them downhill. She sets a fifteen hundred metre pace. Her jeans get in the way and she thinks about taking them off. Running into town in just her pants doesn't appeal. She's so out of condition. Ragged breathing, pulse like a drum.

Two miles in, she stops to throw up. Then off again, elbows in rhythm, mouth wide open, spitting out moisture she desperately needs. At one point she can look over to her left and actually see Snowdon. Or at least she can see its lower hills. The rest disappears into muddy cloud. All the time thinking, when did he leave? How much start has he got on her?

The last mile had been the worst, less than fifteen-hundred-metre pace. At times she's jogged, pain stabbing at her ribs.

As she hits the streets outside the town it occurs to her that he might still be at the bus station. He can't have walked to the mountain, can he?

She passes the police station, down the high street, buses queuing outside the park, a few people around. People watching her, stopping to stare. As the bus stop gets closer she slows to a walk, hands on hips, legs trembling. She's looking for his cap, his shape, any clue.

She checks the timetable and sees that she's missed the bus to Llanberis by thirty minutes. That's if he was even on it. She has another thirty to wait. It's too long. She checks her pockets but can only find the crumpled note. Not a penny, she couldn't get on a bus anyway.

There's a sickening sadness welling up in her chest, hopelessness. Her phone's still got charge, she could call her dad – drop me off on Snowdon Dad, I'm looking for Rhys, who's already dead but might still be trying to kill himself? There are a few people here, swaddled in winter clothes, eyeing her suspiciously. She could ask to borrow money?

The looks she's getting from these people tell Beth that they've all probably seen her fighting with the local beauty queen in the street. Then a bus pulls up and a few people begin to step out. Most are elderly, a young teenage couple; not likely to have the cash.

She sees a woman rising from her seat, the last to get off. She appears to be in her forties, as far as Beth can make out. She's alone and seems to be leaving the bus hesitantly. Beth watches her step off, rooting through the contents of a handbag, head down. As the bus pulls away Beth walks quickly up to the woman, appraising her. Three-quarter-length grey woollen coat. Ash-blonde hair spilling from an attempt to pin it into shape. Long, tapered fingers, ending in bitten-down nails. Beth is by her side and speaks quietly. 'Excuse me?'

The woman looks up at Beth. Deep, green eyes, high cheekbones, a long nose.

'Yes?' the woman says in a soft Welsh accent, taking in Beth's sweaty, bedraggled state.

Beth starts to say something but the words are lost in an insistent series of blasts from a car horn and they both turn to look.

Will grins at Beth from an open car window, waving a

hand, beckoning her in.

Beth looks back at the woman. The woman has a half-smile on her lips. 'I don't think he means me…'

And with that, she turns and walks away, leaving Beth standing stock still, shocked. Another blast from the horn. She looks at Will. Does she have another choice?

The car smells of him; liniment and Lynx.

'You alright?' he asks as she settles down, pulling the seat belt across her shoulders. 'D'you know that woman?'

'No.'

'Oh, right. Looked like you did… where to, miss?'

''Listen, I need a massive favour?'

'Go on.'

'No questions, but take me to Llanberis?'

'What, at the weekend like?'

'No. Now.'

He starts to smile.

'It's halfway up a mountain and it's December. Just be us and the goats… oh, wait, no goats, 'cos even *they're* not so stupid as to be out in Llan–fuckin'–beris in December. And goats are stupid, right?'

He waits for her to laugh and she watches the smile fade from his lips.

'Please?'

He's just watching her, both arms planted on the steering wheel.

'I can pay for your petrol. Not now, but, later?'

'I don't want your money.'

Oh God, has she upset him?

Will looks at her intently for a second more, then reaches

for the gear lever. The engine revs and they're away from the kerb, pulling past the waiting buses.

'Put your window up,' he says, 'gets freezing up past Beddgelert.'

She mumbles a thank you and raises the window, slicing through the chilly air. As she does so, she catches a fleeting glimpse of the woman in the grey coat, striding, head down, past the park. Beth's mind whirrs.

~·~

They're soon weaving into Beddgelert. They pass the bend where her mum died and she looks away. Will nods at the river.

'Sorry, this is the shortest way and I'm guessing you're in a rush?' He sounds angry.

'It's okay. I really appreciate this, Will.'

'You meeting someone up there?'

'Yeah. Kind of.'

'You're not dressed for Llanberis.'

'Well, actually, not Llanberis. There's a car park, on the mountain…'

'Why?'

'That's where we're meeting.'

She can see patches of windblown snow, huddled in drifts against farm walls.

'Am I taking you to see your boyfriend?'

He deserves the truth. 'Yes.'

'Ah right, would've been nice if you'd mentioned that before.'

'You might not have brought me.'

'You're right.'

He sounds hard, like his sister.

'You can drop me anywhere here.'

'Oh yeah, like I'm gonna do that.'

'Really, I shouldn't have asked.'

'But you were desperate?'

'Yes.'

The engine starts to whine as Will drops a gear to climb a hill.

'Long as I know where I stand…'

'You've been really kind to me…'

'Enough, okay?'

She folds her hands into her lap and looks out of the window. More snow now, the hills are laced with it. And then, as they clear a forest of pines, Snowdon looms above them, grey and hostile, disappearing into a shroud of mushrooming clouds.

They practically skid into the car park and Will drives through it, up to its highest corner. The car park is deserted.

'Looks like you've been stood up.' Harshly.

'Thanks for the lift Will.' She starts to open the door and feels a stab of freezing air.

'I can't just let you get out.'

She challenges his look. 'You can't stop me.'

He has twisted sideways in his seat, draping an arm over the top of the wheel. He looks like he might explode and she gets the first stirrings of fear. Then a grin breaks out across his face.

'Now I know why I like you so much.' He reaches into the

back of the car and drags something over to the front. It's a fleece.

'Take this.'

'It's massive…'

'It's mine…'

It has a Porthmadog rugby crest on it and smells just like Will.

'Okay, thanks.'

'You got your phone?'

'Yes.'

'Give it me.'

Surprisingly, she does. Will taps his mobile number into it and hands it back.

'Any problems, yeah..?'

She can't find the words, so nods and slides out of the car. She turns her back on him and jogs over to the first steps out of the car park. She's waiting to hear the car's engine as Will drives away but there's only the moaning of the wind. She doesn't look back.

CHAPTER 48

Beth thrusts her hands deep into the pockets of the fleece and bends her head to the wind. Her calves are still aching after the run into town from Rhys' cottage and she realises that she hasn't eaten in hours.

Yet, here she is – looking like she's the only person on a hostile Snowdon, in a borrowed fleece.

As she reaches the top of the first hill she can see across the fathomless lake beneath her, its dirty green waters flecked with urgent white waves. There's hardly any light spilling through the clouds, just a dull, murky half-dark.

She looks to Crib Goch but can only see where it should be. She has no choice but to go up. Every step burns and reminds her that, at some point, she will need to come back down. As she contemplates this she wonders whether she will be coming back alone, then shakes the thought from her head with a shiver.

Where the path evens out, she attempts to jog, trying to eat up that half hour start he had. Soon, with rasping breath, she enters the cloud base.

Within minutes she's soaking wet, jeans sticking to her legs and chilling her to the bone. Her hair is lank against her cheeks. Old, half frozen snow crunches under her trainers. Then she slips, going down painfully onto one knee.

Not now, she despairs, I haven't got the time to be injured. She clasps her knee, exploring the sides with frozen fingers, rubbing at it. She flexes it carefully and slowly. It's sore but it works, nothing torn.

She's up on her feet again, taking her time, aware of the deepening drop to her right, even if she can't see it. If she hadn't already been up here with Rhys, she'd be lost in minutes, despite what is an unsteady and barely visible path.

She sucks each breath in through gritted teeth, wincing at every step. The wind slaps at her exposed face, stinging her with sleet. Now there are tears mixing with the rain. She's angry and scared and feels stupid. She hates the mountain and she hates her life, what this *gift* has done to her. Her knee is throbbing, her chest is bursting.

She stops and yells into the wind. 'Rhys!'

Again and again, until she's hoarse. There's a large rock in front of her, obscuring the path ahead. She clambers past it, opening her mouth to yell again but the call dies to a croak.

Just at the edge of what she *can* see, down to her right, something twitches in the wind. She climbs closer to the lip of the drop to get a better look. It twitches again and lifts slightly. It's red. It's a cap.

She scrambles down, but suddenly the wind shifts the cloud like drawing back a curtain, and the yawning drop revealed beneath her is terrifying. The fear grabs her stomach, clenching tightly. She's frozen there, almost lying on the rain-slicked rocks.

She slowly inches her way towards the fluttering cap. She can see where the peak has lodged between two smaller rocks. She stretches, fingertips crawling, seeking a grip. She knows that she needs to get lower and is fighting the desire to just lie there and cry. She looks back the way she came and for another horrifying second, can't believe what danger she's in or how she's going to get back.

She screws her eyes tightly shut and tries to get some sense of control, but the wind still tugs at her, trying to rip her off the face of the mountain. The clasp at the back of the cap is clicking against the rock in the wind. Get me, get me, get me, it seems to call.

Maybe Rhys is just the other side of the edge, lying injured. Maybe he needs her, like before. No, she *knows* he needs her. She has to move.

She's been clutching the slippery rocks so tightly that her fingers have begun to cramp. She slowly prises them out of the cracks they've been wedged into. She shifts her weight slightly, testing that her feet are planted on stable rocks. They feel okay, so she places her weight on them and slides into a foetal position, lowering herself inch by inch.

For a second the world seems to pitch sideways and she's sure she's going over. She shuts her eyes again and it passes. When the queasiness has subsided she takes in how far she needs to reach. A metre? Bit more? She tests her weight again, pushing gently through the soles of her feet. Yeah, feels solid. Her right arm is closest to the cap. She can sit up, get it, and see over the lip of the drop. Her left hand has a firm grip, fingertips pushed as far as they will go behind a fair-sized boulder.

She releases her right hand and starts to sit up and reach down. She can feel the touch of the cap's metal clasp flicking through her fingers as it twitches in the wind. Then she grasps it. She cranes her neck as the drop inches into view, hoping she can see him, hoping he's alive.

It's her right foot that goes first, shooting small rocks over the edge. This brings her left knee into her chest and rips her fingers of her left hand off the boulder. She instinctively lets the cap go and claws wildly at the rocks with her flailing right hand. They just scatter from underneath her fingers and she can feel that tilting again, only this time it's real, she's sliding over the edge. She doesn't even have time to scream.

Something digs into her shoulder and she stops, legs dangling over the lip, kicking at nothing. Then there's a hand under her arms and a voice, under the wind.

'Stay still!'

She's lifted easily off the mountain and taken into Rhys' arms. His hair is whipping around his face, eyes like stones.

He drags her back up to the path.

'I dropped your cap...' She sounds pathetic.

He shuts her up by kissing her and she feels like she's spinning at the top of the world as the leaden sky whirls above her. Then his arms are around her and she feels his immense strength almost cracking her ribs.

'What *were* you doing?'

'I thought I'd lost you. I got your note.'

'I'm sorry I did that. I should have just left. It was selfish.'

'You saved my life. Literally, properly...'

'So now we're even?' His face is set hard, serious.

'That's not what I meant.'

'I came here to die, not to put you in danger.'

She starts to flush with anger. 'Oh right, like *that* solves anything!'

She pushes him away with a strength that surprises them both. 'If you'd really wanted to die, you wouldn't have left a note!'

'How was I to know you'd be such a smart-arse that you'd work it out?'

'People don't leave clues unless they want saving!' She has no idea where this fury is coming from, only that she needs to let it out. That she can't stop it.

Rhys is getting just as angry. 'So *this* makes you happy!?'

'*Happy*? Who said anything about being happy?' She is beginning to lose it.

'I did. Your monster. The person who's killed all your happiness.'

'You want to make me happy?' Beth cries, desperate, 'then stay alive! I can't carry on, thinking you're going to throw yourself off the nearest mountain every other day.'

'The note didn't say anything about a mountain.'

'Don't nit-pick.'

He sweeps his hair off his face for a second. 'I'm sorry... I wasn't thinking straight. I just didn't want to go without telling you how I felt.'

'You could have tried talking to me?'

'Then you'd have talked me out of it.'

'Yeah, I would,' she concedes.

'And you'd still have that choice to make.'

'I still do.'

They stand, feet apart with the wind whipping between them, a thousand metres in the air.

The words come from somewhere deep inside her.

'I choose you.'

CHAPTER 49

Rhys slips his hand into hers as they walk down the mountain. Their fingers intertwine easily. They fit. They haven't spoken since she said those words. Beth doesn't feel badly about saying them, although she's not really sure *what* she feels. The late afternoon is now creeping across Snowdon, wiping all the shadows out. Then she has to speak.

'I had a chat with Grandad.'

'Oh yeah?'

'I think I know why we can't… why we have problems *being* together.'

Rhys stops walking. 'Go on…'

'I'm like you. I'm dead too.'

'Fuck off… sorry, didn't actually mean that, but, y'know… *fuck* off!'

'He told me. He saw Grandma Mary bringing me back. It sounds like I'd choked, the umbilical cord was wrapped around my neck…'

Suddenly Beth can't go on. Rhys holds her fiercely. The wind whips their hair together, surrounding them with it.

'Oh God, I'm sorry…' He's slowly massaging her back, strong fingers kneading the knotted muscles there.

'Actually, I'm not sorry,' he continues, 'selfishly, I'm not. You're *here*. I have you. Imagine all the pain your family would have felt if your Grandma hadn't done that?'

'All these years, I had no idea. I feel like I've lived someone else's life.'

He takes her face in his hands. 'Well, now, you start to live your own.'

'I may well have some… *issues*… to get through…'

'I'm here.' He holds her gaze. 'So, your grandad knows then?'

'Not really, he *suspects*, but he said he was afraid to ask the question.'

'Wow. So, your gift, is that only something dead people can do?'

'Oh God, I hadn't thought of that. But that means…' Beth tails off, shaking her head with the creeping insanity of it all.

'It means we have a lot to talk about.' He finishes her sentence. 'Us dead folk need to stick together.'

'I don't like the label "dead",' she states.

'Me neither,' Rhys answers. 'I was starting to think of myself as "reborn".'

'I like that.'

They both begin to shiver simultaneously.

'We should move,' Rhys says. 'Come on, take the first step of that new life…'

They break the embrace and Rhys takes her hand. She takes a step towards him and they walk on, the road clearly in sight.

As they go round the final bend into the car park she sees Will's car. And stops.

'I was wondering how you got here so quickly,' Rhys says.

'It's Will, Susie's brother…'

'Should be a fun drive home…'

'If he lets you in?' She looks up to see if Rhys is going to cause trouble. He smiles easily.

As they approach the car Will starts it up and the lights come on. She bends to his window, which he slowly cranks down.

'Two of you then?'

'I'm Rhys,' she hears from behind her.

'Get in.'

Rhys bounds round to the passenger door and lets himself in. She can't believe his cheek. She has to slide over the rear seat, shuffling Will's rugby stuff into a corner.

'You shouldn't have waited,' she mumbles.

'Both be fucked if I didn't.'

'It's really good of you…' Rhys is beaming at Will.

'Seat belts,' Will orders, shifting the car into gear and, scattering shale from under his tyres, squealing out of the car park onto a deserted road.

She looks back at a disappearing Crib Goch through the gathering dark. She's really not that fussed about visiting again any time soon.

Will speaks something in Welsh. It sounds like water gurgling down a drain.

'*So, ti'n ffwcio hi?*'

To her amazement, Rhys answers instantly and fluently.

'*Meindia dy ffycing fusnas.*'

Of course he speaks Welsh, she just hadn't thought. She tries to sink further into the seat, but Rhys leans over the back of his seat, casually draping an arm there.

'Will just asked me if I was sleeping with you.'

The car twitches round a bend.

'I told him we had something much deeper than that.'

She catches Will's eyes in his rear view mirror. He instantly looks away as her face burns with anger. How dare he?!

Will speaks. 'He actually told me to mind my own fucking business. Which is a fair point, well made.'

'Oh right, and do *I* have a say in all of this?' She's furious.

'Not since I left you out. Sorry.' Will sounds genuine. And equally angry.

Rhys turns back to the front and they drive on in silence. The car's headlights fill the tunnels made by the trees as they swing down and down towards Porthmadog, scattering the odd rabbit.

'Here's just great, thanks,' Rhys speaks suddenly, miles from anywhere.

Will slows, unsure. 'Here?'

'Yeah.' Rhys is already loosening the seat belt and so Beth slips hers off too.

'Keep the fleece,' Will says.

She manages a terse 'thanks' as she closes the door and Will catches her eye; his rugged, tanned face glowing in the dashboard light. She looks away this time and waits as Rhys shuts his door, lightly tapping the car roof, as if dismissing a taxi. Will roars off and they are left alone as the red glow from the brake lights flare once then disappear, leaving them in darkness.

'Bummer…' says Rhys. 'I forgot to tip…'

CHAPTER 50

Once the droning from Will's car has died away, the silence around them becomes heavy with intent. Beth looks at Rhys, his flippancy grating on her a little.

'If it hadn't been for Will, you'd probably be lying at the foot of the mountain.'

'I didn't like the way he spoke about you.'

'I can stand up for myself.'

He holds his hands up, palms towards her. 'Hey, no argument from me there…'

'You're incorrigible.'

'Again, no argument…' He smiles winningly and she smiles back.

'Where are we?' she asks.

''Bout a mile from mine, come on. Rhys waves a hand as he scrambles over a partially fallen stone wall and into a dense patch of woodland.

As soon as they dip under the branches of the first tree, she feels her stomach turning to liquid. She squeezes Rhys' hand tighter. It's almost impossible to see more than a few feet in front of them, but Rhys steps confidently ahead, trailing her behind.

They're going uphill and occasionally a low branch brushes against her and she shudders, swiping it aside. Somewhere an animal screams and she literally jumps on the spot, dragging Rhys to a halt.

'What was *that*!?'

'Fox. I think.' He looks back at her. 'You okay?'

'No. What kind of fox makes a sound like that?'

'One in pain. Probably in a trap.'

'One of yours?'

'Could be.'

They both stand in the dark, breathing slowly. Rhys speaks first. 'Are you angry with me, about that, with Will?'

'No, are you angry with me?'

'No.' He tugs at her hand. 'Right then…'

'There's something out there.'

'Told you, fox…'

She takes out her phone and switches the torch on. It floods their feet with light. She shines it around. Just dense trees and pitch black beyond. And a queasiness that won't go.

'Okay, now I remember – you've got a torch.' This time when he tugs, she follows.

They clear the trees and a glimmer of fading light from the sky paints the field ahead of them a pale grey. She switches the phone off.

'Saving the battery.' The next wall of trees about a hundred metres in front of them looks familiar.

'Where *exactly* are we?'

'Yeah, not my favourite place either. It's where we found that rock.'

She feels like things are sliding into place, things that she can't stop and doesn't understand. Every hair on her arms bristles. They're nearer to the wall of trees now.

'Don't go in there.'

'Jesus Beth, it's miles the other way.'

She's about to argue when her legs start to shake. She pulls

Rhys back, almost leaning away from the woods. There's a lightness at the top of her head, as if it was going to spin and fly off. The world seems off-kilter, unreal.

'Beth?' Rhys' voice comes from the end of a long tunnel. 'Beth… oh shit…'

There's a deep growling behind them.

'Beth, we've got to run. Now.'

She checks over her shoulder. The huge dog is thirty metres behind them. Its shoulders flex with every breath it takes. It has a limp fox clamped between gory, bared teeth. A paralysis fastens her to the ground. And then her head begins to jerk as Rhys drags her along, feet tripping over each other.

'Beth! Run!'

But her feet won't work.

She watches as the dog drops the fox and sits back on its haunches for a second before springing across the field after them. Now she runs.

Side by side they plunge into the darkness of the woods and she knows she's hurtling into a world completely of her own making, horror after horror.

Rhys zigzags between trees and she has to let him lead in order to make it through. All she can hear from behind is the snapping of branches and the whump, whump of the dog's breath as it crashes after them. They skim the boulder where Rhys was buried and she feels a spasm under her ribs, which threatens to bring her down. There's blood in her mouth and she spits it out.

'This way!' Rhys shouts, and they veer suddenly to their right, glancing off a tree. Rhys half turns and takes her by the waist, still running. He's slowing them down and she tries to wriggle free, but his grip is too strong.

The dog is on them. She feels an outstretched leg clawing at her, raking down the back of her calf.

Then, in one fluid movement, Rhys lifts them both off the ground and they are diving forward, hitting the ground hard. Her breath explodes from her lungs as she rolls over, again and again. What is he doing? They're at the dog's mercy.

She tries to scramble up to face whatever's going to happen next. There's a deafening slap of metal and an awful scream. She looks up as the dog is catapulted into the air, turning completely head over tail. It lands with an awful sound at her feet, splattering her with its blood. She can taste the iron, smell its terrible stink.

She tries to crawl backwards, but the weight of the dog on her legs pins her down. It twists its great head towards her and she hears small bones popping. It bares blood-blackened teeth.

She tries to slide away, grabbing at the grass, pulling it loose. The dog is struggling to its feet, and she can feel the pressure loosening on her legs. Its screaming has deepened to a ferocious growl. She's almost free, just her ankles left. Then it lurches at her and she smells its fetid breath, teeth snapping shut inches from her face, covering her in slobber and blood. Something has pulled it back, snagging it.

The dog's trying to yank one of its legs from whatever's holding it fast. Then she sees a glint of metal teeth and the white of bone. The dog pulls hard and the bone begins to splinter. It howls with pain and rage and she wobbles to her feet, knowing that she's spent. She waits for the dog to come for her.

There's a blur of movement as Rhys hurtles from out of the dark, driving himself into the dog's side and bouncing it off a tree. The collision cracks the dog's leg free from the trap, leaving a bloody stump. Rhys ignores the terrible howl coming from the dog and slams into it again, sitting across its rib cage and pinning it to the ground.

He sits astride its shoulders and reaches his hands around its neck. The snap is instant and final. Rhys sits there, chest rising and falling rapidly with the effort. He looks over to her and slowly gets off the dead dog.

'Okay, you did tell me there was a dog…'

She looks down at the metal trap still biting into what's left of the dog's leg.

'One of yours?' she asks.

'Yep.'

'You knew the trap was there?'

'Yep.'

He walks over. 'You're covered in blood.' He reaches up to cradle her chin. 'Some on your face.'

She wipes her nose on her sleeve, not sure whether it's the dog's blood coming off, or hers.

'We need a shower. You more than me.' Rhys smiles.

'I need to get out of these woods.'

'Come on. Not far now.'

She looks back at the fallen dog. 'Are we leaving it there?'

'Well, I'm not eating it and if we stick around here any longer, you'd probably bring it back. Again.'

It's so dark now she flicks her torch on as they pick their way through the undergrowth of dead brambles. Her whole body seems to hurt. She's not sure how much she's got left to give.

Soon Rhys' house starts to take shape out of the gloom. Sightless windows and a crooked hat for a roof. It always sends a pang through her heart to think of him, here, alone.

'We should go back to mine,' she says.

As the adrenaline rush subsides, Beth remembers the woman at the bus and the nagging feeling she's had almost ever since.

'Really? You sure?' he asks.

She stands looking at the dark house and tries to stem the growing unease she now feels. 'Yes.'

Rhys stops in front of her and looks back.

'Okay, you're the boss. I'll just get some stuff…'

She scans the empty house, following Rhys with her torch. 'Why are you looking so pleased with yourself?'

He laughs and walks away from her, pushing his front door open. 'Well, I've seen off my love rival, plucked you off a mountain, in fact, saved your life twice and -'

He stops in the open mouth of the doorway and turns back to her. 'And, well, you chose me…'

She shines the torch into his face, making his green eyes dazzle.

'Rhys,' she says, 'there was this woman…'

Then there's a whirring sound of hollow metal and a movement behind Rhys from out of the dark house. His head snaps forward at the ringing of some dull bell and he hits the floor. Like Grandma, she thinks stupidly, like his strings were cut. She runs forward to him, torch beam swinging wildly. Flashes of light fall across Trev, standing over Rhys, raising a metal pole in both hands.

She throws herself on top of Rhys and feels the full force of the blow across her back. She hears a rib crack. Blood roars through her veins. Powerful hands pick her up and throw her inside the doorway.

She rolls onto her front only to be picked up again and thrown into the kitchen, crashing into the cupboards. Her phone goes spinning out of her grasp, skittering across the floor, its light pointing uselessly at the ceiling.

She can hear a whiny, needling voice from the dark then Susie steps through her torch light and aims a kick at her face. Susie only partly connects, her shoe skidding off the side of Beth's cheek and thudding into a cupboard.

Beth slides up the side of the units, clutching at the rim of the sink. The world spins inside her head. Susie has stepped back and is hissing at Trev. Her voice sounds a million miles away.

'Trev, she knows… she'll have told him…'

'I fucking done it, haven't I?' He's wired, eyes blazing in the torchlight, pupils huge.

'Witch!' Susie practically spits the words at her.

The pressure bursts through Beth's whole body as she wishes them both dead. She pictures them, bloodied and broken. Pictures their hearts, plucked from their writhing, still-warm bodies. Pictures them dead.

Then there's that sticky-Velcro sound coming from somewhere behind Beth and Susie covers her mouth, smothering her own words.

The freshly skinned rabbit stands in the sink. It glistens pink and grey, innards exposed, waxen, pulsing with new life. Its sinews snap back into place with sticky clicks. Its red mouth opens and it starts to scream. Inhuman and piercing.

Trev suddenly lashes out at the rabbit, swinging, again and again until the sink is a mess of pulped guts and splintered bones. Then there is just the sound of metal on metal and the rabbit has stopped screaming.

Trev then turns to Beth, twisting the pole in his bloodied paws, getting a better grip.

'You killed my mum.' Beth holds herself up, back to the window.

She feels a pressure building, that familiar rush. Now, she lets it build, feels it flow from her, drip from her fingertips, spill from her eyes. Let them come, she thinks, let them all come…

There's a shocking crash behind her. The window almost breaks. And another.

'Fuck…' Trev is open mouthed.

Something is thudding against the glass, again and again. She looks back. Birds are looming out of the black night and flying at the window. They leave bloody smears where they hit.

She sees an owl grow swiftly out of the dark, sees it opening its powerful wings and shelters her eyes just in time. It shatters the window with an explosion of jagged shards. Trev and Susie duck, covering their faces as the owl slams against the far wall and drops to the floor, a mess of blood and feathers. It twitches there.

Trev and Susie stand again, slowly lowering their arms. Birds begin to flood through the open window into the kitchen and swirl around their heads, screeching.

Trev swings the pole at them, catching some with glancing blows. Beth feels like she's floating, like she could fly up there with them, crazily, wildly. The air is dense with feathers. A fox clears the window frame and actually uses Beth's shoulder as

364

a springboard, launching itself at a screaming Susie. Susie half turns and the fox takes a bite out of her arm.

'Trev!' Susie screams. 'Make her stop!' Susie shrinks back against the wall as the fox skids on the tiles, ready to attack again.

Trev ignores the birds as they hurtle into his body and raises the pole high above his head, standing over Beth.

There is a splintering of wood and a visceral wail as something huge demolishes the rear door and slams into Trev, completely taking him off his feet and lifting him up, tossing him like a rag doll.

Beth is all blood now, leaking it. She sees as the unmistakeable bulk of a pig bears down on the fallen form of Trev.

A squall of sound rings in her ears and the walls start to close in, all screams merging into one thin scratch of pain.

Beth feels herself sliding down the cupboard, feels the floor accept her useless body, feels her burning, blood-soaked cheek slap softly onto the icy tiles.

She sees a flurry of limbs and feathers, passing, strobe–lit through the torch's gaze. She accepts her fate. Feels her death creeping through her bones.

The darkness shrinks her world, until she can see just one pinpoint of light. Someone kneels beside her and she feels a hand lifting her head off the floor, tilting her towards the torch. A face swirls out of the dark and into the light. She sees one last thing before darkness takes her.

'Mum?'

END OF BOOK ONE

ACKNOWLEDGEMENTS:

A huge debt of gratitude to all who have helped shape this book: my family, sister Lisa and formidable cousins Sue, Shelagh, Sally and Pam, for prompt and encouraging reading. Anne and Dom for their terrifyingly accurate editing. Rhys, Ryan, Tom and Matt for their enthusiasm and creative input. Susan Diek for all things Welsh, especially her skills in profanity, and James, Nat and Rachael and others at The Conrad Press for helping me realise this book. Finally, for the majestic landscape of North Wales for providing my story with a home and a heart.